MW00462203

Poppy Harmon
and the
Shooting Star

Books by Lee Hollis

Hayley Powell Mysteries
DEATH OF A KITCHEN DIVA
DEATH OF A COUNTRY FRIED REDNECK
DEATH OF A COUPON CLIPPER
DEATH OF A CHOCOHOLIC
DEATH OF A CHRISTMAS CATERER
DEATH OF A CUPCAKE QUEEN
DEATH OF A BACON HEIRESS
DEATH OF A PUMPKIN CARVER
DEATH OF A LOBSTER LOVER
DEATH OF A COOKBOOK AUTHOR
DEATH OF A WEDDING CAKE BAKER
DEATH OF A BLUEBERRY TART
DEATH OF A WICKED WITCH
DEATH OF AN ITALIAN CHEF
DEATH OF AN ICE CREAM SCOOPER

Collections
EGGNOG MURDER
(with Leslie Meier and Barbara Ross)
YULE LOG MURDER
(with Leslie Meier and Barbara Ross)
HAUNTED HOUSE MURDER
(with Leslie Meier and Barbara Ross)
CHRISTMAS CARD MURDER
(with Leslie Meier and Peggy Ehrhart)
HALLOWEEN PARTY MURDER
(with Leslie Meier and Barbara Ross)
IRISH COFFEE MURDER
(with Leslie Meier and Barbara Ross)

Poppy Harmon Mysteries
POPPY HARMON INVESTIGATES
POPPY HARMON AND THE HUNG JURY
POPPY HARMON AND THE PILLOW TALK KILLER
POPPY HARMON AND THE BACKSTABBING BACHELOR
POPPY HARMON AND THE SHOOTING STAR

Maya & Sandra Mysteries
MURDER AT THE PTA
MURDER AT THE BAKE SALE
MURDER ON THE CLASS TRIP

Published by Kensington Publishing Corp.

Poppy Harmon and the Shooting Star

LEE HOLLIS

Kensington Publishing Corp.
www.kensingtonbooks.com

KENSINGTON BOOKS are published by

Kensington Publishing Corp.
119 West 40th Street
New York, NY 10018

All Kensington titles, imprints and distributed lines are available at special quantity discounts for bulk purchases for sales promotion, premiums, fund-raising, educational or institutional use. Special book excerpts or customized printings can also be created to fit specific needs. For details, write or phone the office of the Kensington Special Sales Manager: Kensington Publishing Corp., 119 West 40th Street, New York, NY, 10018. Attn. Special Sales Department. Phone: 1-800-221-2647.

The K and Teapot logo is a trademark of Kensington Publishing Corp.

Library of Congress Control Number: 2023930889

ISBN: 978-1-4967-3889-9

First Kensington Hardcover Edition: June 2023

ISBN: 978-1-4967-3891-2 (ebook)

10 9 8 7 6 5 4 3 2 1

Printed in the United States of America

For Joe Dietl & Ben Zook

Chapter 1

Poppy Harmon stopped suddenly in the doorway of the Desert Flowers Detective Agency garage office, her jaw dropping at the sight of Serena Saunders sitting on the couch, her shapely gams crossed, casually sipping a steaming cup of coffee.

"Hello, Poppy!" Serena cooed, waving her immaculately manicured hand adorned with firehouse-red nail polish.

Poppy glanced around the office. Her three partners in her private detective agency—Iris Becker, Violet Hogan, and Matt Cameron aka Matt Flowers—were studying her anxiously, gauging her reaction over the unexpected presence of her former acting rival from the 1980s through the early 1990s.

"I-I don't understand," Poppy sputtered. "I thought we were meeting with a woman named—"

"Karen Hilton," Serena offered.

"We thought so too," Iris snorted in her thick German accent.

"I was afraid if you knew it was me, Poppy, you might refuse to see me, so I used a fake name to set up this appointment. Karen Hilton was a character I played in a very well-received Lifetime movie I did back in 1994 where I played the guidance counselor to a disturbed high school girl who is insanely jealous of her classmate, a popular cheerleader, and plots her murder. It was the highest-rated TV movie of that year. I thought I was a shoo-in for the Best Supporting Actress Emmy, but alas it was not meant to be."

"Okay," Poppy muttered warily.

Serena set her coffee cup on the glass-top coffee table in front of her and then sprang to her feet. "Poppy, it's so good to see you." She circled around, arms outstretched, barreling toward Poppy for a hug.

Poppy thought about backing out the door and running straight for home, but her impeccable manners would not allow it, so resigned she hugged Serena, stiffly patting her on the back as Serena nearly squeezed all the air out of her.

Matt cleared his throat. "Serena wants to hire us."

Matt was the face of the Desert Flowers Agency when they first opened their doors for business nearly five years ago. When Poppy and her two besties, Iris and Violet, decided to become private investigators, ageism, even in a retirement Mecca like Palm Springs, proved to be a major hurdle. No one seemed interested in hiring three highly capable women in their sixties. So Poppy brought in her daughter Heather's ex-boyfriend, an aspiring actor, to play the role of agency founder Matt Flowers. The ploy worked seamlessly. Business began pouring in, and the agency was now one of the top investigative firms in the entire Coachella Valley.

Ironically, Matt's acting career skyrocketed after one particular case involving a Hollywood film by happenstance, and recently he had been only sporadically involved with the cases since he was off shooting films and series around the world. Poppy had given him the option of withdrawing from the agency completely now that they had enough clients to keep the business afloat without his help, but Matt loved playing detective and was adamant about staying on as a part of the team whenever he was in town.

Poppy took a deep breath as she awkwardly pulled away from Serena, who still looked gorgeous. "So you want to hire us? What exactly do you want us to do?"

"I would like for you to conduct a background check," Serena said.

"On who?" Poppy asked.

"My fiancé."

"I didn't know you were engaged," Poppy said.

"Neither did I. Until a week ago, when he suddenly popped the question at Pomme Frite over an escargot appetizer. I nearly choked on my Pinot Noir."

"Congratulations," Violet chirped, willfully ignoring the obvious tension between the two women.

"Thank you," Serena said. "We have not been dating that long. I honestly never dreamed I would *ever* get married again."

Poppy tried to bite her tongue but to no avail. "Five times not enough?"

Serena flashed Poppy a withering smile but did not object to the dig because she knew she was at the moment in need of her professional services.

Poppy immediately regretted the petty comment, quickly adding, "Who's the lucky fella?"

Serena spun around to address the rest of the group, averting her eyes from Iris, who grumpily glared at her. Iris was fiercely protective of Poppy and knew this woman had caused her friend a lot of emotional pain in the past. "Ned Boyce. He's a businessman here in town."

"What kind of business?" Matt asked.

Serena's eyes widened as if she was taking in Matt's muscled frame and flawless face for the first time. "Wealth management. He counsels clients on long-term invest-ments, retirement accounts, that sort of thing. I don't even pretend to understand any of it." She flounced seductively across the room toward Matt, who instinctively took a step back, afraid she might grope him. "By the way, Matt, I saw you in that movie you did with the Rock recently and you were magnificent."

"Thank you," Matt said warily.

"I hope to see a lot more of you," she purred, pausing before continuing with a wink to the ladies in the room, "On the big screen, of course."

Matt cleared his throat again, now very uncomfortable.

Poppy moved to the kitchenette and poured herself a cup of coffee. "Is there a reason you feel the need for a background check? Are there some trust issues?"

Serena shook her head. "Oh no. I just want to be certain there are no skeletons hidden in his closet that I do not al-ready know about."

"If he is an investment manager, then I would assume he is financially secure?" Poppy asked.

"Yes, he's certainly comfortable, but I have seen enough Netflix documentaries to know it could all be a scam. After all, given the fortunes left to me by my"—she stared pointedly at Poppy—"*five* husbands, not to mention my own money from my acting endeavors, I'm not sure if you're aware that I am still working and I have amassed quite an attractive sum of money."

Matt's eyes nearly bulged out of his head. "Wait! All five of your husbands *died*?"

Serena threw her head back and guffawed. "No! Before you get the impression that I am some sort of black widow, only one, Dieter, passed away. The rest, thanks to my crack legal team, were forced to pay up in alimony."

"How did Dieter die?" Iris asked, eyebrow raised, sus-picious.

"Skiing accident," Serena said, brushing it off.

Poppy took a sip of her coffee and gave Serena a considered look before sighing. "Serena, I am very happy for you, but I just don't think we're the right fit for this assignment—"

Serena held up a hand to stop her. "Please. Poppy, I know we have a history, lots of competition and conflicts and unnecessary histrionics . . ."

Mostly on your part, Poppy thought.

"And I am undoubtedly the last person you ever wanted to see again given some of my past egregious behavior toward you . . ."

Well, at least she got that last part right.

"But I am trying to change and become a better person. I promise you that. It's partly why I'm here today. The last five times I tried marriage, I rushed in without thinking. I didn't pay any attention to all the red flags. I refused the advice of my friends, thought I knew best. And none of those relationships worked out in the end. I was even in the middle of divorcing Dieter when he slammed into that tree skiing in Aspen. So this time I just want to make sure I get it right."

"I understand, Serena, and that's commendable," Poppy said in a quiet, measured tone. "But I really don't—"

"I'm sorry," Serena interjected. "I'm sorry for everything."

She managed to quiet the room.

"I take full responsibility for our long-standing feud. I was childish, and mean-spirited, and hopelessly self-destructive, and though I don't expect you to ever forgive me, I ask that you only allow me to help support your business. You have done an amazing thing, Poppy. You have created a whole third act for yourself. Look at you. A successful private investigator with her own firm and partners and employees. And at your age!"

Poppy flinched.

Serena caught herself. "That did not come out right. You know what I mean. Besides, I'm here to admit, here and now, something I have never been able to before—that I am actually older than you. By two years."

"You're right." Poppy chuckled. "You have never admitted that before, but I knew it was true because I snuck a peek at your driver's license back in the eighties when we did that *Valley of the Dolls* TV remake."

Serena smiled. "I'm not proud of the way I behaved back then, and even up to now. It seems the older I got, the more insecure I became, which just made me even more impossible to be around. But meeting Ned, that has changed everything. No more boy toys, no more auditioning for parts I am clearly too old for. I just want to live out the rest of my days happy and content. And I feel I can have that with Ned. I just need to take this one last step to make sure I'm not making another colossal mistake."

Poppy wavered.

She had never seen this vulnerable side of Serena before.

She was all but groveling.

Still, there was a little voice inside Poppy's head that suggested this might all be part of a well-rehearsed act. Serena had, after all, always been a very good actress. Poppy studied her hard, trying to assess her sincerity.

"I will pay double your usual fee," Serena offered as icing on the cake.

"Deal!" Iris blurted out.

Violet nodded her head vigorously in agreement.

Matt smirked. He knew exactly where this conversation would end.

Serena looked at Poppy expectantly, knowing she was the one in the room who had the final word.

"Our research consultant, Wyatt, is out of the office today, but he will be here this weekend, and so we can have him do a preliminary search on your fiancé, Mr. Boyce."

"Is he working on another case today?" Serena asked.

"No, it's his first day of high school," Violet said brightly. "He's my grandson."

"Oh . . ." Serena gasped, a little taken aback.

"Don't worry, Serena," Poppy said with a knowing smile. "He's very good at what he does. If there are any skeletons to discover, our boy Wyatt will find them."

"Lovely," Serena whispered, relieved. "I appreciate you taking this on for me, I really do, Poppy, thank you."

Her words sounded heartfelt, but Poppy was not quite ready to let her guard down.

Not just yet.

Serena made her way over to the door, spinning around to face the group on her way out. "You have a birthday coming up, don't you, Poppy?"

Poppy's mouth dropped open. "Yes, on the twelfth, how did you know?"

"We're both Virgos. I'm the nineteenth, and I remember on the set of *Valley of the Dolls* they brought out a cake to celebrate both our birthdays."

"Yes, but you refused to come out of your trailer for a piece because you did not like the idea of sharing birthdays," Poppy reminded her.

Serena grimaced, now remembering. "I must have blocked that part out. I'm sorry . . ."

"Don't apologize. Water under the bridge," Poppy said.

"Let me make it up to you. I will throw you a party!"

"No!" Poppy yelped. "Serena, I will accept this case, and we will find out everything we need to know about your fiancé, but only on one condition . . . that you do *not* plan a birthday party for me!"

"Why not?" Serena asked, disappointed.

"Because I stopped celebrating them years ago."

Serena nodded. "Understood. Okay, then. No party. Good-bye, everyone." She gave the ladies a friendly wave, and then her eyes lingered on Matt just long enough to make him shift awkwardly, embarrassed by the attention, before she flitted out the door.

Poppy could not believe it.

What an unexpected start to her day.

She was now working for the only person in Hollywood she ever truly despised.

Serena Saunders.

Chapter 2

Ned Boyce's modernist Palm Springs home was built in the late 1960s, a domed concrete structure blending the rock formations into the structure of the hillside it sat upon. At this point on the tour, Poppy had counted at least five bedrooms so far in the upwards of nine thousand square feet of space. The house also featured a spectacular circular living area centerpiece and large curved glass walls that opened onto a terrace and swimming pool, where you could take in the breathtaking views of the Coachella Valley.

When Poppy had asked to meet the subject of their investigation, businessman Ned Boyce, Serena was happy to host a luncheon at Ned's mountaintop home, explaining that Poppy was one of Serena's oldest and dearest friends and it would just not seem right for her to marry Ned before he had a chance to meet someone who was so important to her.

Ned, who probably wondered why Serena had never mentioned Poppy before during their ever-so-brief courtship, had readily agreed, eager to meet anyone close to the woman he loved. A date was set for the next day, and Serena insisted Poppy bring her boyfriend, Sam.

Poppy had initially hesitated about inviting Sam. Their relationship had seemed to cool lately. At least from Poppy's perspective. She could not quite put her finger on why, or even a specific moment that ignited any tension, but she just had the sinking suspicion that Sam, for some reason, was pulling back, starting to distance himself from her. She had asked him about it a week earlier when the two of them were dining on the patio at Spencer's, one of their favorite romantic spots, but he had brushed off her concerns, assuring her that everything was fine.

That's what bothered Poppy. Sam was such a straight shooter. If something was bothering him, there was very little chance he would not come right out with it. He hated playing games. He detested unspoken conflict. Best to get everything out in the open. Which was why Poppy felt such cause for concern. This was so unlike him. She did not even expect him to drive down from his cabin up on Big Bear Mountain to join her, but Serena had been so adamant that this lunch come across as a double date, Poppy was left with no choice but to call him up and explain that she needed him.

Sam did not even hesitate. Of course if Poppy needed him, he would be there. She was enormously relieved. Perhaps she had whipped all of this up in her mind. Maybe she was just being paranoid. But when Sam arrived at her door to pick her up, she instantly sensed his discomfort, this frustrating gnawing distance between them. They hardly spoke the entire ride up to Ned Boyce's home. When they were standing at the door after ringing the bell, Poppy turned to Sam, ready to confront him. But Serena swung open the door and squealed with delight at their arrival before she had the chance.

Serena ushered them inside. Both Poppy and Sam had looked around the insanely opulent property, mightily impressed, their jaws nearly dropping to the floor, as they waited for Ned.

"This place looks eerily familiar," Sam observed.

"I'm sure it does. It was a villain's lair in a James Bond movie back in the early seventies right after it was built."

Sam smiled. "Yes, that's it! Sean Connery had a fight scene out by the pool with two bikini-clad henchwomen!"

"Good memory," Serena said.

Sam winked at her. "It was my favorite part of the movie."

Poppy's attention was drawn to a photographic portrait above the fireplace of a strikingly good-looking couple embracing, taken sometime in the 1950s judging by their wardrobes. His hair was greased back, and he had a pencil-thin mustache and gorgeous brown eyes that offset his intense serious expression. She was auburn-haired, fresh faced, with a playful Rita Hayworth quality about her. "Is that . . . ?"

"Alistair Boyce and Jean Harding," Serena said, nodding. "Ned's parents."

Poppy's eyes nearly bulged out of her head. "Wait, *Ned* is the son of Boyce and Harding?"

"That's right. They shot a film in Palm Springs back in the 1960s. It didn't do very well, but they fell in love with the desert and decided to build a second home here," Serena explained.

"So this palace was their weekend getaway spot?" Sam chuckled, shaking his head.

"I guess they could afford it at the time," Serena said.

There was Hepburn and Tracy. Burton and Taylor. And then, maybe a few rungs down the ladder but still major Hollywood box office stars for a short period in the late 1950s, early 1960s, there was Boyce and Harding. He had been a stage star in London's West End lured across the pond to Hollywood where he played the titular role in a film version of *Henry V* and was rewarded with an Oscar nomination. But it was his second film with a young up-and-coming starlet named Jean Harding, plucked from the chorus line of an MGM musical and groomed to be a star that changed his life. The two fell in love and married, and costarred in a string of romantic comedies that topped the box office, rivaling Rock Hudson and Doris Day at the time. By the early seventies, as their career momentum began to stall, Jean retired from acting to raise their only child, Ned, while Alistair signed on to do a detective series for NBC, part of the old rotating Mystery Movie wheel that featured *Columbo*, *McCloud*, and *McMillan & Wife*. But his effort, about a bounty hunter, failed to catch on and was quickly cancelled by 1973. After that, the couple moved full time to Palm Springs, where they lived out their final days. Alister died in 1984 of lung cancer, Jean followed less than a year later, most assuming from a broken heart.

Given the extravagant surroundings, Poppy wondered why it was not Ned who had come to the Desert Flowers Detective Agency to do a background check on Serena instead of the other way around. Serena stepped forward, almost as if reading her mind, and whispered into Poppy's ear. "He's not as rich as you might think. His parents didn't have much money left when they died, only this house, which they passed on to Ned, who has had to work his fingers to the bone paying for the property taxes and constant repairs."

"Well, he's done a marvelous job keeping it up," Poppy said, glancing around.

"I'm so sorry to keep you waiting," Ned Boyce said as he descended the circular staircase leading up to a guest room that he had converted to a home office, according to Serena. "One of my clients kept me stuck on the phone." He extended a hand to Sam. "Ned Boyce."

"Sam Emerson, nice to meet you," Sam said, pumping his hand before turning to Poppy. "And this is—"

"No introduction needed," Ned said, grinning. "Big *Jack Colt* fan. Correction. Big Daphne fan! Such a pleasure to meet you."

"Thank you. Likewise."

Poppy could feel her face flushing.

And she detected a slight grimace on Serena's face.

"You can count me among the many Daphne admirers who never missed an episode," Ned cooed. "I recorded every episode on my VCR, which back then, was like the size of a smart car."

Poppy shifted uncomfortably. "It was such a long time ago."

"Well, you look just as radiant as you did then," Ned said, turning to Sam. "You're a lucky man, Sam."

Poppy had expected Sam to respond in kind but he was staring outside the large curved glass walls, not even engaged in the conversation.

Poppy cleared her throat.

Still nothing.

Sam was totally lost in thought.

Poppy finally nudged him. "Sam?"

Sam finally snapped back. "I'm sorry?"

"I was just saying how lucky you are to be dating such a TV icon like Daphne from *Jack Colt*," Ned repeated.

"Her name is Poppy, not Daphne," Serena interjected.

"Yes, dear, I know," Ned sighed. "I'm just being silly."

Daphne was the name of the character she had played on the 1980s detective series *Jack Colt, PI* starring Rod Harper, which lasted three seasons. It was the role she was most known for from her decade of acting in Hollywood.

"Welcome to my home, Poppy, Sam. I'm so glad you could come. Are you finished with the tour?"

"Almost," Serena said, her lips pursed. "I need to go check on Helga to see where we are with lunch."

Helga was a part-time cook they had brought in for the occasion, since Serena could barely boil water.

Serena's eyes flashed Ned a sharp warning to stop flirting, at least that's what she intended before dashing off to the kitchen.

"Okay, hon," Ned said, oblivious to his fiancé's jealous streak, before leading Poppy and Sam down a hallway that led to a cabana outside. Poppy stopped midway to gaze upon a large wall mural—a desert landscape, so real in detail it could almost fool anyone into believing it was an actual view from a picture window.

Poppy leaned forward, recognizing the unique style, and gasped. "Dexter Holt?"

A popular artist in the 1960s and '70s, eccentric and remarkably still alive, whose landscape work now fetched millions.

Ned chuckled and reached out and touched Poppy's arm. "Before you get too excited, it's just a copy. Probably worth less than five hundred bucks."

"It's stunning," Poppy muttered.

"My parents loved Dexter Holt when he first came onto the scene as a young artist, but by then their fortune had shrunk quite a bit and they could hardly afford an original, so they hired a local painter to do this knockoff."

"He did an amazing job," Sam offered, finally contributing something to the conversation.

"Yeah, if you look, there's no signature. Dexter Holt always signed at the bottom left corner of all his paintings. But whenever my parents had guests over, they all assumed it was a genuine Holt mural. My parents probably didn't mind at all because they secretly hoped people would think it was real. By then, their careers were pretty much over and their pride had taken quite a beating from

Hollywood's rejection, so they tried to create the impression they were still rich and successful. They were a colorful pair."

"You were still very young when they died," Poppy said quietly.

"College freshman. What little money they had I put toward college and hanging on to this house. This place was their pride and joy, and I made a vow never to sell it."

"I can't imagine what they must have paid to build this place compared with what it's worth now," Poppy said.

Ned shrugged. "Yeah, but the sentimental value of this home is worth a hell of a lot more than any dollar figure I could get."

Serena suddenly appeared. "Lunch is served. We'll be eating out by the pool, so start making your way there."

Ned slapped Sam on the back. "Come on, Sam. Let me make you a ranch water."

"Sounds good," Sam said without missing a beat.

Ned cocked an eyebrow. "You actually know what a ranch water is?"

"Tequila and lime juice over ice with a splash of seltzer," Sam said with a knowing smile. "I spent a lot of time in Texas shooting cowboy movies."

"I like him!" Ned declared before leading him outside.

Poppy hung back as Serena hustled up to her.

"Well? First impressions?" Serena asked, wringing her hands.

"He seems lovely. I am very happy for you," Poppy said.

"No red flags?"

Poppy shook her head. "None that I can see. But we will have to wait and see what Wyatt comes up with."

Poppy turned to follow the men, but Serena stopped her.

"Now that we're friends again, I have to ask . . ."

Poppy braced herself for what might be coming next.

"Is there trouble in paradise? I mean with you and Sam?"

"No. Why do you ask?"

Poppy was not being entirely truthful, of course.

But she was not about to share any concerns regarding her relationship with anyone, especially a client, and more important a loud-mouthed gossip like Serena Saunders.

Serena shrugged. "I don't know, I just sense a little distance between the two of you. But if you say everything's fine, then I will take your word for it. I hope you like Wiener schnitzel. It's Helga's specialty."

Serena turned and flounced down the hall to the sliding glass door that led outside.

"Sounds yummy," Poppy said robotically as she followed her, suddenly worried her relationship was on the rocks like the tequila cocktail Ned had just offered Sam. Because the cold hard truth was, if Serena had picked up on Sam's odd behavior and had noticed something off between him and Poppy, then it was no longer tenable for Poppy to believe that the issue was just a figment of her own imagination.

It was very much real.

Something was definitely wrong.

Chapter 3

If Poppy was certain of one thing by the time she dove into her slice of homemade cherry pie at the end of her lunch with Serena Saunders and her fiancé, Ned Boyce, it was that Ned was hands down head over heels in love with Serena. He sat close to her at the table, hanging on her every word, laughing heartily at every witticism and sarcastic comment she uttered. His eyes danced and twinkled whenever she casually touched his arm during the conversation. Poppy was impressed by how attentive he was to her, making sure that she was perfectly content, her wineglass was filled, and she had everything she needed. The fact was, a part of Poppy felt slightly jealous of Serena since her own boyfriend Sam seemed to be a thousand miles away, even though at the moment he was sitting there right next to her. But she was not here at Ned Boyce's home to analyze the current state of her relationship with Sam Emerson; she had a job to do. When Ned began peppering Sam with questions about his last gig consulting on a cop show that filmed in New York—Sam was still waiting to hear if it would be renewed for another season—Serena seized the opportunity to stand up and move around the table to plop down next to Poppy so she could whisper in her ear, "So, now that you have had more time to get to know Ned better over lunch, do you still like him?"

Poppy nodded. "Yes. I like him a lot. He seems very genuine, especially when it comes to his feelings for you."

"Oh, good! I'm so relieved! I was very nervous what you would think, Poppy." She sipped her Chardonnay, then dabbed her lips with a white linen napkin. "I sensed what a good man he was from the first moment we met, but whenever you're swept up in the headiness of a new romance, you oftentimes can miss any warning signs." She paused thoughtfully. "Or, given my somewhat checkered history with men, willfully ignore them."

"Don't beat yourself up, Serena, I was married to a compulsive gambler for thirty years and did not have a clue," Poppy said with a wry smile. "And I'm supposed to be the detective."

They shared a laugh.

Serena leaned in closer to Poppy, glancing over to make sure Ned was not eavesdropping on their conversation, but luckily he was busy breezily chatting with Sam. "He seems really stable, doesn't he?"

"Yes, very," Poppy assured her.

"Such a radical change for me. A nice, normal man." She crossed her fingers. "Let's just hope the background check doesn't turn up anything unsettling."

Poppy patted the back of Serena's hand. "Don't worry. I have a good feeling."

Serena beamed at her handsome fiancé, who was now laughing at a joke Sam had cracked. She was practically glowing. "You know what? I do, too."

Helga appeared in the sliding glass doorway that led out to the poolside table and spoke in a thick German accent. "Mr. Ashmore is here."

Ned checked his watch. "He's early."

"Yes, he said he can just meet you at the club if you're not ready," Helga said.

"Send him out here, Helga. I'm sure Poppy would love to say hello," Serena said.

"Of course, ma'am," Helga nodded, disappearing back inside the house.

Poppy sat up straight in her chair, surprised. "Ashmore? *Warren* Ashmore?"

"Yes, Warren and Ned are old friends and golfing buddies. Warren directed his parents in a TV movie back in the early nineteen seventies," Serena explained.

Warren Ashmore.

Poppy had not thought about that name in years.

Warren had become a notable up-and-coming film-maker in the 1960s when he was a fresh-faced NYU film school grad who had directed a few well-received features before amassing a fortune directing films made for television in the seventies and eighties. Warren had also been the director of the TV remake of *Valley of the Dolls*, which had starred both Poppy and Serena, the most miserable three weeks of Poppy's career. She and Serena had clashed from the moment the camera started rolling, and as hard as Warren tried to play referee, he was no match for the dueling divas. Poppy had done her best to suppress all the bad memories from that fraught time in her life. Working on that movie was what really pushed her to get out of show business altogether. After appearing in a few more projects, she ultimately retired; married her late husband, Chester; and moved to Palm Springs, although

Serena continued on with her career and to this day was hustling for acting jobs. But now that she had found Ned, perhaps the sun would finally set on her long-storied Hollywood career.

Poppy was shocked by Warren Ashmore's appearance when he sauntered out to greet them. The last time she had seen him, he had probably been in his early forties, fit, muscled, strong, handsome. He was still good looking, but he had aged dramatically. Smaller, balding, wisps of white hair combed to the side, fragile. His bones seemed to creak when he moved. He still had that mischievous grin and ocean blue eyes that had made the women on set swoon, but Poppy wondered if all those years of hard living had finally taken their toll. His leathery weathered skin appeared to have seen too much harsh desert sun. Sam was in his late sixties—not much younger than Warren, in fact—and he was still a force of nature, healthy and energetic, the lines on his face making him even sexier.

Warren's face lit up at the sight of Poppy. "Poppy Harmon, you haven't aged a day!" He teetered toward her and gave her a warm hug.

She instinctively jumped to her feet to meet him halfway, fearful he might trip and take a tumble and obliterate a hip. "Warren, I can't believe it! It's been so long!"

She hugged him lightly, not wanting to squeeze too hard.

He planted a wet kiss on her cheek.

He took a step back and drank in the sight of his two former costars from *Valley of the Dolls* together again. "I never thought I would live to see this day. Poppy Harmon and Serena Saunders peacefully breaking bread and not tearing each other's hair out!"

There was some uncomfortable laughter all around, but mostly from Ned.

"Poppy and I have finally decided to bury the hatchet. The past is the past. Let bygones be bygones and all that jazz. We're both living in Palm Springs now, so why not be friends?"

"Makes perfect sense to me," Warren said with a wink. He then turned to Ned. "I know we don't tee off until three, but I was losing too much money at the casino playing blackjack, so I thought I'd swing by a little early before I went completely broke."

"Not a problem, I just need to go change," Ned said before turning to Sam. "Care to join us, Sam? We can sign you in at the club as our guest."

Sam threw up his hands. "No, thank you. I'm not much of a golfer."

Warren stepped toward Sam, staring at him, trying to focus, as if he was struggling with bad eyesight. "Sam? Sam Emerson?"

"I was wondering when you would recognize me," Sam responded, grinning.

Sam stood up, and the two men pumped hands.

"I'll be damned, you're still alive!" Warren joked.

Sam turned to the ladies. "Warren and I worked together on a Stallone picture back in the early nineties."

"Sam did a polish on the script," Warren said. "Stallone had been starring in a string of action movies, all of them big box-office hits. Then we came along and broke his winning streak."

"Yeah, it was a dud all right. But we had fun." Sam shrugged.

Ned headed into the house.

"Can I offer you a drink, Sam? Helga will make you a plate if you're hungry," Serena said.

"No, I'm good. I already ate at the casino. I lost so much today, they took pity on me and let me eat for free at the lunch buffet," Warren said, shaking his head.

"You working on anything these days, Warren, or are you fully retired now?" Sam asked.

"No, I'm always working on something. You know me. I can't get my head around the concept of retirement. I just secured financing for a small independent feature I plan to direct. Good script by some kid who just won a screenwriting contest."

Serena's ears perked up. "Oh? Is there a role for a beautiful and vibrant mature woman aging ever so gracefully?"

"Afraid not, love," Warren said, almost relieved. "The one role you might be right for is already cast with the wife of the guy kicking in most of the budget. It was pretty much a package deal that I couldn't refuse if I wanted to actually make this movie. We're still looking for our male lead though. We can't afford a big name, but I'm looking at a few young actors on the rise." He turned to Poppy. "I think you may know one of the names on the list. Matt Cameron?"

Poppy gasped. "Yes, Matt is like a son to me. And he's a wonderful actor."

"I hear good things. And he was a hoot in that movie he did last year with Dwayne Johnson. This role has a lot more depth, however; it's not a light comedy, so I would need him to audition to make sure he's got the chops."

"He does. Trust me," Poppy said confidently.

Poppy was ecstatic.

This could be a potential game changer for Matt.

A part that challenged him and allowed him to show off what he could do with a meaty role. Poppy believed in Matt's talent more than anyone. And although she loved having him as part of the Desert Flowers Detective Agency, she knew it was only a matter of time before he rightfully bowed out to build his acting career. But in the meantime, Poppy, Iris, and Violet would enjoy having him around as an integral part of their crime-solving clan.

"I'm going to go see what's keeping Helga with the coffee. Warren, promise me you won't keep Ned at the nineteenth hole too long after your game. I don't want him coming home drunk."

"No promises," Warren said playfully.

Serena flashed him an admonishing look and then disappeared inside. Once she was out of earshot, Warren's smile slowly faded.

"Honestly, Poppy, I was not kidding. I never thought I would ever see the day that you two would be within a two-mile radius of each other."

"What is it they say, time heals all wounds?" Poppy shrugged.

He eyed her suspiciously.

He was definitely not buying it.

And she was not about to admit that Serena was a client and she was there to vet her fiancé, Ned Boyce.

"How long have you and Serena been back in contact, Warren?" Sam asked.

"Not long. Just since she started dating Ned. Knowing her like I do, I will admit I did try warning him at first, but he fell so hard and fast, there was just no convincing him." He sighed. "So I decided that if I wanted to hold on to my friendship with him, I would have to keep my mouth shut and just let it happen."

"So you don't approve," Poppy said quietly.

"Maybe she's changed, maybe she hasn't. It's hard to tell. Let's face it, despite her massive flaws, she's still a good actress. I just wish it wasn't all happening so fast." He glanced at Poppy. "You know what she was like, how she used men, chewed them up and spit them out. It's hard to trust her. And Ned's a sweet guy, very low key, no drama."

"Opposites attract," Sam offered.

"You're right, Sam," Warren said ruefully. "But Ned's a good friend. I would hate to see him get hurt."

Poppy could hardly argue with Warren.

It suddenly seemed strange that Ned was the one she was investigating. If anyone in this marriage union should be carefully examined, it was the bride herself.

Chapter 4

Matt was practically bouncing off the walls when Poppy delivered the exciting news that Warren Ashmore was interested in him playing the lead in his next film. When the Desert Flowers team gathered at the garage office attached to Iris's house for a debriefing on the Serena Saunders case, Matt was far more interested in discussing the script his agent had managed to get ahold of and e-mail to him rather than any information that computer whiz Wyatt had come up with regarding Ned Boyce.

"It's a modern-day neo-Western, and I play a Wyoming ranch hand on the run after getting accused of murdering my abusive boss who had it out for me. The twist is, I'm not even sure I'm innocent since I guzzled a whole bottle of whiskey and blacked out. When I wake up the next morning, I literally have blood on my hands and the cops are on their way to the bunkhouse to arrest me, so I hightail it out of there in a pickup truck with a shotgun and the boss's daughter who I'm in love with and the only one who believes I didn't do it. Of course, everyone assumes I've taken her hostage. This guy's got so many levels, I've never played such a richly drawn character before. I couldn't sleep a wink last night after reading the script."

"Before you write your Oscar acceptance speech, perhaps you should wait to get an audition first," Iris snorted, always the blunt realist.

Matt nodded. "You're right, of course, Iris, but a part like this really could change the trajectory of my career."

"Oh, we are so proud of you, Matt," Violet gushed.

"Thank you, Violet. Let's just hope I don't tank the audition. I mean, if I even get to do it. I've been glued to my phone all morning waiting for my agent to text me."

Poppy sat on the couch, sipping coffee from a mug. "If the script is as good as you say it is, I am a bit surprised Warren Ashmore is the one directing it. He's not exactly on par with Spielberg, and he's certainly not a fresh-faced new director. He's mostly been toiling in cheesy TV movies the past few decades."

"Yeah, my agent says the same thing, but apparently he's close buddies with the producer who is putting up most of the money, so it was Ashmore or nothing. Same with the guy's wife. Sure, I'd love to work with someone who's not . . ."

"A has-been?" Iris offered.

"No, I wouldn't put it that way, I'm certainly not an ageist, but his recent films definitely have been somewhat workmanlike, a little pedestrian . . ."

"It does seem he takes a lot of projects for the money," Poppy concurred. "But what he does have going for him is a breadth of experience behind the camera."

"Yes, that's got to count for something! And who knows, maybe he will surprise everybody. It would make a great Hollywood story. Put out to pasture by the cruel film industry only to claw his way back and win Best Director at the Academy Awards."

"And direct his leading man to a Best Actor win as well," Poppy said with a wink.

"It would be an honor just to be nominated," Matt said, staring off into space, smiling.

"You are picturing yourself in a tuxedo standing at a podium holding your award and thanking us for all our support, are you not?" Iris said, laughing.

Matt snapped out of his daydreaming. "Like you said, I still have to get through the audition."

"And I need to get to soccer practice!" Wyatt exclaimed, tapping his foot impatiently on the floor in front of his computer.

Violet's grandson Wyatt had just started high school and, much to their surprise, was starting to play sports. He had never shown any interest in physical activity during his preadolescence, mostly preferring to play video games, but according to Violet there was a rumor circulating that he had his eye on a female classmate who was "into jocks," which might explain his newfound passion for bending it like Beckham.

"What have you got for us, Wyatt?" Poppy asked.

Wyatt spun around in circles in his office chair as he talked. "It's pretty clear this Ned Boyce guy is not marrying the Saunders lady for her money. He's got more cash on hand than one of Putin's Russian oligarchs."

Poppy gasped. "What? Are you sure? Serena left me with the impression that he was not very rich, that his wealth management company draws a modest income and the house is a money pit."

"He does all right with the business, but that's not where most of his fortune comes from. His second wife, Cecily, was apparently loaded. She left him everything when she died six years ago," Wyatt said, still spinning.

"I was not aware he was a widower," Poppy said. "Or

super rich, for that matter. Except for the house, he certainly doesn't flaunt it."

Iris marched over and grabbed a hold of Wyatt's chair, stopping it midspin. "Stop it. You are making me dizzy."

"Sorry, Aunt Iris," Wyatt said. "He donates a lot to various charities and humanitarian causes. Seems like a really generous and cool dude."

"I am sure Serena will be happy to hear that," Poppy said, ready to close the case.

"Except for one teeny tiny detail," Wyatt said.

Poppy put her coffee mug down, bracing herself for what was about to come. "And what's that?"

Wyatt tried to spin himself again, but Iris kept a firm grip on the back of his chair to make sure he did not go anywhere. He gave her a resigned look and sighed. "Cecily drowned in a boating accident. They took their yacht out on a Fourth of July weekend to Dana Point and apparently one night she had too much to drink and somehow fell overboard. Ned claimed he had already gone to bed and didn't hear a thing. The captain called the Coast Guard the next morning when they realized she was missing, and they recovered her body a few miles down the coast two days later."

"How awful," Violet moaned.

"Why didn't she call for help? Or if she did, why didn't anyone hear her?" Poppy asked.

"Because she had a gash on her head, like she might have hit it on something when she fell. The cops assumed she was unconscious when she hit the water," Wyatt said. "They ruled her death an accident."

Matt folded his arms, curious. "So there was never any suspicion of foul play?"

"I didn't say that. There was plenty of it. Still is. Just go online and google Cecily Loudon-Boyce. All her friends and family think Ned did it. According to her sister, Cecily was planning on divorcing Ned, and she believes he killed her before she had the chance, leaving him all her money."

"*Ned?* I find that difficult to believe. When I met him at lunch yesterday, he seemed like such a sweet, gentle man," Poppy said.

"Yeah, so do most serial killers!" Matt piped in.

"There's a whole bunch of true crime fanatics on Twitter and Instagram trying to get the police to reopen the case, but the police claim there just isn't enough evidence to justify it," Wyatt said.

"Do you think Serena knows about all this?" Violet wondered.

"She must. How could she not?" Poppy muttered, mystified. "Why didn't she mention this to us when she hired us?"

"Maybe she doesn't believe any of the people who suspect Ned of foul play. She could have just dismissed all the rumors as ridiculous," Matt suggested.

Poppy nodded.

That was the most plausible explanation.

Serena was in love with the man and balked at any notion that he was some sort of scheming murderer.

But Serena must have known that this information would ultimately turn up in their investigation.

Wyatt jumped up from his chair. "So are we done? Is the case closed? Can I get my cut of Ms. Saunders's fee so I can buy some new Air Jordans after soccer practice?"

"Not quite," Poppy said, her mind racing. "I'd like to look into these allegations a bit more before we wrap anything up."

They heard a phone buzzing.

Matt snapped to attention, reached into his pocket, and pulled out his phone. He closed his eyes and took a deep breath before glancing at the screen.

His expression was unreadable for a few seconds, then his eyes lit up and he looked up at the heavens, a wide grin now plastered on his face.

He did not have to explain.

They all knew he had just landed the audition for Warren Ashmore's upcoming neo-Western film.

Chapter 5

The Thunderbird Country Club in Rancho Mirage opened in 1946 and immediately attracted a predominantly Hollywood crowd with its dude ranch activities like shooting, horseback riding, and chuck wagon meals. A number of show biz luminaries such as Frank Sinatra, Ginger Rogers, and Bob Hope snapped up Thunderbird real estate, and US presidents were also drawn to the club when the owners constructed a world-class golf course a few years later. Dwight D. Eisenhower became a member in 1961, and Gerald Ford and First Lady Betty Ford had a home custom-built on the thirteenth fairway. And in more recent years, Barack Obama played the course. The homeowners were an exclusive bunch to this day, which is why it was no surprise when Poppy learned that the sister of Ned Boyce's late wife Cecily was a resident. Carina had also inherited great wealth from her family, spending most of it on funding the arts in the Coachella Valley. Once an aspiring opera singer, according to Wyatt's research, Carina came to the conclusion after years of training, even with millions of dollars at her disposal, that all her money simply could not buy her serious talent. So after decades of lessons and commitment, she quietly stopped trying to be an artist and transitioned to a more suitable role as patron of the arts.

Poppy had read a few articles in the press package Wyatt had assembled of the news coverage following Cecily's drowning. There were several quotes from Cecily's grieving sister Carina suggesting that the police had not done a thorough enough job investigating her sister's death. Poppy was curious to know if Carina still felt that way.

Wyatt had managed to scrounge up a phone number, and when Poppy called, Carina answered after the first ring. Poppy had barely begun her spiel about vetting Ned Boyce before Carina was inviting Poppy to visit her home as soon as possible so they could sit down and talk.

Apparently Carina Loudon had a lot to say.

Iris was eager to drive her new used Jaguar she had recently bought, so Poppy and Violet piled in for the fifteen-minute drive to Rancho Mirage. After stopping to check in with a security guard, they were directed to pass through the large wrought iron gates and take two left turns to Carina's street. As they pulled up in front of the stunning Spanish Colonial architectural masterpiece, they saw a grand four-tier fountain in the front courtyard that evoked Old Europe.

Iris shifted the car into the park position, staring at the expansive house. "I deserve to live in a place like this!"

"I think you might be about four million short if you want to buy a home here," Violet said.

They all got out of the Jaguar and walked up to the front door. Before Poppy had a chance to ring the bell, the door swung open and they were greeted by Carina Loudon herself. She was a striking woman in her late fifties, very well put together, not a hair out of place. She was casually dressed in a turquoise button-up top with the sleeves rolled up halfway to her elbow and white Capri pants. She smiled, welcoming the three women into her home.

Inside was just as elegant as the outside, with custom stonework and crystal chandeliers.

After declining an offer for some coffee or tea, Poppy, Iris, and Violet were led to the large open living room, where Carina asked them all to take a seat. She didn't seem to want to waste any time. She sat down in an antique chair opposite them. Iris and Violet were still gaping at the opulent surroundings.

"What a beautiful fireplace," Violet observed.

Carina glanced at it. "One of five."

"This home has *five* fireplaces?" Iris gasped.

Carina nodded, slightly embarrassed. "I know, it's a bit much."

"Not for me," Iris sniffed. "I would be perfectly happy here. How many bedrooms?"

"Six bedrooms, eight baths," Carina answered.

Iris shook her head. "That's too many bedrooms. I don't want to be hosting houseguests all the time. You know how my friends back in Germany are. They would come here and stay for months on end!"

Poppy decided they had spent enough time gushing over Carina's home. "I saw a photo of you and your sister hanging in the entryway as we came in. You two could have been twins."

"Cecily was five years older than me, but I will take that as a compliment. She was a gorgeous woman. Inside and out." Her voice suddenly became very quiet. "I think about her every day. I miss her so much."

"I'm sorry," Poppy said.

It appeared as if Carina was about to cry. Her eyes

welled up with tears, but she swiftly grabbed a tissue from her shirt pocket, dabbed at her eyes, then wadded it up, collected herself, and managed to avoid any kind of emotional breakdown. "So Ned is getting married again?"

"Yes, to Serena Saunders, our client. Serena is a famous actress," Poppy explained.

"Semi-famous," Iris barked. "She's not exactly Helen Mirren!"

"I'm afraid I have never heard of her. But I don't watch many movies or any television, except the news."

"Consider yourself lucky then," Iris couldn't resist cracking.

"Iris!" Poppy sighed, flashing her a look of consternation before turning her attention back to Carina. "Did you know Ned well?"

"Well enough." Carina shrugged. "We were never close, especially after . . ." Her voice trailed off. "But when he and Cecily first met, I liked him. He seemed nice, and I could tell he made my sister happy—in the beginning anyway."

"What do you think happened?" Violet asked.

"He killed her," Carina said so nonchalantly she might have been reciting the weather report. "Cecily wanted a divorce and Ned panicked that he was going to be left with nothing because our family's lawyers made him sign an airtight prenup before they got married. The only way Ned would get any of her money was if she died while they were still married. It was pretty cut-and-dry."

"Why do you think the marriage was on the rocks?" Poppy asked.

"She got bored. My sister and I have a history of chasing after the bad boys, the ones destined to break your heart in the end. The pop stars and NFL players. We were like the Kardashians but without the reality show, just the money. Both of us tried living in this fantasy that we were real-life heroines of some romance novel. But it was all just an illusion. In the end, the two of us realized we just made very bad choices. And then Ned came along. Steady, kind, quiet. And ready to take care of her. I think Cecily loved him, but in a father figure sort of way, someone who she knew would always be there. A rock. She took comfort in knowing he would never surprise her. But quite frankly, after a decade of that, her life felt pretty dull."

"She missed the excitement of unpredictable, unreliable men," Poppy surmised.

"Yes. She wanted to travel, see the world, hobnob with interesting people. Ned wanted to stay home in that house on the mountain his parents built. She hated that place. She felt trapped there. She told me a week before she died that she was going to finally divorce Ned and start over, try to inject her life with more fun and glamour. She certainly had the means to do it."

"I assume you no longer have any contact with Ned?" Poppy asked.

"No, just through our lawyers."

"Lawyers?"

"Ned is trying to sue me. He has absolutely no case, but he's trying to scare me."

Violet looked at her curiously. "Scare you?"

"I'm writing a book. About my life with my sister. Our globe-trotting adventures in our twenties and thirties. And what really happened to her on board that boat. I told Ned I was writing a tell-all, but he didn't seem too worried about it at first, that is until I found an agent who sold it to a big New York publisher. That's when the cease and desist letters began pouring in. But they can threaten me all they want. It's not going to stop me from publishing the book. I have my own team of very expensive sharks making sure my voice gets heard. I want everybody to know what a dangerous menace Ned Boyce is."

Poppy studied Carina, whose face was taut, her eyes dark with rage as she discussed her estranged former brother-in-law. Her description of the man seemed so incongruous to the impression Poppy had gotten of Boyce when she'd had lunch with him just the other day. But it was clear that Carina Loudon was 100 percent convinced that he was capable of murder.

Carina locked her gaze on Poppy. "This client of yours, Serena something . . . ?"

"Saunders," Poppy said.

"Serena Saunders. You tell her to watch out. Ned is a danger to her. If it doesn't work out between them, there is no telling what he might do."

Poppy stood up. "We will most certainly tell her. Thank you for your time. If you think of anything else, please don't hesitate to call me." She produced a Desert Flowers business card and handed it to Carina.

"You should talk to Jack," Carina said.

Poppy noticed a beautiful white rag doll cat stroll in and rub up against Carina's left leg. "Who's Jack?"

Carina casually reached down to scratch the top of the cat's head, causing him to purr. "Jack O'Connell. Captain Jack. He was on the boat the night Cecily supposedly drowned by accident."

"But he corroborated Ned's story. He was a big reason the police so quickly closed the investigation," Violet said.

"Well, I just interviewed him for my book," Carina said, picking the cat up and setting it down on her lap, where she continued to stroke its fur. "He's telling an entirely different story these days." She glanced down at her cat. "Right, Camilla?" She bent down and kissed the top of the cat's head. Then she looked back up at Poppy, Iris, and Violet, eyes narrowing. "You will definitely be surprised by what he has to say."

Poppy frowned.

The case against Ned Boyce was starting to get worse.

Chapter 6

As Violet leaned over the pool table in the dive bar they had driven to in Indio, Poppy held her breath.

Violet gripped the shaft of the pool cue with fierce concentration and lined up her shot after chalking the cue. All eyes in the bar were fixed upon her. "Eight ball, left corner pocket." She closed one eye, aimed the tip at the center of the cue ball, and tapped it, sending it hurtling across the green table and dropping the eight ball into the left corner pocket.

That was it.

Game over.

Violet had beat her opponent twice in a row in a two out of three game challenge.

Captain Jack O'Connell sighed, tossed his cue down on the table, and threw his hands up in surrender. "Okay, you win. I'll talk with ya." Then he reached for his mug of beer and guzzled it down, some foam spilling onto his scraggly brown beard. He was smaller than Poppy had expected, only about five feet seven, and wore a Miami Dolphins baseball cap from the city where he had been raised. He was wiry, with dark leathery skin from too much time in the sun and bleary eyes from too many beers in this little out-of-the-way bar, the Rusty Nail, deep in the heart of Indio, California, a hot, dusty working-class town in the Coachella Valley. Carina Loudon had been right. If they wanted to discuss the Cecily Loudon-Boyce case, then the man to talk to, the only other person on the boat that fateful night besides Ned and Cecily, was Captain Jack.

But when Poppy, Iris, and Violet had swept into the Rusty Nail, they were met with confused stares from the patrons, who were wondering why three well-dressed classy ladies were ordering Manhattans at the bar from the grizzled, grunting, huge silver-bearded bartender.

Especially Captain Jack, who studied them warily.

Poppy had approached him first, having recognized him from a news report Wyatt had brought up on his computer of the drowning five years ago. She had noticed just how much Captain Jack had aged in those ensuing five years. After introducing herself as a private detective, Captain Jack had waved her off dismissively, refusing to engage with her. Then he went back to signaling the bartender for another beer.

Iris, who did not suffer fools or rude people lightly, had marched up behind him, tapping on his shoulder and trying more forcefully to explain what they needed from him. He just kept his back to her, not even bothering to turn around and acknowledge her presence.

Poppy had physically pulled Iris back before she had the chance to spin him around and pop him one in the nose.

They knew they would need to try another tactic.

When another younger patron in his early twenties had challenged Captain Jack to a game of pool, the three women watched in awe as the obviously tipsy Captain beat the pants off the kid who was half his age and far more sober. Violet had jumped down from her bar stool and sauntered over and loudly challenged him to a best out of three games.

At first he had refused. "I don't like humiliating women."

Violet giggled. "Oh, don't you worry about that. You certainly will not humiliate me."

He was still eyeing her dubiously when she giggled again and purred, "Are you scared I might win?"

Captain Jack then slammed down his beer on the bar and started vigorously chalking his cue. "Let's play."

What followed was in the true spirit of that glorious day back in 1973 when Billie Jean King crushed Bobby Riggs in a highly publicized tennis match, striking a blow to sexism and ugly male chauvinism.

They didn't even have to play a third game.

The wager had been planned before they had racked the balls for the first game. If Captain Jack won, they would pay him two hundred dollars. If Violet won, Captain Jack would buy them another round of Manhattans and sit down and talk to them about the night Cecily Loudon-Boyce drowned.

Little did Captain Jack know but he was about to go up against the Minnesota Fats of Palm Springs. Much to the utter surprise of Poppy and Iris, Violet was a formidable pool player with a fervent competitive streak.

She annihilated him.

And to his credit, Captain Jack kept his word.

And now, with fresh drinks, they all sat at a quiet corner table away from the noise and chatter with only the music of the country group Boy Named Banjo playing in the background.

Captain Jack scratched his beard. "So Carina sent you to me? She's a good egg. I hope that book she's writing blows the lid off this entire case. People need to start talking about it again, find out what really went down that night."

"You initially told police the same story as Ned Boyce. You corroborated his claim that you had both gone to bed and did not hear anything," Poppy said, locking eyes with him.

Captain Jack nodded slightly. "Yeah, what can I say? Ned was paying my salary. I didn't want to make waves, and I had been drinking a lot that night, so maybe I just imagined what I had heard."

Iris leaned forward. "Which was?"

"I had just gone down to my cabin after going through my check list, making sure the anchor was secure, things like that. I took a sleeping pill because I have terrible insomnia, got in my bunk, and had barely closed my eyes when I heard them fighting up on deck."

"Ned and Cecily?" Poppy asked.

"They were the only other two on board. It was pretty loud and heated. I heard a couple of glasses smashing. It got so intense at one point I almost went up on deck to break it up, but then I heard a splash and it got real quiet. It was eerie. I was so drowsy at that point from the rum and pill, I thought I might have dreamt the whole thing. Next thing I knew, I was waking up, the sun was up, and I heard someone pacing back and forth up on deck. I went up and that's where I found Mr. Boyce worried about Cecily. He said she had never come to bed after he left her the night before and that she wasn't on the boat. I suggested that maybe she had slept in the guest stateroom and taken the dinghy to shore for breakfast early, but Mr. Boyce had already called the restaurant and the manager told him she had not seen Mrs. Boyce since yesterday. That's when I started to worry and told Mr. Boyce we should call the Coast Guard or police, but he said no, they wouldn't do anything until it had been twenty-four hours. But by noon, he finally gave in and we called to report her missing."

Poppy frowned. "Did you ever ask Ned about the fight you had heard the night before?"

Captain Jack shook his head and splayed his fingers on the table. "I know, I should have, but this was my first hire as a captain, and I was desperate to stay on the boss's good side, and like I said, he was paying me well. Very well. I hadn't made that kind of money in my whole life. I'm not saying it was right, that's just where my head was at the time."

"Have you stayed in contact with Ned Boyce?"

"I spoke to him only once after that day. He called me to make sure we were telling the police the same story. When I told him I was a little foggy about the whole night, he helped me fill in the blanks . . ."

"To line up exactly with what *he* was telling the police," Poppy noted.

"Yeah, pretty much. After his wife's funeral, he sold the boat. Too many painful memories, he said. So I was out of a job."

"Why change your story now after all these years?" Poppy asked.

Captain Jack shrugged. "I don't know, maybe I should've spoken up earlier, but I think I had convinced myself that the memories from that night, hearing the two of them arguing and then the splash, that they weren't real. They were just somehow conjured up in my intoxicated brain. But now, after reliving the events of that night so many times in my head for all these years, I've come to the conclusion that they *were* real, they really did happen, and I can no longer stay silent."

"Did you go to the police?" Iris asked.

"Yes, but they weren't very interested in what I had to say. The case was closed and now I was trying to change my story. They didn't take me seriously at all, which is

why I'm hoping Carina's book might generate some renewed interest."

Poppy sipped her Manhattan, set the glass down, and
then stared intensely at Captain Jack, who gave her a half
smile. "So now you believe Ned Boyce killed his wife."

"Without a doubt."

He didn't even hesitate.

Chapter 7

Not even the considerable acting talent of Meryl Streep could disguise the shock on Serena Saunders's face when Poppy rattled off Ned Boyce's financial net worth in the outdoor garden patio where they were having Sunday brunch with Iris and Violet.

Serena shot out an arm, grabbed for her Bloody Mary, and guzzled it down, wiping some tomato juice off her upper lip with the white linen napkin that had been resting in her lap. She then cleared her throat. "I beg your pardon?"

Poppy repeated the figure.

Serena sat back and placed a hand over her rapidly beating heart.

"Surely you knew," Iris said skeptically.

Serena shook her head. "No, I did not. Of course I knew he was well off. The house alone is worth millions, but . . ." She stared off into space, then turned and zeroed in on Poppy again. "How much did you say?"

Poppy repeated the number for a third time.

Serena patted her chest lightly with her hand, trying to calm herself down. "One point three billion? Billion? With a *B*?"

"Yes, give or take a million or two," Poppy said.

"I-I had no idea," Serena sputtered. "And here I thought he might be marrying me for my money so he could pay the hefty property taxes on that humungous house."

"You two never discussed money *ever*? How much you're both worth?" Poppy asked.

Serena forcefully shook her head again. "No. Never. We both assumed the other was financially independent so it was never really going to be an issue." She paused, staring at the stately, light-adorned ficus tree that stood a few feet away from them before returning her gaze to Poppy one more time. "You're absolutely certain? *B*? As in *billion*?"

Iris sighed, annoyed. "How many times must she say it?"

Violet, who was sitting next to her at the table, nudged Iris's shoulder. "Until it finally sinks in. Give her a break, will you, Iris? It is quite a lot to take in at once."

Serena flagged down a passing waiter and raised her empty Bloody Mary glass. "I'm going to need another one of these. And bring these ladies more champagne. We need to celebrate."

"Yes, ma'am," the young good-looking waiter said, smiling as he headed off, and Serena's eyes lingered perhaps a moment too long on his impressive youthful derrière.

Poppy, Iris, and Violet all took notice but wisely said nothing.

"Well, given this new information you three have brought to my attention, I guess brunch is on me," Serena said giddily.

Poppy could see the news was finally settling in from the perceptible dollar signs in Serena's eyes.

"That scamp," Serena chuckled playfully. "I mean, I always knew he was well off, but he's always been a bit cagey in discussing just how well off. Now I know!"

"You're an heiress!" Violet chirped.

Serena took a sip of her chilled gazpacho with Maine lobster with her soup spoon. A wide smile crept across her face. "I suppose I am. I never thought at my age I would ever marry again, let alone become an insanely rich woman. Can you imagine?"

"Just to be clear, the bulk of his money is not from his business. He inherited from his late wife, Cecily. He must have told you about her," Poppy pressed.

Serena waved her off. "Yes. In passing. But at the risk of sounding crass, I honestly couldn't care less where it comes from."

Poppy's inclination was to suspect that this had all been a ruse, a plan put into motion by Serena to give everyone the strong impression that she had been completely clueless about Ned's massive wealth, when in fact she had known all along and was just covering her tracks to fend off any accusations that might come her way that she was just a gold digger.

But Poppy could sense Serena was not faking it.

She was genuinely surprised.

Stunned, even.

And now her imagination was exploding with all the exciting possibilities this newfound wealth could bring into her life.

The waiter returned with their drinks, setting them down in front of each of them.

"Enjoy, ladies," he said, sliding the drink tray under his arm and turning to leave. Serena could not resist stealing another quick peek of his backside as he went to take an order at a nearby table. Then she snapped out of her lascivious thoughts and raised her glass.

"Shall we toast a job well done? I must say, the Desert Flowers Detective Agency has exceeded my expectations."

Iris and Violet lifted their flutes of champagne, but Poppy abstained for the moment.

"There is one more thing we need to discuss," Poppy said, trying not to sound ominous but not succeeding entirely.

Serena raised an eyebrow. "Oh?"

Poppy took a deep breath. "How much do you know about Cecily?"

Serena shrugged. "Not much. I know she drowned in a tragic boating accident a while back. It took a long time for Ned to get over her. He loved her deeply. But now, I'm happy to report, he's ready to move on . . ." She held her Bloody Mary in the air, eager to toast to something. "With me!"

"Cheers," Violet cooed, clinking her flute with Serena's glass. They all took a sip except for Poppy, who left her flute sitting on the table in front of her.

Serena sighed. "What's wrong, Poppy?"

"Are you aware of the disturbing rumors that are floating around out there?"

Serena's whole body stiffened. "Rumors are not facts."

Iris and Violet nervously went back to eating their crab cake Benedict and banana-stuffed French toast, respectively.

Poppy nodded. "Yes, I agree. But we have talked to enough people involved who have very strong opinions about Ned's role in his late wife's death that I believe, at the very least, are worth a little more investigation."

"To what end?" Serena sniffed, her breezy tone vanishing.

"So we can be absolutely certain that Ned Boyce had nothing to do with Cecily's drowning."

"The police ruled her death an accident. Why shouldn't we take their word over a bunch of gossipy strangers?" Serena huffed.

"I would hardly call the captain of the boat who was there that night and Cecily's own sister strangers," Poppy said, trying not to push Serena too hard.

"What exactly are you getting at here, Poppy? Just come out with it," Serena groaned, a little annoyed. "What do you want?"

"I would like a little more time to look into these allegations, uncover some more definitive information, so you can proceed without any doubt in your mind whatsoever."

"The wedding is next week," Serena said in a clipped tone.

Poppy hesitated before plowing ahead. "Which is why I think it might be prudent to postpone the wedding, at least until we—"

Serena had heard enough. "Absolutely not! I paid you to satisfy my concerns about Ned, and you have done just that. All you need to do now is email me the bill and I will Venmo you your fee and then we will be all squared away."

Poppy knew she should stop talking, but the little voice inside her head just would not allow her to do it. "Serena, I'm only thinking of your well-being."

"And I appreciate that. Especially given our checkered history. But read my lips, Poppy. I am marrying Ned. It's full steam ahead. This boat captain and the sister, they're obviously lying! Who knows what their game plan is? Maybe it's a scheme to extort money from Ned in order to make them go away. That's a real possibility, especially if he's as rich as you say he is. He might pay a healthy sum just to get them out of his life. It's not worth the nuisance of their obviously false accusations."

"You're right. But wouldn't it be worth it just to—?"

Serena was having none of it. She wanted this matter closed. She slammed the palm of her hand down on the table, startling all of them into silence. She took a deep breath before she spoke. "Like I said. Full steam ahead, Poppy. I am marrying Ned, as planned. And if you disapprove, then don't come to the wedding. But it's happening. On schedule. In Ned's grand and marvelous backyard." She then turned to Iris and Violet. "I hope you two will still come."

Poppy reached out and touched Serena's hand. "Serena, I would never boycott your wedding. Of course I will be there."

Serena gave her a relieved smile. "Good. I'm happy to hear that. And don't worry. I know Ned's heart and he's a kind, loving, adoring man."

Iris gulped down the rest of her champagne. "A kind, loving, adoring man with a billion dollars."

Serena could not stop herself from erupting in a fit of euphoric giggles.

How could she not?

She was on the verge of becoming a billionairess.

Chapter 8

"Matt, I feel utterly ridiculous accompanying you to your audition with Warren Ashmore," Poppy scoffed, sitting in the passenger seat of Matt's Prius as they tooled up the winding road in the Las Palmas area of Palm Springs to Warren's home.

"I'll tell him you're my good luck charm," Matt said, unfazed. "He won't care. He adores you. And who knows, maybe there's a part in the movie for you, like last time."

He was referring to another case the team had worked on a couple years ago when they were trying to smoke out the stalker of the star of a Netflix remake of *Palm Springs Weekend*, and the director, a longtime Poppy Harmon fan, had cast her in a meaty supporting role.

"Absolutely not! Never!" Poppy insisted. "My days behind the camera are officially over!"

"Never say never," Matt said with a side wink.

It had been Matt's idea to bring Poppy along when she expressed the desire to talk to Warren Ashmore about his best golfing buddy, Ned Boyce. Despite Serena's insistence that as far as she was concerned the case was closed, Poppy could not resist pressing on, at least until she was reasonably certain Serena was not marrying a murderer.

Warren's vintage Spanish Colonial–style home was not nearly as opulent or expansive as the neighboring properties, which dwarfed it, but the house had charm to spare and a lovely front yard landscape dotted with palm trees, aloes, and potted prickly pears in front of the structure's white-washed walls adorned with lush bougainvillea. To Poppy's surprise, pounded into the decomposed granite walkway leading to the house was a For Sale sign. Matt pulled up to the curb and then hopped out, mentally preparing himself for his audition. Poppy followed close behind, remaining silent, not wishing to interrupt his process.

After Matt rang the bell, the door swung open almost immediately. They were greeted by Warren himself, who lit up. "Poppy, what a lovely surprise!"

"I am just here for moral support. I promise to stay out of the way," Poppy said.

"Nonsense, I'm happy you're here! We can relive old times once I'm done with Matt," he said, ushering them both through the door.

The inside of the home was sparse. Most of the walls were bare. There was very little furniture in the large open living room, just a white leather couch and a flat screen TV on the wall. Some moving boxes were stacked in a corner.

Warren seemed to read Poppy's mind. "I'm in the middle of moving. It's time for a change. I wouldn't mind finding a home in Thunderbird where I'll be closer to my favorite golf course."

"I'm sure this place will be snapped up in no time," Matt said.

"No doubt. I'm already entertaining a few offers."

Poppy glanced around, taking in the sweeping square footage, speculating this property could sell for at least two and a half million. Depending on how much Warren owed on the mortgage, he could be in line to net a fortune.

"Can I offer either of you a drink?" Warren asked.

"No, thank you, Warren, I'm fine," Poppy said.

"I'll take a water, if you've got one. Sometimes I get dry mouth when I'm nervous," Matt said.

Warren chuckled. "There's no need to be nervous, Matt. I've seen your work. And I'm mightily impressed. This is just a formality the investors are insisting upon."

Warren's reassuring words did not have the desired effect. Poppy could see Matt fidgeting and starting to sweat. He desperately wanted this part.

Warren gently took Matt by the arm. "Why don't we go into my office? I've got a camera set up in there. Poppy, make yourself at home. This won't take long."

"Of course. Take all the time you need."

The two men disappeared down the hall.

Poppy wandered around a bit, marveling at the elegant porcelain Moroccan backsplash in the kitchen, making her way into a lovely dining area with a view of the backyard, which boasted a luxury pool and spa and soothing waterfall against the backdrop of the soaring San Jacinto Mountains. On the Spanish-style solid oak handcrafted dining table were more moving boxes. One was open, and unable to resist, Poppy stole a glance to see what was packed inside. There were stacks of framed pictures and on top, much to her delight, was an old photograph from 1987, the year she had shot the *Valley of the Dolls* remake co-starring Serena and directed by Warren. Warren sat in his director's chair, legs crossed, a cigarette dangling from his mouth, flanked by Poppy and Serena.

It had been taken almost forty years ago.

My God, Poppy thought to herself, *I look so young.*

As she stared at the photo, memories began flooding

back of that tense and fraught time in her life, and one traumatic afternoon in particular, which changed the course of her relationship with Serena, an incident she had tried for so long to bury and forget. But now, looking at this photo, she could not help but go back to that fateful day in her mind.

Hollywood, California
January 1987

Poppy had already soured on what she thought might be a career-boosting role playing the bright-eyed Anne Welles originally played by Barbara Parkins in the 1967 adaptation of Jacqueline Susann's smash hit novel. Although the critics had lambasted the film mercilessly, audiences flocked to see it, making a financial windfall for 20th Century Fox. ABC was now hoping to create ratings magic with an all-new TV version to celebrate the upcoming twentieth anniversary of the film. When her agent called with the good news that the network, studio, and director all wanted her to play Anne, it was like a gift from the Hollywood gods. She had just wrapped three seasons playing loyal secretary Daphne on Jack Colt, PI, and this would be an opportunity to show her range in a more dramatic role, prove to casting agents that she could do more than just furrow her brow and say, "Please be careful, Jack" as her handsome mustachioed boss set out to take down the bad guys every week in prime time. She was also excited to bond with her two co-stars, Serena Saunders playing Neely O'Hara and Kate Farrell playing the naive sex kitten Jennifer North. On their first day on set, Kate had sent Poppy a beautiful bouquet of roses with the note "Looking forward to working with a living Doll!"
It was a lovely gesture, from a lovely new friend.

Poppy and Kate had dinner together whenever Poppy had found herself in Beverly Hills where Kate and her studio executive husband still lived to this day.

But if Poppy had hoped for the three women to form a sisterly bond, those dreams were dashed the moment the mercurial Serena Saunders blew onto the set like a Category 5 hurricane, making outrageous demands and alienating the crew with her tardiness and tantrums. But she reserved most of her venom for Poppy. Serena had arrived already carrying a grudge, and Poppy could not understand why. Serena was pleasant enough, or at least tolerant of Kate, but whenever Poppy was around, Serena's mood instantly darkened.

When Poppy came out of her trailer that first morning of shooting to film the scene where Anne brings Neely some talent agency papers to sign, she simply said to everyone, "Good morning! Isn't it a lovely day?" Serena had rolled her eyes and spit out, "There's nothing good about a day when we have to listen to your prissy Pollyanna good manners!"

It was as if she were channeling Bette Davis, who barked some similarly rude comment to Celeste Holm on the set of All About Eve.

Poppy guessed Serena wanted to emulate the difficult but talented iconic Davis by abusing her co-stars, and it appeared Poppy was to serve as the perfect punching bag.

After an entire morning complaining about her lighting and her itchy costume and Poppy's lackluster line readings, it was time for lunch, and Poppy retreated to her trailer to catch her breath and cry her eyes out without giving Serena the satisfaction of seeing her tears, which Serena would have considered a victory.

Poppy opened her tiny fridge and took out her tiny plastic container of tuna salad and began stabbing at it with her plastic fork as she turned on the small color TV and watched news coverage of President Reagan at the Berlin Wall, demanding the Soviet leader end the era of a divided Germany "Mr. Gorbachev, tear down this wall!" She had barely taken a bite of her tuna fish when there was a knock on the door.

"Come in, it's open."

The door swung open and Warren Ashmore poked his head in. "I just wanted to check on you and make sure you're not rattled by this morning."

Poppy felt a wave of relief.

At least she was not alone in noticing Serena's incorrigible behavior.

She was also not going to let anyone know just how deeply upset she truly was. She wanted to be considered a professional, there to get the job done, no matter what was thrown at her. So she was determined to reinforce her steely resolve.

"I have dealt with my share of divas, Warren. Serena's nowhere near the worst."

Warren smiled. "I'm happy to hear that. I heard the rumors, but you never fully prepare yourself until you are confronted with the reality. She's an even bigger bitch than even I had expected."

"Why did you hire her?"

"Because in many ways she is Neely—insecure, a little unstable, certainly unpredictable . . ."

"And with an undeniable mean streak," Poppy sniffed.

"You're not wrong. But if she can deliver all of those qualities on film like she does in real life, then I've done my job. No matter what hell she puts us all through, at the end of the day, it's all about the final film."

He was right.

Poppy wanted this movie to succeed just as much as anyone else. She yearned to be the Queen of the TV Miniseries in the 1980s like Jaclyn Smith, Lindsay Wagner, and Valerie Bertinelli.

Warren vaulted up the rickety metal steps and inside Poppy's Star Waggon, slamming the door behind him. She was a bit taken aback by the sudden move and sprang to her feet, setting down the container and fork on the Formica table.

Warren took another step closer. "I just want you to know, Poppy, that whatever happens, I have your back."

"Thank you, Warren," Poppy said hesitantly.

He took another step closer.

"And if you ever need anything, anything at all, I'm here for you."

She did not feel the situation warranted another thank you, but his face was so close to hers and he did not seem to have any sense of personal space. Poppy felt uncomfortable and awkward and just repeated again, "Thank you, Warren."

She was about to take a step back, away from him, when she felt his arm sliding around the small of her back, pulling her toward him. Before she had a moment to react, his lips were pressed onto hers and he was forcing his tongue into her mouth.

She found everything about this revolting.

Just then, she heard the door to her trailer swing open and a woman's voice chirp, "I'm sorry if we got off on the wrong foot this morning, dear . . ."

Then just horrified silence.

Poppy instantly pushed Warren away, who had this unsettling grin on his face. Her eyes darted to Serena, who stood in the doorway, trembling, enraged. Without saying another word, she backed away and stalked off.

Poppy shoved Warren even farther away. "What were you thinking? Now you've done it!"

Warren's grin faded, replaced with mortification. "I am so sorry, I thought—"

"Whatever you thought, you thought wrong."

"Poppy, please forgive me. I completely misread the situation. I feel so embarrassed."

Poppy wracked her brain, trying to remember a moment, any moment, when she gave her director the slightest impression that she was romantically interested in him. She had endured this type of behavior before. There were a string of lecherous directors on Jack Colt who assumed just because Poppy was a young single woman, she was ripe to be plucked. The Casting Couch was like a game in Hollywood, expected to be played. But Poppy was having none of it. If her career depended on how many times she had to lie on her back, then she would chuck it all and go work as a bank teller.

The reason she did not quit was Warren Ashmore.

Unlike most powerful men in Hollywood, he truly showed remorse over misinterpreting the signals. Most spurned directors would sabotage her performance or cut down her role in the editing room, bad-mouth her as difficult all over town, do everything in their power to blackball her in the industry, all to soothe their wounded egos. But not Warren Ashmore. He bent over backward trying to be on his best behavior for the remainder of the shoot. He even called Poppy's agent to explain what had happened and how it had been all his fault. It was a noble gesture and a much needed boost because Serena Saunders spent the rest of her time shooting Valley of the Dolls spreading malicious rumors about Poppy, how she was sleeping not only with her director but half the male cast and crew, how the director was favoring Poppy over her and Kate because of his illicit affair with her. When the production wrapped three weeks later, Poppy had completely forgiven Warren and vowed never to speak to Serena Saunders ever again.

Present Day.

Poppy smiled, staring at the photo.

That's why she still had a soft spot for Warren Ashmore, despite the ill-advised pass he had made in her trailer all those years ago. He was a gentleman who was not afraid to admit his mistake.

"How old were you in that picture?" Warren said, hovering behind her.

Startled, Poppy spun around.

Warren stood a few feet away, Matt just behind him.

"Twenty-eight, twenty-nine. I remember at the time I was so terrified of turning thirty. I was so worried my career would be over. It was such a different time in Hollywood."

"You were gorgeous then, you're gorgeous now," Warren said, smiling.

It did not come off as creepy.

His comment seemed genuine.

Friendly.

Not the least bit suggestive.

Poppy's eyes flicked to Matt. "How did it go?"

Warren answered for him. "He nailed it. As expected."

Poppy lit up. "Then?"

"I just need to get the investors to sign off and then we can negotiate a contract."

Poppy raced to Matt and gave him a warm hug. "Oh, Matt, I'm so proud of you!"

"I still can't believe this is all happening," Matt said. "I better go call my agent. Warren, do you mind—?"

"Of course not. Go outside by the pool so you can have some privacy."

Matt giddily bounded outside.

Poppy set the framed photograph of her, Warren, and Serena from the 1980s back in the moving box. "That photo brings back a lot of memories."

"Not all bad, I hope."

Poppy smiled. "Of course not."

"Who would have thought that Serena Saunders would someday come roaring back into my life and marry my best friend?" Warren laughed, shaking his head.

"She treated you just as badly as she treated me, so how do you feel about that?"

Warren shrugged. "Frankly I had forgotten all about her awful behavior on that set. Maybe I mentally blocked it. Trauma victims will sometimes do that."

Poppy smiled knowingly.

"Serena and I ran into each other at a charity event a few months ago and I introduced her to Ned, so basically this whole wedding is my fault."

Poppy raised an eyebrow. "So you really don't approve of the marriage?"

Warren gave a wry smile. "Like I said before, Ned's a good friend."

"Do you put any stock in the rumors swirling around about Ned's involvement in the death of his wife Cecily?"

"Ha! Absolutely not! Ned's one of the most honest and upstanding men I've ever had the privilege to know, and I am not going to listen to the rantings of a couple of kooks! The captain's a hopeless drunk, and the sister, have you met her? She needs to be locked up in a loony bin!"

Harsh words indeed.

But Warren was going to stand by his buddy Ned no matter what. Poppy, on the other hand, was decidedly on the fence, which meant this whole ugly business warranted further examination, in her opinion.

Matt had returned to the living room from outside where he had just finished the victorious call with his agent in LA, having overheard the latter part of their conversation. "Well, for what it's worth, it's pretty obvious to me that Ned Boyce is madly in love with Serena, so I don't suspect she is in any real danger from him."

"At least not yet," Poppy muttered. "But I agree. His feelings do appear genuine. I just hope they will stay happy together."

Warren clicked his tongue and shook his head woefully. "Frankly, I worry less about how Ned will treat Serena and more about how that old battle-ax Serena will treat sweet old Ned. Poor sod has no clue what he's in for after he says I do."

Poppy could not have agreed more.

Chapter 9

Poppy could hardly imagine that this was the same Captain Jack, the bleary-eyed downtrodden drunk they had encountered at the Rusty Nail just days earlier. But here he was, hair combed, face shaved, wearing a clean polo shirt and tan chino shorts and deck shoes. There was even a whiff of cologne in the air. Possibly Eternity for Men, if Poppy had her fragrance right. He actually cleaned up pretty nice.

Even more surprisingly, Captain Jack appeared, at least on the surface, stone-cold sober.

When Captain Jack had contacted Poppy by phone the previous day, imploring her to set up a meeting between him and her client Serena Saunders, his words were slurred and she could hear loud music playing in the background. He was obviously calling from a bar. She had declined his request and hung up. But he proved persistent, leaving four messages begging her to let Serena know that he wished to speak with her before her wedding day. Poppy had not returned any of his messages until she finally spoke to Serena, who had been unexpectedly open to the idea.

"Why not hear what that broken-down old slippery sardine has to say? It might be fun!"

Poppy had advised against it, but like old times when they were bitter rivals and could not agree on anything, the more Poppy pleaded her case, warning her Captain Jack might have some hidden agenda, the more Serena warmed to the idea of getting in the same room with him. After all, she was dying of curiosity to know anything about her husband-to-be, even the sticky, uncomfortable parts.

So Poppy had arranged an afternoon sit-down at the Desert Flowers garage office. Matt was waiting at home on pins and needles for his deal to appear in Warren Ashmore's new film to close and had begged off, but Iris and Violet, along with tech whiz Wyatt, were all eagerly in attendance in case there were any unexpected fireworks.

Poppy had been careful not to offer any alcohol as they sat down, and to his credit, Captain Jack did not ask for any, just a bottle of water, which she happily delivered to him. Once he screwed off the cap and took a swig, wiping his mouth with his bare forearm, did he finally get down to business.

He offered a crooked smile to Serena, who sat opposite him on a couch flanked by Iris and Violet, who stared at Jack with blank expressions like an on-duty Secret Service detail. Wyatt sat at the desk in the corner of the room, quietly observing. Poppy perched on a stool next to Captain Jack.

There was a marked tension in the room.

"Thank you for seeing me, Ms. Saunders. I sure do appreciate you giving me a little bit of your valuable time. I know you must be very busy preparing for your—"

"You are right, Captain. I am a very busy woman, so why don't you just get to the point?" Serena sniffed.

Captain Jack nodded. "Right. Yes. Sorry. I'm a little nervous. I've never met someone so famous before."

Poppy tried not to take offense, but it hardly worked. He was most definitely dissing her. And at this moment, she liked him even less, if that was possible.

Serena, for her part, softened a bit and Poppy could see a slight uptick in the far corners of her mouth. She was desperately trying not to succumb to the flattery, but a few more considered compliments from the captain and her efforts would be for naught.

"And may I say you have not aged a bit since I first saw you in that TV movie you did about the killer bees with Richard Chamberlain way back when," he said shyly.

"You may," Serena cooed, blushing slightly. "Now, you wanted to speak with me about my fiancé, Ned?"

"Uh, yes," he said, clearing his throat.

He sounded like a smoker, too.

"Ms. Saunders, I have known Ned Boyce many years. As an employee and, yes, even a friend. We shared a lot of good times, bad times, a number of ups and downs, and I always stayed loyal. But what went down that night on the boat with his wife Cecily . . . Well, I just can't stay silent anymore."

"You did for five years," Iris noted with a stinging tone.

"Yes, yes I did. And I will have to live with the consequences of that. Ned convinced me it was part of my job as captain, as his friend, to keep my mouth shut, tow the party line. I know it was wrong now. In fact, I knew it was wrong back then. But I was heavily into the sauce, in debt to a loan shark. I needed that job so badly, I couldn't risk losing it, so I went along with Ned's version of events . . ."

Serena arched her back and frowned. "I think I have heard enough . . ."

"No, wait, please!" Captain Jack begged, holding out

his rough, calloused hands. "I'm not here to hurt you. That's the last thing I would ever want to do. I'm a big fan . . ."

"As you have already told us," Poppy snapped, quickly losing patience.

"I just want you to hear me out, get an idea of my side of the story, just so you have all the facts before you walk down that aisle."

Serena bit her lip, contemplating.

But like Poppy and her Desert Flowers cohorts, her curiosity got the better of her.

"Go on," Serena whispered.

"He's a bad man, self-serving and manipulative . . ."

"Ned? *My* Ned?" Serena scoffed. "I find that very difficult to believe."

"You've known him for what, like three, four months? I've known him for seven years. He's very good in the beginning, draws you in with his generosity and effortless charm, but then, when he's got your trust, that's when things start taking a dark turn."

"It sounds like you saw *The Tinder Swindler* on Netflix," Wyatt chimed in from across the room.

Captain Jack ignored him. "I'm not here to scam you. I don't want anything from you. I just want to caution you, that's all. . . . Look for small signs that will prove what I'm telling you about Ned is on the money."

Poppy could tell that Captain Jack's vigorous attempt at sincerity was slowly starting to work. She could see with her own eyes, Serena beginning to waver ever so slightly. There was a questioning look in her eye. A slight tremble in her lips.

Poppy was more resolute in the fact that something hinky was going on here but she could not yet figure out exactly what.

"He just seems so genuine . . . But maybe I don't know

him as much as I thought . . ." Serena muttered, barely audible.

Captain Jack's ears perked up. "What was that? I couldn't hear you."

"I said he seems so genuine," Serena repeated, a bit louder but still almost unintelligible.

Captain Jack leaned forward. "Yes, good. You said something about not knowing him as well as you thought. Could you repeat that one more time? I got a hearing aid and it's acting up."

Poppy thought his behavior was very odd, but she still could not pinpoint what exactly he was up to.

Wyatt hopped off his desk chair and scurried over to his grandmother Violet and whispered something in her ear. Violet's eyes widened and she smiled at her grandson before turning to face Captain Jack.

Violet's face darkened, a decidedly rare occurrence. "Captain Jack, are you secretly recording this meeting?"

His eyes bulged out. "What? No! Of course not!"

"My grandson seems to think you are. May we see your phone?"

Captain Jack shifted uncomfortably in his chair. "I forgot it in the car. Trust me, I am *not* recording anything!"

Wyatt whipped out his phone and made a call.

Suddenly they could hear the Black Eyed Peas singing a muffled version of their hit "I Gotta Feeling."

Iris sat up straight. "Where is that coming from?"

"His back pocket," Wyatt pointed out. "I'm calling his phone. I took his number when he called Aunt Poppy to set up this meeting."

"My grandson is a genius, don't you agree?" Violet said, smirking.

Poppy held out her hand. "May I please see your phone, Captain?"

"I told you—"

"Now, Captain!" Poppy demanded.

He was outnumbered.

These ladies were not fooling around.

Resigned, he reached into his back pocket and pulled out his phone, tossing it to Poppy, who caught it in her right hand. She glanced down at the screen and saw the audio-recording app in use, and then, frowning, looked up and announced to the group, "Wyatt's right. He's been recording our every word."

"Why? For what purpose?" Violet asked.

"I bet he's making some kind of documentary!" Wyatt chimed in. "Like *The Tinder Swindler* only in this one Ned Boyce is the villain and he's like the hero out to rescue one of his con victims!"

Poppy swung around to confront Captain Jack. "Is that true?"

"It's not like that. Yes, I'm working on a documentary about the drowning, but it's because I'm trying to get the truth out there!"

"By lying to us. By secretly coaxing Serena into becoming suspicious of her fiancé," Poppy growled, sneering at him.

He blanched, then rose to his feet, defensive. "Every word I told her is one hundred percent true!"

"So you're a cheap showman out to make a fast buck at the expense of my happiness," Serena snorted. "You are a hideous, heartless man, Captain Jack, and I never want to see or hear from you ever again."

"I'm telling you, Ned Boyce is not what you—"

Poppy interrupted him. "Iris, would you please show our guest to the door?"

Iris stood up and gripped his arm tightly. "This way . . ."

"I'm not leaving, at least not until you listen—"

Iris squeezed his arm tighter until he visibly flinched. "Either I show you the door or I show you my fist."

There was no doubt in anyone's mind, especially Captain Jack's, that Iris was dead serious, and with her sturdy build and hammy fist, she could probably take him out with one quick punch to the face.

He was not about to test her.

Captain Jack shook his arm free. "No need. I can show myself out."

Then he stalked out the door, slamming it hard behind him.

Serena forced a smile but was on the edge of tears.

Poppy felt sorry for her.

Her resolve to marry Ned had been utterly unshakeable. And yet, with all of these people coming out of the woodwork with unsettling and disturbing tales about him, Poppy could detect a slight hint of uncertainty behind Serena's moist eyes.

It had to be taking a toll.

Chapter 10

Poppy spotted them immediately after parking her car in the lot adjacent to Koffi, a tiny coffee house, part of a chain in the Coachella Valley, set just off Highway 111 in Rancho Mirage. They were seated at a table near the back of the patio, side by side, sipping coffees. Instead of walking over and introducing herself first, Poppy made a beeline inside the store without making eye contact with them to order a double espresso. She felt strongly that she might need a big boost of caffeine for this last minute meeting.

After paying for her drink and picking it up at the counter, Poppy made her way back outside. This time they spotted her. The man waved at her. Poppy sauntered over to them with a warm smile.

She was about to meet Ned Boyce's two adult children from his first marriage.

The man stood up and spoke in an English accent. "Poppy, thank you for taking the time to meet with us. We both really do appreciate it. I'm Gavin."

"Nice to meet you, Gavin," Poppy said, shaking his hand.

"And this is my sister, Willa Boyce-Havens."

Willa smiled and gave Poppy a curt nod but made no attempt to shake hands or verbally greet her.

They were both in their late thirties, early forties, attractive. Gavin struck Poppy as the friendly one, more gregarious. He had a dark tan and resembled his father Ned in looks and how he carried himself. Willa, on the other hand, must have taken after her mother. Blonde, pale face heavily made up, cool, brittle, every movement and look carefully considered. They hardly looked like siblings in Poppy's opinion.

"Please, have a seat," Gavin said, pulling a chair out for her.

"Thank you," Poppy said, sitting down. She took a quick sip of her espresso. "I must say, I was surprised when I received your email. I wasn't aware Ned had children."

"That's probably because Serena likes to pretend we don't exist," Willa sniffed, her words dripping with disdain.

Gavin shot her a sharp look, then turned to Poppy. "Dad married our mother, Catherine, shortly after they met at Leeds University in the UK. He was there studying for his masters and she was an undergraduate. The marriage only lasted a few years. After Willa was born, they divorced and Dad moved back to the States. We stayed in Bristol with Mum, who raised us."

"Does your mother still live in Bristol?" Poppy asked.

"She's dead," Willa blurted out.

"Oh, I'm terribly sorry," Poppy said.

Willa stared at her paper coffee cup with a sour expression on her face.

"Dad was five thousand miles away when it happened, so no one can try to blame him for that one," Gavin cracked.

"I see you've heard the rumors regarding your father's second wife, Cecily," Poppy said.

"Of course, how could we avoid them? Complete rubbish," Gavin snapped. "Our mother died of a rare form of cancer. It was insidious and merciless and took Mum way too soon. We miss her every day, don't we, Willa?"

Willa moved her head slightly, but Poppy could not tell if she was nodding yes or just acknowledging that she had heard her brother speak. Poppy could feel her coldness even in the ninety-five-degree desert heat.

Poppy opted to just converse with the far more amiable brother. "Did you have a good relationship with Cecily?"

"We hardly knew her. Met her once, I think, when I was stateside on business. I don't think Willa ever did meet her, did you, Wills?"

"No, never," she whispered.

"The thing is, we didn't have much of a relationship with Dad before Mum passed. Once he moved back to America, we hardly saw him. After he married Cecily, they came across the pond on a vacation and I met them in London. Willa refused to come."

"Why should I make an effort? He most certainly did not," Willa said bitterly.

"After he left us, Mum struggled a bit financially. I think she thought Dad might help out more, given who his parents were, these famous American film stars, but the truth was, he seemed to forget about us. Years later, after Mum died, he reached out to us and tried to explain that it was Mum who had kept us apart, that he had tried to stay a part of our lives but she wanted nothing to do with him."

"At least that's *his* story," Willa spit out, her eyes devoid of emotion. "And she was conveniently no longer around to defend herself."

"By the time Dad married Cecily, who was fantastically wealthy, he was much more generous with his time and money. If it had not been for his initial investment, I never would have been able to get my own business off the ground. I owe him everything."

Willa pursed her lips and scoffed.

It was obvious she felt she owed her father nothing.

Gavin glanced nervously at his sister, then back to Poppy. "When Cecily died so tragically, Dad was all alone again, and I knew he was hurting, so I came over to spend some time with him and make sure he was okay."

"I am sure that meant a lot to him," Poppy said.

"It did. It turned out to be the best decision I ever made. A real bonding experience. Now, we're closer than ever. It's taking a little more time with Willa to thaw the ice, but she's getting there."

"It's more difficult for me. I have a husband and two toddlers back in Bristol. But I'm here now for his wedding, number *three*, so that's *something*."

"You're right, sis. Baby steps," Gavin said.

Poppy was eager to get to the point of this requested meeting, and she suspected who Gavin and Willa wished to discuss with her. "So I take it you have met Serena?"

"Unfortunately, yes," Willa said, full of scorn.

"Willa, please," Gavin scolded.

Poppy smiled at the sulking Willa. "You're not a fan?"

Willa's icy gaze turned to Poppy. "Those Yelp reviews are correct. You are a very good detective."

So she had a sense of humor.

Would wonders never cease?

Gavin brushed off his sister's comment. "Actually, Ms. Harmon, that's why we contacted you to set up this meeting. We are specifically interested in your new career as a private investigator, and yes, my sister's right, we have done our research and you appear to be a very accomplished one."

"I have a lot of help. I work with an excellent team," Poppy said.

"Yes, well, we, my sister and I, would like to hire the services of you and your team as quickly as possible."

Poppy raised a curious eyebrow. "To do what exactly?"

"We want you to prove that Serena Saunders is a gold digger who is only marrying our father for his money," Willa said matter-of-factly.

Poppy sat back and folded her arms. "You already seem quite convinced. Why do you need me?"

"Because there is always the possibility we could be wrong. But after meeting Serena and getting to know her a bit, we fear her motives for marrying him are rather suspect," Gavin said.

"Serena has her own money," Poppy reminded them.

Willa scoffed again, something she must have perfected over the years. "Not nearly as much as he has thanks to Cecily."

"We were hoping you might do a deep dive into Serena's life in order to prove our suspicions. That way we can present the evidence to Dad before the wedding and he can make his own decision. We just want him going forward with eyes wide open. We're *not* trying to break them up."

Willa's sullen sulky face spoke volumes.

She did not agree with her brother at all.

As far as she was concerned, this whole meeting with Poppy was specifically designed to break them up.

Poppy took a deep breath. "I must confess, Serena is already one of my clients."

"Why does *she* need a private investigator?" Gavin asked, befuddled.

"She hired my firm to investigate your father, dig up any

skeletons in his closet she ought to know about before walking down the aisle."

Willa's mouth dropped open in shock, her first outward show of emotion other than annoyed detachment. "Are you serious? That's the most absurd thing I have ever heard! Serena is afraid Dad was out to take advantage of *her*?"

"Yes, and to be honest, she had no idea just how wealthy Ned was after Cecily's death, which does suggest she is *not* marrying him for his money," Poppy said.

"So why not just do for us what you did for her? A quick background check in order to put our minds at ease," Gavin suggested.

"I am afraid that would a conflict of interest. I'm sorry. I wish I could help you," Poppy said.

"I see," Gavin said, disappointed.

"Perhaps I can refer you to someone else who would be willing to take this on," Poppy offered.

Gavin forced a smile.

This was not the outcome he had been hoping for.

Finding another detective would eat up valuable time.

And unlike Poppy, he or she would be starting from scratch. The whole point of hiring Poppy was because she already had a history with the subject of the investigation.

Poppy downed the rest of her espresso and told the siblings that she would most likely see them again at the wedding. If they did not somehow manage to put a stop to it beforehand.

Because one thing was perfectly clear in Poppy's mind.

Gavin and Willa may have reconciled with their father after many years of estrangement and their incentive to expose Serena Saunders as an opportunistic fortune hunter out to get her hands on their father's money could be purely out of loving concern for his well-being.

But the fact remained, if Ned Boyce did not marry Serena, there would be no greedy stepmother standing in the
way of his two grown children, now a big part of his life,
from inheriting the vast sum left to him from his fabu-
lously rich late second wife, Cecily.

No, they had every reason in the world to push Serena
out of the family portrait.

Permanently.

Chapter 11

Poppy had no clue when she arrived at Ned Boyce's home that she was walking straight into an ambush. When Serena had texted her earlier in the day asking if Poppy could come around after lunch and saying that it was very important, Poppy had just assumed it must have something to do with the wedding since she was no longer working for Serena as a private investigator.

But when Serena opened the door to greet her, Poppy immediately sensed something was up. After giving her a brief hug, Serena grabbed her hand and practically yanked her inside, leading her into the living room where she saw Gavin and Willa sitting nervously on the couch while Ned stood near the fireplace, a perturbed look on his face.

"Hello," Poppy chirped.

It was all she could think to say at the moment.

Gavin forced a smile.

Willa just sat tight-lipped and staring at the floor.

"Thank you for taking time out of your busy day to come see us, Poppy. I know how busy you are," Serena said cagily.

"Not at all," Poppy said, glancing around at all the miserable faces. "Is something wrong?"

Serena huffily folded her arms across her chest. "Yes, as a matter of fact, there is. I requested that Gavin and Willa come here today because I want to ask them a direct question, and I want you here to make sure they don't try lying outright to my face."

"Okay," Poppy said warily.

Gavin sighed and turned to his father. "Dad, come on, why are you allowing her to talk to us like—"

Ned abruptly cut him off. "Shut up and let her speak, Gavin."

His uncharacteristically peeved tone startled both of Ned's adult children, and they both sat back and remained silent.

Serena paused for dramatic effect.

She had always relished keeping people on their toes.

Poppy could hardly stand the suspense.

Finally, Serena took a step toward Gavin and Willa, her eyes narrowing, and asked in a low gravelly voice, "Did you two actually go to my best friend Poppy and ask her to dig up dirt on me? Were you that stupid?"

Both Gavin and Willa shot Poppy furious looks, assuming she had squealed about their meeting, which she most certainly had not. She made it a hard rule that all communication with clients and meetings with prospective clients remain strictly confidential.

"Don't look at her, look at me," Serena growled. "I asked you a question."

Gavin studied Poppy, trying to figure out her role in this unexpected confrontation. He then glanced over at his father by the fireplace, who just glared at him and his sister.

"H-How did you know?" Gavin stammered. "Did Ms. Harmon—"

"For the record, I did no such thing," Poppy insisted. "It is not my place to say anything to anyone about who wants to enlist my services."

Serena gave her a snakish smile. "You have always been the utmost professional in whatever endeavor you choose to do. Frankly I find it maddening. You're my best friend. You should have told me."

"That's not how I operate," Poppy snapped, annoyed at having been dragged into the middle of this knotty family drama.

Serena returned her gaze to Gavin and Willa. She looked as if she was enjoying toying with them like a cat playing with two cornered frightened mice. "It just so happens my hairdresser, Lyla, who also happens to be one of my closest confidantes, is addicted to the lavender black tea latte at Koffi. She goes there every single day to pick one up."

They had been spotted.

Poppy imagined Serena had spies all over Palm Springs.

"B-But how did she know what we were—" Gavin sputtered.

"She was sitting right at the next table. How could she not eavesdrop?" Serena sneered.

Willa had heard enough. "What does it matter? Poppy turned us down!"

"That's not the point," Serena spit out. "I understand you don't like me, that you suspect my motives for marrying your father. I have lived with people making false assumptions about me for my whole life. But what I cannot tolerate is you so cruelly going behind your father's back!"

Oh, she was good.

Turning it around and making the kids feel guilty.

Insinuating that they had somehow betrayed their adoring father's trust.

Poppy could not tell whether Ned was agreeing with her or not because he remained disconcertingly quiet and stone-faced.

"We were just trying to protect him," Gavin squeaked,

keeping one apprehensive eye on his father, trying to gauge where he stood in all this.

"You could have just cut out the middle man and come straight to me," Serena said. "I would have happily provided you with all the financial documents you required in order to put your suspicious minds at ease about me being some desperate debt-ridden harlot chasing after a gravy train!"

Gavin let out a heavy sigh. "Now don't play the martyr, Serena, we never meant to suggest—"

"I have heard enough!" Ned bellowed.

Everyone in the room suddenly froze in place.

Ned marched over so he was towering over his children. "Gavin, Willa, I know I haven't been the best father. I missed out on a lot of your childhoods and I'm going to have to live with that. But I have tried, in recent years anyway, to make up for all that lost time. And we've made a lot of progress. We're so much closer now than we've ever been. Am I at least right about that?"

"Of course, Dad!" Gavin cried.

Willa shrugged. "I suppose so."

"I love you two with all my heart and I always will."

Poppy could feel the "but" coming.

"But," he continued, "I also love Serena. She has given me a whole new lease on life. I never thought I would ever love again after Cecily died. But fate has smiled down on me and brought this incredible woman into my life. And I'm going to do everything I possibly can to hold on to her and protect her. Like it or not, I *am* marrying this woman and she *will* be a part of our lives. And if you can't accept her, if you can't accept *us*, then you might as well leave right now."

Gavin stood up and frantically moved toward his father as if he was going to embrace him. "Dad, believe me, we certainly did not intend to upset—"

"And if you don't, I will cut both of you out of the will in short order," Ned said, eyes blazing.

This stopped Gavin in his tracks.

Neither of them had ever expected a threat like this one.

A tiny, barely audible gasp escaped from Willa's lips.

Then more silence.

Poppy caught Serena trying to suppress a self-satisfied grin.

Gavin took a moment to collect his bearings and then followed through with a hug. "Dad, we just want you to be happy, and if Serena makes you happy, then we can't ask for anything more."

Except for a permanent place in Ned's will.

Gavin turned to his sister. "Don't you agree, Willa?"

"Yes," she mumbled halfheartedly, her cheeks reddening.

"Good. Then this discussion is over," Ned announced. "I have a golf date with Warren and I'm late."

He bounded out of the room, leaving behind his two shell-shocked children and a victorious fiancée who was trying with all her might not to break out into a celebratory jig.

And then there was Poppy, who was still confused as to what she was even doing here, and wondering how soon she could make her escape.

Chapter 12

"Hi, it's me."

Poppy closed her eyes.

It was Sam calling.

She knew what was coming.

"You're cancelling," she sighed.

"Yes, I'm sorry."

"Sam, everyone's already here. We were just waiting for you," Poppy said evenly, determined not to lose her temper.

This was the second time in a week he had pulled out of plans at the last minute.

Poppy had decided after wrapping up the Serena Saunders case that she would host a small dinner party at her home. Just a light Salmon with Bowtie Pasta, a summer salad, a nice bottle of Chardonnay, and her homemade Key Lime Pie for dessert. Given her dining room table only sat six, she had kept the guest list exclusive to her inner circle. Her partners at the Desert Flowers Agency, Iris and Violet and Matt and their crack IT expert, Violet's grandson Wyatt, whom she was watching while his parents were out of town. And then of course there was Sam, her boyfriend. How could she not include him? And yet, deep down, she suspected this might happen.

Why not? He had been cancelling every date they had scheduled on the calendar. And always with a good excuse. So she was looking forward to hearing what he would come up with this time.

"Engine trouble with your truck again?" Poppy asked skeptically.

"No, nothing like that. I've had a pounding headache all day that I just can't shake. I've been popping Tylenol like breath mints, but it just won't go away. I think I might just head back to Big Bear tonight."

Sam's cabin in Big Bear was his solitary retreat away from all the troubles in the world.

And apparently from Poppy.

"I'm sorry this is so last minute. I was really looking forward to seeing everyone and relaxing, but I'm afraid I won't be much fun to be around."

"I understand," Poppy said.

It was a fib.

She actually did not understand.

She wanted to confront him right now and find out exactly what was going on with him. But she had four hungry guests in her living room and she needed to play hostess.

Their serious talk would just have to wait.

"Are you still planning on being my date to Serena Saunders's wedding next week?"

"Of course. I'm sure I will be fine by then."

"Let's hope so," Poppy said with a twinge of sarcasm.

It was not lost on Sam.

"I won't let you down. I promise," Sam said, a little more forceful in his tone. He obviously sensed Poppy's frustration with him.

"Feel better, Sam," she said curtly, ending the call.

Poppy wanted to believe him.

She really did.

But he had been acting so strange lately.

She knew something was up with him, and she was annoyed that he was not willing to just come out with what was bothering him.

She had a sickening feeling in the pit of her stomach.

Thoughts of another woman kept nagging at her.

She had seen no clues or signs that Sam might be seeing someone else, but she had worked enough cases following straying spouses all over the Coachella Valley not to at least entertain the possibility.

Poppy set her phone down on the counter, finished shredding the salmon and adding it to the pasta, and then opened a fresh bottle of Chardonnay and headed into the living room to make sure everyone's wineglasses were full.

Violet was blushing when Poppy crossed over to her and poured her some Chardonnay. Iris was snickering and Wyatt grinning impishly, so it was not difficult to deduce that Matt had just told another one of his off-color jokes. She would have scolded him about doing it in front of Wyatt, but she was reasonably sure that Wyatt had heard much worse at school.

Poppy went around the room, stopping at Wyatt, who was on the couch next to Matt. "More lemonade?"

"No, thanks, Aunt Poppy, it's way too sweet for me. But I wouldn't mind trying a little bit of that wine."

"Uh huh," Poppy said. "There's a can of lime seltzer in the fridge. You can have that."

"Who was that on the phone?" Violet asked.

"Sam," Poppy muttered.

Violet suddenly looked worried. "Is everything all right? He should've been here by now."

"He's not coming," Poppy sighed.

There was a long silence, which made Poppy uncomfortable, and so she quickly continued, "He's not feeling well. He has a headache, so he's decided to drive home."

"All the way to Big Bear?" Iris barked.

Poppy caught Iris and Violet exchanging concerned looks.

Matt leaned forward on the couch, clasping his hands together. "Where was he calling from?"

"I don't know," Poppy said quietly.

"Is he here in Palm Springs?" Matt asked.

"Honestly, I don't know," Poppy repeated, slightly irritated.

Another painful silence.

She knew they were all thinking exactly what she had just been thinking.

He was sneaking around with another woman and had just not worked up the nerve to confess it to her yet.

Or he had some terminal illness and could not bring himself to tell her he had only weeks to live.

Frankly she could not decide which would be worse.

No, dying was much worse.

She was just feeling sorry for herself.

Poppy plastered a bright smile on her face. She was not about to allow her fears to ruin this evening. She had spent way too much time preparing this lovely dinner.

"If you'll come to the table now, we can start with our salads," Poppy said.

Wyatt eyed his grandmother's full wineglass but Violet noticed, frowned at the boy, then scooped it up out of his reach. Matt grabbed the stem of his own glass too when Wyatt's gaze wandered over to it after his grandmother shuffled off to the dining area.

"Better luck next time, bro," Matt joked.

Matt's phone buzzed. He grabbed it from his back pocket and stared at the screen. "It's my agent. Excuse me."

He nervously headed out the sliding glass door to the backyard for some privacy.

Poppy, Iris, and Violet all took their seats at the dining table but could still see Matt outside pacing back and forth, in deep discussion with his agent.

Then there was whooping and hollering and Matt doing a little dance at the edge of Poppy's swimming pool. She half expected him to fall in. Then he came bounding back inside, euphoric.

They all knew what had just happened.

"You got the part!" Poppy exclaimed.

Matt nodded excitedly. "Yes! Warren didn't even have to fight for me. The studio signed off on me after seeing my audition tape. They're closing the deal tomorrow and we start shooting in a month in Colorado!"

Violet jumped to her feet, ran around the table, and threw her arms around Matt's neck. "Oh, honey, I am so proud of you!"

"We all are! Now we can say we know a real movie star!" Iris boasted.

Poppy could see Matt's mind racing.

He probably had a thousand people he wanted to tell.

But he did not want to be rude.

Poppy decided to give him an out. "Matt, we will all understand if you want to skip dinner and call your family and friends with the good news.

Matt gave her a puzzled look. "You are my family. The people I most care about are right here in this room, so let's celebrate together!"

They all raised their glasses.

Wyatt begrudgingly picked up the can of lime seltzer Poppy had just put in front of him.

"To Matt," Poppy cheered. "The next Benedict Cumberbatch!"

"Matt is much cuter than him!" Iris protested.

Poppy noticed Wyatt pouting.

"You can sulk all you want, Wyatt. You're not getting any wine."

"It's not that. I begged Matt to let me negotiate his contract. I know I would've gotten him a much better deal than his agent."

Matt guffawed.

But Poppy knew the kid was right.

With his ingenuity and tenacity, Poppy had no doubt in her mind that Wyatt definitely would have scored a much larger pay day for Matt.

The boy was a genius in so many ways.

A fact his grandmother always loved to tout.

And Poppy was happy to have the enterprising four-teen-year-old on the Desert Flowers team.

Chapter 13

Because Matt's acting career was really starting to take off and he was now becoming more recognizable to the general public with each project, it was becoming more difficult to send him out on undercover assignments for the Desert Flowers Detective Agency. However, Matt still relished the opportunity at every turn, and so when the team decided to take another crack at Captain Jack O'Connell, Matt was ready to suit up.

Captain Jack's story of what had happened the night Cecily Loudon-Boyce drowned was beginning to look a little wobbly with every TV interview he did. He had told Poppy he had been drunk and taken a sleeping pill that night. But on a recent TMZ-type expose show, he claimed to have been clear-eyed and stone-cold sober. He had told Poppy he had spoken to Ned only once after the incident because Ned wanted to get their stories straight. To others, they had been in contact for weeks, if not months later. He had claimed to a reporter to have never met Carina Loudon, Cecily's sister, and yet Carina herself told the Desert Flowers team that not only had Captain Jack done an interview with her for her forthcoming book, she had been the one to point them in his direction to get his version of events.

Captain Jack was either a confused drunk or a terrible liar.

Then there was the handwritten note sent anonymously to Ned that Serena had stumbled across promising that the media attacks on his good name would stop if he just paid fifty thousand in cash. Details of the drop-off would follow. After Serena turned the note over to Poppy, the first name that had popped into her head was, of course, Captain Jack. Carina Loudon would have no need to try to extort any money from Ned, because she was just as rich as he was. It *had* to be Jack. He was wallowing in a dive bar every night, desperate to turn his fortunes around. It *had* to be him!

They just needed to prove it.

Poppy suggested Matt pose as a reporter for one of those *Dateline* true crime TV shows and arrange an interview with Captain Jack. So Matt placed a call to him, pretending to be Tyler Jones with *Top Story*, a real online news site with millions of viewers. There was even a real reporter named Tyler Jones who looked similar to Matt in height and build, but with a buzz cut and goatee, so Matt took a razor to his head and slapped on fake facial hair. Wyatt wired him up so Poppy, Iris, and Violet could listen in on the interview from inside a van parked outside the Rusty Nail bar, where they had agreed to meet.

"I did my research, and you've got a lot of Instagram followers," Captain Jack told Matt as they greeted each other and presumably took a seat at the bar.

"He sounds drunk!" Iris sniffed.

"He's always drunk," Poppy concurred.

"Wyatt, honey, can you turn up the volume? I can barely make out what they're saying," Violet asked.

"I told you to go get your hearing checked, Violet. Why don't you ever do what I tell you?" Iris sighed.

"My hearing is fine, Iris! It just needs to be a little louder! And what about your eyes? You're too proud to get a vision test! You nearly walked into a door yesterday!"

"Shhhh, both of you!" Poppy scolded. "There is nothing wrong with Violet's hearing or the volume! If you both just stopped talking, we could actually hear what's going on inside the bar."

Wyatt snickered. He always found Iris and Violet's constant bickering hilarious.

"I'm happy you agreed to talk to me, Captain," Matt said through the listening device. "And I promise to help get your story out there. I just need for you to sign this waiver that when the time comes, we can put you on camera."

"Oh, sure, yeah, that makes sense," Jack slurred.

They heard some scribbling on a piece of paper.

"Now, why don't you start from the beginning. Tell me what happened that night."

Captain Jack launched into his spiel, the same one he had rattled off to Poppy, but again, there were discrepancies, new details, embellishments from when he had previously recounted the tale to Poppy. First, he was back to having had "a few" cocktails, but no sleeping pill. In this latest version, he actually heard a woman scream before the splash. And although he had told Poppy he and Ned had called the restaurant on shore the next morning to see if Cecily had gone there for breakfast, now he claimed they had not, that Ned had refused to allow Jack to even look for her.

Matt knew all of this.

"That's odd," he said. "Because you told *Dateline* you called the restaurant and they had not seen her that morning."

"No, I didn't," Jack protested. "I wanted to, but Ned wouldn't let me."

"I have it on tape."

"It's not me. You know how they have all these deep fakes now!"

"It's you."

"So I'm a little fuzzy on some details, but I never said I was sober that night!"

"Um, yes you did, to several news sources."

"No, I'm pretty sure I did not. Excuse me. Hal, could I get another drink, please?"

He was starting to get nervous.

Exactly where the Desert Flowers team wanted him.

"I want to help you, Jack, really I do. If Ned Boyce murdered his wife, it's important to all of us that he be held accountable," Matt said.

"Yes, yes, that's right! He does need to be held accountable! That's why I'm doing all of this! I'm doing it for Cecily!" Jack cried.

"Are you?"

Poppy envisioned Matt arching his eyebrow.

"Yes! Of course! Why else?"

"Because my producers tell me that you have been working on a documentary about the case from your point of view that you hope to sell to a major streaming service for a lot of money."

"Oh, that! Well, that went away! There isn't going to be a documentary. The whole thing kind of fell apart, so sorry to blow a hole in your producers' ridiculous theory!"

"I see, so money is not your motive," Matt said.

They could hear Captain Jack gasp at the idea of his character being called into question by some muckraking online reporter.

"I thought this was supposed to be a friendly interview! Your producer, the one with the weird accent, who called me, she promised me you were interested in telling *my* side of the story! If this is how it's going to be, then you can just forget about me going on camera with you!"

The producer in question had actually been Iris on the phone trying to disguise her German accent obviously with middling success.

"This is just a little pre-interview, Jack, just to make sure we are all on the same page, a chance for us to get to know each other a bit before we sit down for the real interview. The last thing in the world I want to do is make you feel uncomfortable."

There was a pause, then a clink as another drink was put in front of him at the bar.

They could hear a slurp as Captain Jack quickly gulped it down.

"Well, good then, it's important we see eye to eye. I don't want any surprises that might throw me off when I'm on camera, you understand?"

"Completely. Which is why it is so important we get everything out in the open now, nail down all the details, so you don't have to deal with any curve balls. Like *this* for instance."

Another pause.

Matt must have slid the note Ned had received in front of Captain Jack, who was now looking at it.

"What's this?"

"The note you wrote to extort money from Ned Boyce."

"I don't know what you're talking about! I wasn't trying to extort anything!"

"It says right there you will stop promoting your false stories about what happened the night Cecily died if Ned pays up."

"*What*? It doesn't say any of that!"

"Your documentary didn't work out, so you decided to

try out a textbook extortion scheme, and once we prove it was you who wrote that note, and trust me, Ned, we *will* prove it, then that's all the cops are going to need."

"Anyone could have written that note! You can't possibly prove it was me!"

"Wrong again. You signed this waiver agreement. Look closely. It's the same handwriting. There are a lot of experts out there who will be able to confirm it in a court of law. You might as well come clean now, because nobody's going to ever believe your version of events after this gets out."

"Who are you? You're not a reporter! Are you some kind of cop?"

Poppy threw open the back doors of the van. "That's our cue!"

"Stay put, Wyatt! We'll be right back!" Violet cried as she scrambled out of the van after Poppy and Iris.

"I never get to do any of the fun stuff!" Wyatt yelled after them.

Poppy, Iris, and Violet hurried inside the Rusty Nail, where they found Captain Jack in mid-meltdown, shouting and pointing a crooked calloused finger at Matt, who had removed his glasses and fake goatee, revealing himself to Captain Jack.

"Calm down, buddy," Matt said, taking a step back in case Jack decided to lash out and take a swing at him. "It's over."

Desperate, Captain Jack reached out to snatch the waiver form he had signed out of Matt's hand, but Matt anticipated the move and quickly plucked it out of reach.

"Give me that!" Jack demanded.

"Take this instead," Poppy said, holding out a business card.

Noticing her for the first time, Captain Jack squinted his eyes, confused. "What—What are you doing here?"

"I came to give you this. Please, be a good boy and just take it."

Captain Jack didn't make a move at first; he was still busy trying to assess the situation, and what was happening to him. Finally, he grabbed the business card out of Poppy's hand and stared at it. "Who's Lamar Jordan?"

"He's a police detective. He's going to be showing up on your doorstep tomorrow morning, probably with an arrest warrant, so make sure you're dressed, your teeth are brushed, and you're ready to go," Poppy said with a smile.

Chapter 14

After a quick debriefing back at the Desert Flowers garage office at Iris's house, where Poppy reassured the staff that it was highly unlikely that Captain Jack would make a break for it because he was so broke he didn't even own a car, Poppy then headed home, exhausted and ready for bed.

She debated calling Sam to check in, but just thinking about him seemed to get her ire up. No, if he wanted to speak with her, he should make the effort to call her himself. She was finished pussyfooting around him and trying to figure out what was on his mind. He would tell her when he was ready, and in the meantime, it was time to just get on with her life.

Poppy was about to turn off Highway 111 on her way to her house in the Movie Colony when it occurred to her that she should call Serena and fill her in on what had happened at the Rusty Nail and how their plan to nail Captain Jack to the wall had gone off without a hitch. Any way you sliced it, this was good news, which she was eager to share.

Serena would undoubtedly be pleased that there was at least one less person working against her happily-ever-after ending with Ned Boyce. She still had Cecily's sister, Carina, and his two suspicious offspring, Gavin and Willa, to contend with, but at least when it came to the loud-mouthed, drunken pain in the butt Captain Jack, his role in the drama was essentially kaput.

Poppy asked Siri to ring Serena's number.

The call went directly to voicemail.

"Hi, Serena, it's Poppy. I have some interesting news I want to share with you. Captain Jack O'Connell will no longer be all over the media spouting his lies about Ned. Call me when you get the chance and I will happily fill you in on all the details."

She ended the call.

Poppy pulled her car over to the curb, still a few blocks from her house. She decided to send Serena a text.

I just left you a voicemail message. I have big news regarding Captain Jack. Call me when you can.

She waited a few minutes.

Still no response.

This was highly unusual for Serena.

She was always glued to her phone and typically responded within seconds no matter what she was doing.

It was almost eleven o'clock at night according to her car's dashboard. Poppy thought Serena had planned to spend the evening at home alone since Ned was out of town on business. She waited some more, her stomach in knots.

This was silly.

There could be a dozen reasons why Serena was not calling her back.

She could be at a dinner party regaling the guests with her spicy Hollywood gossip. Or maybe she was enjoying a late night massage. Or perhaps she had just fallen asleep in front of the TV.

Any of those scenarios was entirely possible.

But just not plausible.

Poppy knew Serena Saunders well enough to know that none of those reasons made any sense.

Serena never stopped glancing at her phone, because she constantly feared she might miss an important call from her manager, who could have a lead on a new acting job.

Poppy found herself pulling the car into a U-turn and heading back east on Highway 111 and up the winding road that led to Ned Boyce's mountaintop home. Serena had given her the gate code when she had first hired her, and luckily Poppy had a very good, if not photographic, memory.

She punched it in, and the massive wrought iron gate slowly swung open. She drove farther up the hill until she was rounding the expansive circular driveway.

There were lights on in the house.

But it was eerily quiet.

Poppy got out of her car and marched up to the front door. She glanced down at her phone in the palm of her hand.

Still no text or call from Serena.

She was about to ring the doorbell but before she had the chance, a loud noise, like the sound of a car backfiring, startled her.

She looked around, confused.

What was that?

Then she heard it again.

It wasn't a car.

Or fireworks.

It was a gunshot.

Two of them.

And they both had come from inside the house.

Poppy frantically tried turning the door handle.

The door was unlocked.

She pushed her way inside the house, heels click-clacking

across the tiled floor of the entryway, as she screamed at the top of her lungs, "Serena! Serena! Where are you?"

Still nothing.

Then, quite suddenly, she heard a third shot, this one much louder coming from the back of the house.

She made her way down the hall to the main bedroom, stopping suddenly in the doorway, gasping as she threw a hand to her mouth.

Serena stood in the middle of the bedroom, in a pink nightgown, staring vacantly into space while clutching a revolver in her right hand.

Just a few feet away, a man's body lay crumpled on the floor, facedown, arms stretched out, his body twisted to one side.

"Serena, what happened?" Poppy cried.

Serena's eyes slowly moved toward Poppy.

She looked at her blankly for a moment, as if she was confused as to where she was or what she was doing.

"Serena!"

Finally, Serena snapped out of her trance-like state and gazed down at the lifeless man on the floor. Her eyes suddenly filled with tears and with a guttural cry, she wailed, "He's dead! I shot him!"

Chapter 15

"Poppy Harmon," Detective Lamar Jordan sighed as he walked through the front door of Ned Boyce's house and spotted Poppy sitting on the couch in the living area next to a distraught Serena. "I would say what a surprise it is to see you here, but to be honest, it's never a surprise when I show up at a crime scene and there you are right in the middle of everything."

"Lovely to see you, too, Detective Jordan," Poppy said. "How is your gorgeous wife, Lynn?"

"Probably wrapping up and freezing the delicious pot roast I had just sat down to eat when I got the call to come up here," he grumbled.

"Please, do give her my best," Poppy said with a smile.

Jordan nodded, then rubbed his eyes with his right thumb and forefinger. "What are you doing here?"

"Serena Saunders is a friend, and I just happened to be coming by for a visit when I heard the gunshots."

"Of course you just happened to come by," Jordan sighed. He turned to one of the uniformed officers by his side. "Where's the vic?"

"In the main bedroom down the hall. Forensics are

already here," the young wide-eyed, wet-behind-the ears policeman reported.

"Who called 911?" Jordan asked the officer.

"I did," Poppy answered before the young cop had the chance. "I found Serena in the bedroom holding the gun and a man sprawled out on the floor . . . dead."

"Okay, Ms. Saunders, would you mind accompanying me to the kitchen so I can ask you a few questions?"

Serena was slumped over on the couch with her hands covering her face, so her words were a bit muddled when she spoke. "Why can't we just do it here?"

"I thought you might prefer a little privacy instead of all the commotion around here," Jordan said, trying to be a little more thoughtful than his typical gruff, hard-nosed demeanor.

"Well, I don't," Serena sniffed. "I want to do it right here." She reached out and grasped Poppy's hand. "And I want Poppy by my side for emotional support."

"Okay, then," Detective Jordan said with another heavy sigh before sitting down in a chair opposite the two women. He reached into his sports coat pocket for a pen and pad of paper. "Can you tell me exactly what happened?"

Serena looked frightened. She glanced at Poppy, who gave her an encouraging smile.

"Go on, Serena," Poppy whispered. "He's here to help."

Serena sat straight up, closed her eyes as if trying to clear her mind, recalling the events as best she could manage in the heat of the moment. "I was just getting ready for bed . . ."

Jordan was scribbling on his pad and then flicked his eyes up toward them. "What time was that?"

"I don't recall, nine, nine-thirty. I usually don't retire until around eleven, but it had been a very long day going over wedding plans and seating arrangements and I was bone-tired. I had already changed into my nightgown and was brushing my teeth in the bathroom when I thought I heard a noise. The water in the sink was running, so I turned it off and listened but I didn't hear anything. When I came back into the bedroom, I decided to call Ned, my fiancé—he's out of town on business . . ."

Jordan stopped scribbling and looked up again. "Where?"

"San Francisco, I believe. He went to see one of his clients. He has a wealth management company."

"Where is he staying?" Jordan asked.

"I believe the Palace, in the financial district. That's his favorite place to stay when he has to go up to the Bay Area."

"Have you called him yet to let him know what's going on?"

Serena slowly shook her head. "No. Everything has been happening so fast. I can barely catch my breath right now."

Jordan went back to scribbling. "Understood."

"I took the liberty of calling Ned when we were waiting for the police to arrive," Poppy interjected. "He's at the airport now, trying to catch the last flight home to Palm Springs."

Lamar grimaced, then turned his attention back to Serena. "And then what happened?"

"I was reaching for my phone on the nightstand when I suddenly heard a loud banging sound coming from out here in the living room."

"Like someone breaking in?"

"No, more like someone bumping into something in the

dark. I had turned off all the lights when I went to bed," Serena explained. That detail stuck with Poppy. She had noticed lights on when she had arrived.

Jordan swiveled his head toward the front door. "I don't see any signs of forced entry."

"That's because I sometimes forget to lock the door. Ned's always getting after me for it. He says it's careless, but we're so far up the hill, who would bother to come all the way up here?"

"It's a ritzy house. I can think of plenty of robbers who would love a crack at this place," Jordan said.

"Plus we have a gate," Serena added.

"That someone athletic could easily climb," Jordan noted.

"Just so you know, the door was unlocked when I arrived as well, Detective," Poppy explained.

Jordan stared at her, almost as if warning her not to speak, but thought better of it because she was obviously keeping Serena from losing it completely. He took a stab at a softer, more compassionate tone with mixed results. "Okay. After you heard the bang, could you tell me what you did next, Ms. Saunders?"

"Yes. I knew Ned kept a loaded revolver in the bedroom closet. On the top shelf in a gun case in the corner. I never thought in a million years I would ever need it, but it was the first thing that popped into my head when I heard a stranger in the house. So I ran to get it. I remember I was having trouble snapping the case open, but the second I got my hands on the gun I heard a rustling sound directly behind me."

"The intruder?" Jordan asked quietly.

Serena, eyes brimming with tears, nodded. "I spun around and he was just standing there, a shocked look on his face, like he was surprised I was there. Me, in my own home. Well, soon to be mine. Right now it still just belongs to Ned."

Poppy thought that was an odd detail for Serena to include.

Who cares if the house technically still did not belong to her? It suggested she may have been spending a lot of time thinking about all the expensive possessions she was about to acquire after tying the knot with Ned.

"He could have thought no one was home and just lucked out that someone forgot to lock the front door," Jordan suggested. "Is there an alarm system?"

Serena nodded. "Yes, but . . ."

"You forgot to arm it."

"Ned's always going on about my forgetfulness."

"Just for the record, did you know the man when you saw him standing in the bedroom?" Jordan asked.

"Of course not! I had never seen him before."

Jordan scratched the dark beard stubble on his face. "Did he say anything?"

"He demanded I give him all my jewelry," Serena sniffed. "Which I found a little funny."

Jordan cocked an eyebrow. "Funny, how?"

"Well, he didn't appear to be armed and I had a loaded gun in my hand. I think I laughed in the moment. Like I would just hand over all my valuables when I clearly had the upper hand in the situation."

Jordan studied Serena's face with his suspicious brown eyes, trying to read what kind of woman he was dealing with, whether she was telling him the truth or not. "If you had the upper hand in the situation, how did he wind up dead on the floor?"

"Because when I laughed, he got angry and took a step toward me. I raised the gun and warned him to stay back. We just stood there for a few seconds, and then he just came charging at me. I thought he was going to try to wrestle the gun away from me, and so I guess I just panicked and pulled the trigger!"

"You shot him and he fell to the floor?" Jordan asked.

"Yes, yes, that's what happened. And then the next thing I knew Poppy came rushing in."

"You shot him once?"

"Yes, I believe so," Serena moaned, wringing her hands in despair.

"There was more than one bullet wound," Jordan said pointedly.

"M-maybe twice," Serena sputtered.

"He had three bullet wounds," Jordan said, eyes narrowing.

"Okay, three times! I don't remember! I was practically catatonic with fear! I could have shot him five or six times! I am sorry I did not take the time to count, Detective! I was terrified he was going to kill me!" She broke down in gasping sobs as tears streamed down her cheeks.

Poppy put a comforting arm around Serena. "It's okay, Serena, he's just trying to get all the facts."

"He's making it sound like I murdered him, the man who broke into this house to rob and maybe murder *me*! I don't know how many times I fired that gun! When he came at me, I just started firing wildly! I wasn't sure I even hit him!"

"Actually, your aim was perfect. Three times squarely in the chest," Jordan said with a sharp look.

Poppy could tell Detective Jordan was not completely buying Serena's story. And with good reason. Serena had just claimed she fired the gun wildly. If she had fired three quick rounds in the chest, the shots would have been in much faster succession. But Poppy distinctly remembered there being a few seconds between shots before she arrived in the bedroom and found Serena standing over the man's body.

After the first shot in the chest, the man would have most likely dropped to the floor immediately. Then why shoot him again? And was she standing over him as she plugged him with the next two bullets?

Poppy feared there was much more to this story than Serena Saunders was at the moment willing to divulge.

Chapter 16

The young newbie officer cleared his throat as he gingerly approached Jordan, who was still jotting down a few notes on his pad. "Sorry to interrupt, Detective Jordan, but Higgins would like to have a word in the . . . other room?" He was flicking his eyes toward the main bedroom where the dead body was still sprawled out on the floor.

"Excuse me, ladies. Don't go anywhere. I will be right back," Jordan said, rising to his feet, stuffing the pad and pen in the inside pocket of his jacket, and marching down the hall.

Poppy, her arm still around Serena, gently squeezed her shoulders. "Can I get you anything?"

Serena, her eyes bloodshot, her mascara smeared, glumly shook her head.

Poppy thought it strange that Serena still had makeup on. She had told Detective Jordan she was going to bed. Would she not have removed her makeup? Or perhaps there was a simple, reasonable explanation. She just did not have the opportunity to wash her face clean before she heard the man breaking into the house. Poppy decided not to make an issue of it for the time being.

Poppy stood up. "You sit tight. I'm just going to take a quick peek at the crime scene."

Serena was dabbing at her eyes with some tissue. "Are you allowed to do that?"

"I guess I am going to find out," Poppy said, casually strolling past several officers, who were so busy chatting about an LA Dodgers baseball game that they barely noticed her. She tiptoed down the hall, acting as if she was going to make a sharp right into one of the bathrooms but continued on to the door to the main bedroom and poked her head in. Detective Jordan's back was to her as he spoke with another plainclothes detective. Jordan towered over the much shorter Detective Higgins, a little pudgy with a kind face.

Poppy's eyes scanned the body on the floor.

He was probably in his late twenties.

Classically good-looking with dark hair and angular features.

And he was extremely well-built.

His tight black T-shirt accentuated his arm and chest muscles and six-pack abs.

He undoubtedly spent a lot of time at the gym.

Before Serena Saunders shot him three times.

Poppy desperately wanted to eavesdrop on Jordan's conversation with his fellow detective, Higgins, but they were both speaking in low voices and it was difficult to make out exactly what they were saying. Poppy took a tentative step inside the bedroom and then moved silently across the carpeted floor, just a little closer to Jordan.

Poppy could finally hear the two men talking.

"No identification?" Jordan asked.

"No wallet, no driver's license, nothing. And no car outside. Either he hiked up the hill or someone dropped him off. We did recover a gym membership card that might help us identify him." Detective Higgins pressed the card in the palm of Jordan's hand. Jordan squinted as he looked at it, and then reached into his pants pocket to extract some portable readers. Once he slid them up the bridge of his nose, he was able to see what was on the card. "Muscle Buddies in Rancho Mirage. No name on the card, just a membership number. Should be enough to ID him."

Muscle Buddies.

Poppy made a mental note of it.

"May I help you, ma'am?"

Startled, Poppy swiveled around to find herself face-to-face with the young officer whose job it was to keep everybody away from the crime scene.

Poppy had to think fast on her feet. "It's been a very stressful evening, and I just wanted to freshen up a bit in the bathroom."

The officer pointed a thumb over his shoulder. "You passed it. It's back that way."

"Is it?" Poppy asked, acting all wide-eyed and innocent. "This is such a big house, I guess I just got turned around."

"I can escort you there if you want," the officer said sternly.

"Thank you, you're very kind, but that won't be necessary," Poppy said before glancing back to see Detective Jordan glaring at her, fully aware of what she was doing.

"Officer Healey would be more than happy to take you out of here, right, Don?"

The young officer gave a vigorous nod and then gripped Poppy by the upper arm and quickly led her out of the bedroom. He practically frog-marched her back down the hall, but before they reached the bathroom they heard the front door slamming and Ned Boyce's booming voice.

"Serena, my God, are you all right?"

Poppy scurried toward the living room.

Officer Healey called after her. "I thought you were going to freshen up!"

Poppy stopped in her tracks, then slowly turned around, eyes fuming. "Young man, do you wish to imply that I do not look presentable?"

He gave her a sudden confused, apprehensive look. "W-what? N-No, ma'am, I just thought you wanted . . . You look fine, more than fine, you look lovely, ma'am."

She nodded approvingly, then spun back around and hurried to the living room, where she found Ned with his arms wrapped around Serena, holding her tight and comforting her.

"It's all right, love, I'm here," he said, slowly stroking her back with his hand.

"It was just so awful. I have never been more scared in all my life!" Serena choked out between sobs. "I was sure he was going to kill me!"

"I'm just relieved you knew where I keep my gun. Otherwise the outcome might have been very different."

"I wasn't even sure how to use it. I just closed my eyes and started pulling the trigger!" Serena wailed.

That was not quite true.

Poppy clearly remembered Serena telling her once that she had guest-starred as a teenager in the last season of Barbara Stanwyck's classic Western *The Big Valley*, in which she played the rebellious daughter of a wanted gunslinger. The Barkley family, led by matriarch Victoria Barkley, played by Ms. Stanwyck, takes her in and she causes quite a ruckus becoming obsessed with handsome half-brother Heath, played by Lee Majors, and accidentally shooting younger sister Audra, played by Linda Evans, while taking target practice on the ranch. Serena always boasted that she had learned how to use firearms for that role, and according to the stunt coordinator, she had turned out to be quite a good shot.

But Poppy found no reason to call her out on this right now when Serena was such a fragile mess.

But she certainly would make a point of doing so at a later time.

Serena rested her head on Ned's chest, sniffing and quietly crying. Ned had moved his hand up from her back and was now delicately stroking her hair.

Serena closed her eyes as she desperately held on to her fiancé. "Darling, do you think it might be a good idea to postpone the wedding?"

Ned stopped petting her and took a step back, shocked. "What?"

"I don't want this casting a dark cloud over anything. Maybe we should wait until things die down, at least until the police figure out who that man is and how he came to pick this house—"

Ned cut her off. "Absolutely not. I know who he is. He's just a dumb, two-bit thug who thought he could get away with robbing my house, but now he's dead and we no longer have to worry about him."

"I just don't want this incident to be the only thing people are talking about on our wedding day."

"I have long stopped caring what other people think, my love. I have been waiting forever to find my true soulmate, and I'm not going to put up with any more delays. I love you and I want to make it official. I will not allow some random burglar, or my greedy children, or my unhinged ex-sister-in-law, to disrupt our special day. The wedding is going ahead as planned. And that's my final word."

Poppy could see Serena's eyes suddenly glisten with adoration as she threw her arms around Ned's neck. "I love you, darling!"

"I love you more!" Ned cooed.

And then they kissed passionately.

It would have been the perfect scene from the ending of a mushy romance novel if not for the disconcerting fact that the bride-to-be had plugged a man with three bullets, a man who was now lying dead on the floor of the loving couple's bedroom.

Poppy knew in her gut that this was far from Serena's much desired happy ending.

This story was just beginning.

And was about to take a very dark turn.

Chapter 17

Lying flat on her back on a fixed incline bench, hands gripping the barbell, Poppy took a deep breath and, using all her strength, lifted the sixty-five pounds up over her head. Her arms were on fire. She had not exercised like this in years. She maintained her figure with a weekly yoga class and a couple of swimming aerobics sessions at her usual gym. And of course, she loved to hike the many walking trails in Palm Springs during the season before the temperatures got too hot, but this sweaty workout was definitely a challenge.

Her arms suddenly got a little wobbly and she thought for a moment she might lose her grip and drop the heavy weight, driving the steel bar down on top of her and crushing her windpipe, but suddenly she felt the presence of a man standing close behind her. His tanned fingers closed over hers, helping her steady the barbell.

"Looks like you need a spotter," the man said in a deep, soothing voice.

Her eyes fluttered upward and stared at a young man in his late twenties, dark hair and features, in a tight-fitting red tank top and black Speedos, both of which highlighted his Greek-god-like muscled chest, legs, and arms.

"Thank you," Poppy gasped, sitting up on the bench. "You arrived just in time. I think I bit off a little more than I could chew."

"Always happy to help such an attractive lady," he said with a playful wink. He relieved her of the barbell and effortlessly set it down in its rack like it was made of plastic and not heavy steel. "I'm Amir."

"Hello, Amir. I'm Poppy," she said, reaching down for her towel and dabbing the sweat off her face.

"I haven't seen you around here before," Amir said, flashing a stunning smile of perfectly white teeth.

"I just joined today," Poppy said. "I'm trying to get back into shape."

"You look lovely to me, but it's always a good idea as we get older to keep those muscles strengthened."

He certainly was a charmer.

But that was no surprise.

Muscle Buddies was full of young handsome trainers who were especially attentive to their older female clientele, which made up about 95 percent of the gym's core membership.

"Have you found a personal trainer yet? Because I would be happy to work with you," Amir said, reaching out and taking Poppy's hand, helping her stand up from the bench.

"That's very sweet. It's only my first day. I'm still getting the lay of the land, but I will certainly keep you in mind."

He held on to her hand, like he did not want to let go, then he plucked a card from the inside seam of his Speedos and pressed it into the palm of her hand, folding her fingers closed with his and squeezing it slightly. "Here is my number. Call me anytime. Day or night."

Then with another wink he sauntered off, spying another woman, this one in her seventies, who had just blown through the front door, a little frazzled, late for her session. "Amir, I am so sorry, I got a flat tire and Triple A took forever!"

Amir bussed her cheek. "You're fine, love. I got your text." He gently caressed her back. "Relax, you're here now. We have plenty of time."

Poppy watched as Amir laid his hands all over the woman, gently massaging her shoulders. She seemed to relish the attention. They whispered in each other's ears as she pulled a bottled water out of her purse, and then they strolled over to the row of treadmills to warm up.

"That's Addie Harold," a woman said. "Her husband, Carl, owns half the grocery stores in Alabama. Big, big bucks."

Poppy turned to find a friendly blond woman, about the same age as Poppy, hovering behind her right shoulder. She was a little chunky, with a cherubic face decorated with hot pink lipstick, very cute and perky. Before Poppy had a chance to introduce herself, the woman shot out a hand. "Carol Blansky. Snowbird from Toronto. Are you a new member?"

"Yes, as of today," Poppy said, shaking her hand. Poppy glanced around at all the members working out. "I had no idea this was a women-only facility."

"Technically, it's not," Carol said. "But you only have to take a look at the trainers to understand why so many women sign up. There are men who train here, but they're mostly gay."

Poppy glanced around at the five trainers working with their clients. Although Addie was now huffing and puffing on the treadmill, her cheeks flushed as Amir cheered her on, stroking her arm that grasped the side bars, most of the other women in the gym were just standing around chatting with the young men like it was a singles bar for "cougars," a term referring to older women who preferred the company of younger men. Poppy despised the

term and found it degrading to women. It was not like
they labeled men who liked younger women as anything
other than just men.

In the far corner, Matt, also in tank top and Speedos
and looking just as fit as all the professional trainers, was
in the middle of doing a series of chin-ups, counting off to
himself, already at 110. He had been the first to join Muscle Buddies after the police had found that membership
card on the body of the John Doe whom Serena had shot
at Ned Boyce's house. Although certain Detective Jordan
already had the name of the dead man, he certainly was
not about to share what he knew with Poppy, so she had
decided to do a little independent investigation to find out
just what he was doing at the Boyce house that night.
And if there was some kind of connection, to either Serena or even Ned, Poppy was determined to find out exactly what it was. Unless he was just a supremely unlucky
burglar who had the misfortune of picking the wrong
house to rob.

The gym's owner, Kal, had enrolled Matt, complimenting his looks and sparkling personality. At first Matt
thought the owner was hitting on him but then quickly realized it was more of an assessment, an observation he
seemed to be filing away in his mind for future use. After
working out two days at Muscle Buddies, Matt had reported to the Desert Flowers team that he had a weird vibe
from most of the trainers, who all seemed to be vying for
the attention of the older female clients. Matt kept to himself for the most part during his first two workouts,
watching the trainers fall all over themselves to flirt with
the women and keep them engaged as they flitted through
their training sessions, with less of an emphasis on muscle
toning and more of a focus on keeping up a festive party
atmosphere.

That's when they decided it might behoove their progress if Poppy applied for membership at Muscle Buddies in order to zero in on exactly what was going on at this gym/social club.

"See anything you like?" Carol asked, giggling. "They have all types here. Dark and handsome. Blond and frisky. Bald and domineering. It's like an all-you-can-eat buffet. A little something for everyone."

Poppy surreptitiously pointed at Matt. "He looks nice."

"He's not a trainer. He just joined the gym a couple of days ago. But Kal has his eye on him. I think he may be grooming him."

Poppy cocked an eyebrow. "Grooming him for what?"

"To be a trainer. In case you hadn't noticed, you basically have to be a young man with movie star looks in order to work here."

"Yes, I can certainly see that. Why is that so important?"

Carol shrugged. "Eye candy is good for business, I guess. But get ready. If they see you working out alone, they will be all over you like bees to honey wanting to, quote unquote, help you be the best you that you can be."

A six-foot-five Adonis blew through the door with shoulder-length brown hair and waved in their direction.

"I gotta go! Nicholas is here! Look at him! It's like he just walked off the set of *Game of Thrones* after slaying a dragon. Chat with you later!"

Carol bounced over to give her gladiator a warm hug.

Poppy continued with some hand weights but was constantly interrupted by trainers introducing themselves. There was Mick with the ocean-blue eyes. Julio with a woody-spicy scent from his cologne. Even the gym owner himself, Kal, made a play for Poppy's attention, running down a list of exercises that would enhance Poppy's already shapely figure.

"I have an opening on Wednesday, if that works for

you," Kal said. Like his trainers, Kal too was exceedingly handsome. She guessed he was of East Indian descent, on the shorter side, compact, buff, and gorgeous.

"If you don't mind," Poppy said, eyes flicking toward Matt working out in the corner alone. "I want *him*."

Kal glanced over. "Oh, that's Matt. I'm afraid he's not a trainer here. He's just a client."

Poppy bit her bottom lip. "How disappointing. I've been watching him all morning. I had my heart set on him."

"I suppose I could talk to him. He certainly knows his way around a gym. Maybe he's looking for some kind of arrangement."

"He certainly would be worth the drive every day from the Thunderbird Estates."

Poppy's instinct was to paint the picture that she was a wealthy woman willing to pay anything to get what she wanted. And mentioning the Thunderbird Estates, where the wealthy Carina Loudon lived, would certainly go a long way toward achieving that objective.

Kal's friendly smile widened.

Her comment had landed just where she wanted.

He placed a hand on the small of her back, rubbing it slightly. "Let me see what I can do."

Then he bounded over to talk to Matt.

Matt was on the payroll in less than an hour.

And by the time of their first session playing trainer and client the following morning, Matt had already used his access as an employee to log on to the gym's computer and find the member ID of the man Serena Saunders had gunned down in her bedroom just a couple of nights earlier.

Justin Cambry.

Chapter 18

Poppy huffed and puffed on a treadmill alongside Carol Blansky, who was glued to her phone reading a text message. Poppy was at the moment busy eyeballing Addie Harold, who seemed to be having an intense conversation in the corner of the gym with her impossibly sexy trainer, Amir. Addie had her arms around a big green medicine ball, and she appeared distressed as Amir quietly tried to calm her down. He took her by the arm, attempting to steer her through the gym exit so they could go outside for some privacy while they talked. But Addie was having none of it. She shoved the medicine ball into Amir's stomach, nearly knocking the wind out of him, and fled the gym. Poppy could see through the large picture windows Addie running to her classic Porsche, hopping in, and after a few false starts trying to rev it up, backing out of her parking space, nearly clipping a passing Volvo, and then speeding off down Sunrise Way.

"What do you suppose is going on with Addie? She looked very upset just now," Poppy said casually.

Carol glanced up from her phone. "She did?"

"Yes, I think she had some sort of disagreement with Amir."

Carol shrugged. "Probably just a lover's quarrel."

Poppy turned to Carol, surprised. "I thought Addie was married."

"She is. But word around the gym is, Addie's head over heels in love with Amir and has been sneaking around seeing him behind her poor husband Carl's back."

"Do you think she's going to leave her husband?"

Carol threw her head back and howled. "Are you kidding me? And throw away her rich and famous lifestyle that she's enjoyed these past thirty years? No way! I'm sure this whole sordid affair is just a temporary distraction! She's too spoiled to leave everything Carl has to offer. It would be a totally stupid move on her part!"

"If that's the case, then she should be more careful. There are a lot of loose lips around here. Word could get back to Carl," Poppy said.

"Are you married, Poppy? I don't see a ring."

Poppy glanced at her hand and thought carefully before answering. "I am. I just take it off when I exercise."

"Is he as rich as Addie's Carl?"

"We're comfortable."

"That means *uber* rich. It's just so unfair," Carol pouted. "Why?"

"My dear departed husband, Oscar, has been dead and buried nearly a decade, I'm footloose and fancy free, I can date whomever I want, and do you think any one of these trainers has bothered giving me the time of day? Of course not! I think I'm at least as pretty as Addie Harold, for goodness sakes! What does she got that I haven't got?"

About forty million dollars in the bank, Poppy surmised in her head.

"I've been dropping hints to Nicholas ever since I hired him as my trainer, but once he heard I was on the market and totally available, now he won't give me the time of day! It's always strictly professional. How annoying is that?"

"Consider yourself lucky. Younger men can be quite a handful."

"It sounds like you speak from experience," Carol cooed, excited to hear more.

"I worked in Hollywood for years. Sexy young men were a dime a dozen, many with questionable motives. You have to be careful, especially if you're an older woman with means."

"Speaking of actors, I saw a movie on Netflix last night. I could've sworn your trainer, Matt, is it? There was an actor in it who looked *exactly* like him!"

Poppy's guard suddenly went up.

It had to be Matt.

Probably the remake of the campy 1960s classic *Palm Springs Weekend* that he had done a couple of years ago. Poppy had played a minor role in the film as well during a case, but Carol had not seemed to notice her at all. Instead of lying, Poppy thought it best to confront this wrinkle head on.

"I'm sure it was him. Lots of struggling actors have second jobs to make ends meet until they get their big break."

"I suppose you're right." Carol's eyes twinkled. "Speak of the devil."

Matt, in a tight-fitting tank top and short shorts, strolled over to them, winking at Poppy. "Hey, beautiful, ready to work up a sweat?"

Carol giggled. "Does it have to involve cardio? I can think of plenty of creative ways we can accomplish the same goal!"

Matt gave her an impish smile.

"I know, I know, you were talking to your client," Carol moaned, punching a button and slowing her treadmill down to a stop. "I'm going to grab a water before Nicholas gets here. Enjoy your workout, Poppy. Don't do anything I wouldn't do."

"I'm sure that gives us a wide berth then," Poppy joked.

"Later," Carol sang as she bounced off.

Poppy leaned in and whispered in Matt's ear. "Just so you know, I told Carol I have a husband, so now that's part of my cover."

"Good because Kal's been hounding me to find out your marital status. The moment you requested me as your trainer, he's been a whole lot nicer, taking me under his wing and showing me the ropes. He told me to get to know you better, flatter you, become an indispensable confidante."

"What for?"

Matt shrugged. "I don't know. He won't say just yet. I think he wants to wait until he knows he can trust me. But I get the feeling he's grooming me for something, so we just have to keep flirting until we figure out what the game is."

Matt playfully stroked Poppy's cheek.

She instantly recoiled. "Matt! I think of you as my son!"

Matt leaned in and whispered, "We're undercover, Poppy. We have to make it look convincing."

Poppy glanced around to see Kal by the reception desk staring at them. She quickly covered by tossing her head back and giggling coquettishly, then teasingly slapping away Matt's hand and saying loud enough for Kal to hear, "You are incorrigible."

Kal had a self-satisfied smile on his face as he walked back into his office. In his mind, Matt was making progress with charming the client.

Matt waited for Carol and her Adonis trainer, Nicholas, to pass by them to a rubber mat, where Nicholas ordered Carol to do a hundred sit-ups, pressing his hands down on her sneakers as she tried lifting herself up off the floor, heaving as he counted off, "One . . . Two . . ."

Matt turned his back to them and checked the time on Poppy's treadmill. "Another five minutes, Poppy."

Poppy sighed and continued marching at a brisk pace.

"I sent Wyatt the password to the gym's computer system. He downloaded the entire client list from the past two years. Serena Saunders was not on it."

"So if Serena is lying and actually did know the man she shot, she did not meet him here."

Matt nodded. "But he picked up on a curious trend. The majority of the clientele here do seem to be women, but there is a very high turnover."

"Don't most gyms have people sign up to get fit and then drop out when they can't and don't want to commit the time it takes to get into shape?"

"Absolutely, but nothing like this. Scores of women have signed up here but then cancel their memberships just a few months later. It's odd. Normally people drop out after a year or so, but not at this rate. And there were no refunds issued to any of them who purchased a yearlong membership. It's like they just wanted to wash their hands of this place and didn't care about the money."

"What do you suppose happened?"

"Beats me. But Iris and Violet are out right now paying a visit to a few of them, hoping to find out."

Much to Poppy's chagrin, Matt completely committed to his role of badass personal trainer, forcing Poppy through a rigorous hour of weight lifting, jumping jacks, and push-ups. Then, when her time was up, Poppy, exhausted, grabbed her bag from the ladies' locker room and, with every muscle on fire, stumbled out of the gym to her car.

Matt lingered, chatting with a few of the other trainers so it would not appear as if the two of them were leaving together. They had agreed to meet back at the Desert Flowers office.

Poppy had arrived first with Matt following just a few minutes later. Iris and Violet were already there waiting for them, enjoying a tasty chilled glass of Chablis to celebrate the end of a tiring workday.

As Poppy poured herself a glass in the kitchenette and Matt grabbed a sparkling water from the fridge, Violet recounted what they had learned. "We paid a visit to four recent clients of Muscle Buddies, all of whom cancelled their memberships, and not one of them wanted to talk to us."

"One rude woman slammed the door in my face and nicked my nose. I may have a lawsuit!" Iris bellowed.

"We asked why they left the gym so abruptly, but all of them seemed scared to say anything," Violet said, sipping her wine. "One woman actually started to hyperventilate when her husband came to the door and asked what we were doing there. She had this look of terror on her face."

"That's the one who nearly broke my nose!" Iris snorted.

"So whatever the reason was, they definitely do not want their husbands to find out," Poppy said.

"This is sounding more and more like some kind of blackmailing scheme," Matt suggested. "A band of gym training gigolos seducing wealthy older married women, then threatening to tell their husbands if they don't pay up."

"It all makes sense. And maybe Justin Cambry was a part of the operation," Violet piped in.

"Until Serena Saunders plugged him full of holes!" Iris exclaimed.

"Do you think Justin was blackmailing Serena and she decided to bump him off before he had a chance to expose her to Ned?" Violet asked.

"It's possible," Poppy said, her mind wandering.

But if that was the case, why wasn't Serena's name in

the membership directory? Or had she somehow managed to delete it? Or did she hire someone else to erase any evidence of her connection to Justin Cambry? Or was she telling the truth about the random break-in and had no connection to Cambry at all?

So many questions were still left unanswered.

And Serena's wedding to Ned Boyce was now only days away.

Chapter 19

Ten years ago, when Poppy was still with her now late husband, Chester, retired and already living in Palm Springs, long before she had the notion of getting her private investigator's license, she had walked into Alvin Albertson Jewelers on El Paseo in Palm Desert with her diamond wedding ring looking to get it repaired. She had taken it off her finger while getting a manicure at a local beauty salon and accidentally dropped it on the floor just as a woman passed by her and stepped on it with the heel of her shoe, heavily damaging it.

Of course the rock-hard diamonds were still intact. But the prongs that held it were crushed, the setting warped, and the shank or band was bent out of shape. Her manicurist assured her that Alvin Albertson was the best person in the Coachella Valley to repair it. Poppy wasted no time and drove straight to his shop, hoping Alvin might be able to return the ring to its former glory before Chester found out what had happened.

When she had swept through the front door of the shop, Alvin's jaw had nearly dropped to the floor. That's when Poppy knew he recognized her from her work in television. The response was usually the same. Both men and women had fond memories of her character Daphne, the spunky, loyal secretary to the macho, mustachioed *Jack Colt, PI*. But Alvin had been a superfan. He gushed that he had recorded the entire series on VHS and watched them over and over again whenever he was depressed or anxious. He even claimed that if you gave him a number between one and sixty-eight, he could tell you exactly which episode it was, although Poppy declined to test him on this rather disturbing skill. His favorite episode was number thirty-two in the second season, the one where Daphne went undercover in a women's prison to help an old sorority sister from college who was railroaded on a trumped-up drug charge by a judge with a vendetta against her father, an arch rival who was on the short list to become a State Supreme Court justice. It was a very dramatic episode with a breathless prison escape scene involving trigger-happy deputies and barking bloodhounds, but all Poppy could remember from shooting that particular show was trudging through muddy waters handcuffed to Judith Light, who was guest-starring as her college friend. It was unusually cold that day in Burbank and neither Poppy nor Judith could stop shivering, and yet, both professionals, neither ever complained.

Alvin was beside himself that such a big TV star was in his tiny jewelry shop tucked away in a near deserted mini-mall, which Poppy found charming. Her manicurist was proven to be right. Alvin was a miracle worker. She had her ring back the next day, looking the same as it did when Chester officially slid it on her finger on their wedding day. Since then, Poppy had been one of his most loyal clients. Whatever the task, earring post replacement, broken clasp on her string of pearls, Alvin attended to all her jewelry needs.

But as she arrived today, she knew her request would most certainly test Alvin's love and loyalty toward his favorite TV actress of all time. And she was fully prepared to be turned down flat.

Alvin was behind a glass case examining a gemstone under his microscope while an expectant customer eagerly awaited the verdict. She noticed the customer's body tense up when Alvin frowned, picked up the stone, and handed it back to her. "I'm afraid it's a fake. Costume jewelry. One hundred percent silver-plated brass."

The woman flushed with anger. "That lying SOB! I knew he was trying to convince me he was rich! Never date anyone you meet at a swap meet!" She hurled the piece into the trash can. "Thank you, Mr. Albertson!" Then she stormed out past Poppy, the bell on top of the door ringing as she slammed it shut behind her.

Alvin lit up at the sight of Poppy. "Look who is gracing my shop with her blinding beauty. It's as if the clouds just lifted and the sun is shining brightly."

"You're such a smooth talker, Alvin."

"What can I do for you today? Is that necklace clasp giving you trouble again?"

"No, I don't need anything repaired. I'm looking for a necklace. An expensive one."

"How expensive?" Alvin asked, curious.

"The most expensive one you've got."

"I have just the piece," Alvin said excitedly, running into the back and returning a few moments later with a black case, gently setting it down and opening it.

Poppy gasped at the sight of a dazzling necklace made of small ovals, teardrops, rounds, and candy-shaped gemstones such as London blue topaz, rock crystal mother of pearl, and black onyx triplet. A genuinely breathtaking piece of jewelry. After gazing lovingly at it, she glanced up at Alvin, who seemed to be reading her mind.

"Eighteen karat. Worth about twenty-five thousand dollars, give or take a few hundred."

"My goodness, it's absolutely stunning," Poppy whispered admiringly.

"Is this a gift? I surely hope not. That would be an utter shame. I can think of no better place where this piece belongs than around your pretty neck."

"It's for me."

"Excellent! Now you have the option of paying with an installment plan, or I can charge the whole amount to your credit card right now."

Poppy was not even sure there was enough credit on her card to put down half that amount. "I would love nothing more than to be able to buy it, but I simply can't afford it."

Alvin shot her a confused look. "I'm afraid I don't understand."

"I was hoping I could borrow it."

The blood drained from his face. "Borrow it?"

"Just for a day. Less than a day. A few hours at most."

"Why do you need it for such a short time? Is it for some kind of an acting job?"

"You might say that."

She was not lying. It was an acting role of sorts. She wanted to convince Kal, the owner of Muscle Buddies, that she was a very wealthy woman with very expensive taste in jewelry, a fact that might put her in the crosshairs of this potential blackmailing scheme that she and the Desert Flowers team suspected might be operating out of the gym.

"Are there any big stars in the movie?" Alvin asked before quickly adding, "I mean, besides you, of course!"

"Yes, but I can't talk about it. The project is very hush hush."

Matt had just done a co-starring part in another big Dwayne Johnson Hollywood action movie in Europe that had yet to be released, so he might be considered a big star.

There was no point in elaborating until she had Alvin on the hook.

She could see he was wavering.

He was enamored with show business. She watched his eyes flick back and forth as he debated with himself how smart a move it was to be lending her the most valuable piece of jewelry in his entire shop. Poppy's instincts told her he would ultimately bend to her will. After all, it was not just anyone asking this huge favor. It was Daphne, his favorite character from *Jack Colt*.

"I suppose it would be all right for just one afternoon. It's insured, after all, in case anything catastrophic happens."

"Nothing will happen. I promise to guard it with my life."

He carefully picked up the necklace and handed it to her. "Why don't you go in back and try it on in front of the mirror in my office?"

She took the necklace and draped it delicately over her hand as she walked through the black curtain leading to the back. She stood in front of the mirror and gently put it around her neck, snapping the clasp closed. She felt like the Queen of England wearing the crown jewels.

This would be perfect.

If this did not make her Kal's next mark, nothing would.

Suddenly she heard the bell on the door ring as someone entered the shop.

"Good afternoon, sir, how may I help you?" Alvin chirped.

"I'm looking to buy a necklace for a special someone."

It was a man's voice.

A voice she clearly recognized.

Sam.

What was he doing here?

"There's a lady in the back trying one on that's worth twenty-five grand."

She heard Sam's distinctive laugh. "That's a little out of my price range. My budget's a grand, fifteen hundred tops. You have a really pretty gold pendant on sale here I heard about. Let me take a look," Sam said.

Poppy crept over to the black curtains separating the office from the shop and peeked through.

It was definitely Sam.

And he was browsing all the jewelry in Alvin's expansive glass case of inventory.

She saw Alvin pull out a gorgeous necklace and present it to Sam. "Is this the one? A solitaire pendant pear-shaped necklace, yellow gold, will set you back twelve hundred dollars."

"That's it. Perfect. Can you wrap it up? It's a gift."

Sam was not the type to haggle.

A gift?

Her birthday was coming up.

Sam was obviously going all out buying her a present.

She could not believe how romantic this gesture was, which made her now feel foolish for thinking their relationship was in trouble. Any man about to break up with a woman would not buy her a twelve-hundred-dollar necklace.

Chapter 20

Poppy and Matt sat across from Detective Jordan, who was in his office at his desk, hands clasped together, a half-eaten roast beef sandwich and cold cup of coffee next to him. Matt had placed his phone on the desk in front of Jordan and pressed the play button on the screen as the recording began.

"So what's the game?" Matt's voice asked on the recording.

"It's simple, really," Kal explained. "You get friendly with your wealthier married clients, lure them in with a little flattery, and then, when the time is right, go in for the kill, get them into a compromising position and make sure you get it on video."

"What if they resist?"

"You move on to the next mark. But trust me," Kal assured him. "Nine times out of ten they're willing to play. Most of them can't stand their husbands and crave any kind of romantic attention."

"Then you threaten to tell their husbands if they don't pay up?" Matt asked on the recording.

"We don't ask for a check. Too easily traceable. Plus there is a good chance their husbands would notice the money missing. So we have them claim they lost something valuable, usually jewelry, like an expensive pair of earrings or that flashy necklace I saw your client wearing this morning."

The ploy had worked perfectly.

When Poppy had sashayed into Muscle Buddies flaunting Alvin's necklace worth twenty-five grand and Matt had mentioned to Kal that he would be willing to do anything to get his hands on some extra cash to pay off his mounting debts, Kal had made the calculation that Matt was ready to be brought into his blackmailing operation. When Kal had asked Matt to meet him at a bar around the corner so they could talk, Matt made sure the recording app on his phone was already running so they would have a full confession to present to Detective Jordan.

Detective Jordan grimaced, shaking his head, disgusted by the whole scheme.

Kal continued on the recording. "Then they file a claim for the lost valuable and when the insurance company pays up, they hand the money over to us. They're not out anything, they still have the jewelry, and their husband is none the wiser. So no one gets hurt."

"Genius. Has anyone ever threatened to go to the police?"

"Not yet. If they do, they're basically fessing up to insurance fraud and could go to jail. That's not a good outcome after a short-lived fling with your personal trainer. So they've all obediently kept their mouths shut and just moved on with their lives."

Which would explain the high cancellation rate of gym memberships.

"So what's the next step?" Matt asked on the recording.

"How open do you think your client is to a more physical relationship?"

"It's been pretty innocent so far, but I think I can get her there," Matt assured him. "She's always complaining about how her husband is always out of town, and how lonely she gets. The best part is, she suspects he has a mistress so I can work the whole 'this is a way to get even' angle."

Poppy winced while listening to the recording. It was disturbing to hear Matt sound so cold and wicked, the opposite of his true personality.

He was a very good actor.

"Perfect," Kal said. "The key is to make her feel special, like you never entertained the idea of dating a client before, that she's the first woman you would ever consider breaking the gym's code of conduct by getting into a romantic relationship with a client. So how much do you think that necklace she was wearing is worth?"

"Twenty-five grand."

There was a pause.

"That much?"

"I asked her. She was happy to tell me. I get the feeling she's got a lot more where that came from."

Poppy could picture Kal beaming.

"Welcome to the team, Matt."

Matt reached across Detective Jordan's desk and pressed the stop button on his phone app. "That's pretty much it. I will email you the whole recording so you have it as evidence."

"Thank you," Detective Jordan said. "This is very helpful. I will, however, ignore the fact that you two staged your own undercover sting operation without consulting me, but it wouldn't be the first time you Desert Flowers people have taken matters into your own hands."

"We were investigating another matter and just coincidentally stumbled across this. It happens," Poppy said with a sly smile.

"Yes, I am constantly reminded of that fact," Jordan said, grimacing. "But this is good. I think I might drive over to Muscle Buddies myself once I get an arrest warrant issued."

"And please, Detective, when you interrogate Kal, be sure to ask him about Justin Cambry."

"The kid Serena Saunders shot, yes. We know he worked out there for a brief time. You think he might have been a part of the operation and Serena was a target?"

"There is no record of Serena ever being a member of the gym, but Kal might know something more," Matt said.

"Got it," Jordan said, eyeing his roast beef sandwich. "Now would you two get out of here so I can finish my lunch?"

Poppy and Matt stood up and filed out of the office as Jordan tore off a hunk of roast beef with his mouth.

Matt drove Poppy home, where she tried calling Sam. She got his voicemail. Then she puttered around the house doing some light housework before taking a much needed nap. When she awoke, it was already dusk and she checked her phone to see if Sam had called her back.

He had not.

But there was a message from Detective Jordan.

"Hi, Poppy, Lamar Jordan here. We got Kal in a holding cell. He tried lying when we arrested him, pretending not to know why he was being put in handcuffs, but when we played the recording for him, he saw no other way out than to cop to the whole thing. So good work. Oh, and as for Justin Cambry, Kal admitted he was a gym member but never a personal trainer, nor did he play any part in the whole blackmail scheme. I ran a check on him, and he does have a rap sheet, mostly petty theft and fraud, but I don't see any reason why Kal would lie to protect him. So my gut's telling me that he probably broke into Ned Boyce's house to rob it, expecting no one to be home, but found a very scared Serena Saunders in the bedroom with a gun. In my opinion, it sounds like a simple case of self-defense."

Serena would be thrilled to know that, at least where the police were concerned, she was in the clear.

Chapter 21

"Surprise!"

Poppy stood startled, mouth agape, in the threshold of Ned Boyce's house as at least thirty people, many of whom she did not personally know, beamed excitedly, knowing she had not suspected a thing.

And she definitely had not.

In fact, she specifically remembered asking Serena not to acknowledge or celebrate her upcoming birthday, which was still a few days away.

But Serena had gleefully ignored her wishes, and just when Poppy had arrived home and was planning to call Serena with the good news that Lieutenant Jordan had no plans to investigate her further in the death of Justin Cambry, Serena had called her first. She sounded a bit frantic and out of breath, asking Poppy to come to the house right away, that it was an urgent matter they had to deal with and it just could not wait until morning. Poppy was exhausted and just wanted to go to bed, but she was also curious as to what was so important it required her immediate attention. So she got in her car and drove straight up the hillside to Ned Boyce's home, just as she had the night she had heard the gunshots and found Serena standing over the body of Justin Cambry.

She had pulled up in the circular driveway, and jumped out, scurrying to the front door. All the lights were on in the house. There were several cars parked nearby that she did not recognize. She rang the bell and when Serena opened the door, ushering her inside, she was suddenly assaulted by a loud crowd yelling, "Surprise!"

Serena jumped up and down quite happy with herself for successfully keeping Poppy in the dark about her plan to throw her a surprise birthday party.

"Did you suspect anything?" Serena asked, gleefully clapping her hands.

"No, I most certainly did not," Poppy said, trying to keep her cool, noticing a catering company buzzing about hard at work setting out a feast of food and a handsome man with a white shirt and bowtie tending an open bar. Serena and Ned had certainly gone all out.

"Let me get you a drink," Serena purred, flitting off toward the bar.

Poppy spied Iris and Violet hovering in the back of the crowd and made a beeline for them. Violet wilted when she saw the frustrated look on Poppy's face.

"We had nothing to do with this, we swear. Right, Iris?" Violet cried.

"I told her no party!" Iris insisted. "But she just would not listen."

"We tried to stop it, we really did, but her check had not cleared yet and we didn't want to upset her and risk not getting paid for the work we did," Violet explained.

Poppy glanced around at the expectant crowd waiting for her to mingle before turning back to Iris and Violet. "I don't have a clue who half these people are."

"They're mostly Serena and Ned's friends. Matt's not

even here yet, and besides the two of us, the only other important person in your life who is here is Sam," Iris said.

Poppy perked up. "Sam's here?"

Iris nodded. "Yes, I saw him talking to Ned earlier."

Poppy scanned the crowd, searching for him, but she did not immediately spot him.

Serena returned, handing Poppy a glass of champagne, then raised her own glass in the air. "May I have your attention, everyone? I would like to make a toast to my dear friend Poppy, whom I have known for too many years to count. And we won't count them because we want this to be a *happy* birthday!" Serena cackled as the crowd smiled and nodded appreciatively. "Here's to Poppy, my *best* friend!"

Everyone clinked and gulped down the expensive champagne.

Iris bristled. "*Best friend*? Who does she think she is? She barely knows you. Clearly Violet and I are your best friends. How dare she try to usurp our position. You don't even like her that much!"

"It's fine, Iris, let her say what she wants as long as the three of us know the real truth," Poppy assured her.

"Excuse me!" Serena shouted to her guests.

The chatter died down, allowing Serena to take center stage again. She was clearly not done speaking.

"I would also like to take this opportunity to make an announcement. As of today, I have been officially cleared in that nasty business involving that awful young man who broke into this house. The police have informed me that they have concluded that the unfortunate shooting was completely justified."

Maybe the first shot.

But all three?

In Poppy's mind, it was overkill.

But it was not her job to say so.

"Now there is nothing standing in the way of me marrying this amazing man of my dreams, Ned Boyce!"

Ned gazed lovingly at his bride-to-be, saluting her with a whiskey on the rocks.

"So . . . Here's to *me*!" Serena cooed, guzzling down the rest of her champagne.

More clinking and drinking.

People began descending upon Poppy, wishing her a happy birthday, trying to make small talk. Out of the corner of her eye she spotted Sam smiling, giving her a little wave. He would not approach her when she was busy hobnobbing with Serena's party guests, although she wished he would. All she wanted was to enjoy a quiet dinner with Sam at one of their favorite Palm Springs restaurants, John Henry's Cafe or Johanne's. But no, Serena Saunders had had other ideas. And like it or not, Poppy was going to have to endure dozens of unfamiliar well-wishers for at least the next few hours.

Poppy was already embarrassed by all the fuss Serena had sprung on her, but it only got worse when she was led outside on the patio, where a long table had been set up with a pile of beautifully wrapped birthday gifts. Not only had Serena strong-armed all of these people into showing up, she also made them bring gifts. It was humiliating, especially since Poppy did not know any of them. It was painfully excruciating to sit there under the stars opening presents and pretending to be thrilled by an expensive coffeemaker, a spa package, a sundress that she would never be caught wearing. Since she did not know anyone's name, she would read the card attached out loud, then search the crowd to put the name with a face by gauging their reactions.

She finally protested when she opened the gift from Ned and Serena, a mini Lady Dior bag made in blush cannage lambskin, which she knew must have set them back about five grand. She begged them to return it, but they would not hear of it.

Then came the final gift.

From Sam.

Serena made a big show of making sure everyone knew this one was from Poppy's boyfriend.

Poppy cringed at Serena's description of Sam as her boyfriend.

He seemed so much more than that.

At least until lately when he started to become so distant and unavailable.

The box was thin and angular, decorated with ocean-blue wrapping paper and a yellow ribbon.

The box was the perfect size for that stunning solitaire pendant pear-shaped necklace she had seen him buy at Alvin's jewelry shop. Sam stood shyly off to the side, but Serena ferreted him out, grabbing his arm and frog marching him up to Poppy in time for her to open his gift.

"Sam, you shouldn't have . . ." Poppy heard herself saying as she carefully untied the yellow ribbon.

"Don't be so delicate, Poppy, we're all dying of curiosity, just tear the damn thing open!" Serena howled as everyone chuckled.

Poppy ripped the tape off the paper, sliding the box out, and then setting the paper down on the glass patio table. "I cannot imagine what it could be . . ."

Of course she was fibbing.

She knew she was going to have to deliver a convincing performance, pretending she had not expected to find this absolutely stunning necklace.

When she opened the box, she had to instantly shift her facial expression from shock to jubilant. She lifted a lovely blue flower kaleidoscope Italian silk scarf out of the box and held it up for all see. "Sam, it's gorgeous. I love it."

She tried her best, but her words came off forced and mechanical.

The scarf was indeed gorgeous.

But she had been expecting the solitaire pendant pear-shaped necklace.

The one Sam had told Alvin was for someone special.

It was time to employ her best acting skills.

She flung the scarf around her neck and modeled it in front of the crowd as everyone offered Sam compliments on his beautiful taste.

Sam bent down to kiss Poppy on the cheek. "Happy birthday."

"Thank you, Sam," Poppy said, trying hard to sound sincere but still coming across a bit robotic.

She could see Iris and Violet tensing.

They knew Poppy well enough to know something was up.

Poppy squeezed Sam's hand as her mind raced with worry.

If the necklace had not been meant for her, then who had Sam bought it for?

Chapter 22

The bride and groom could not have asked for more beautiful weather on their wedding day. The sun was already setting and the temperature had already topped out at a comfortable eighty-seven degrees and was continuing to cool down. The large circular wedding arch made of white roses set up in the expansive backyard and the quintet ensemble playing Vivaldi's *Four Seasons* classed up the affair quite nicely. Serena was staying hidden in the bedroom, not wanting to be seen before her grand entrance. Poppy hoped that she would not be wearing white given the long winding road behind her was littered with a slew of ex-husbands. Although with four marriages under her own belt, Poppy was not about to judge.

Sam had begged off earlier that day as Poppy's date. He said he had woken up with a bad head cold, but Sam rarely got sidelined by a stuffy nose or scratchy throat. Poppy suspected he just did not want to come. Iris and Violet also chose not to attend, both struggling to come up with excuses, although Poppy knew neither of them particularly liked or wanted to support Serena, especially now that she was no longer a client. As for Matt, he had bowed out at the last minute too, citing a meeting in Hollywood with the producers putting up the money for his new neo-Western film.

So Poppy was on her own.

She mingled with a few of the guests, mostly friends and colleagues of Ned. Serena had so few people to invite—a former assistant, her agent and manager, one cousin out of seven in total, who was the only one she said she could tolerate for any long period of time. Poppy wandered over to the empty bar to order a drink, noticing the lavish spread of gourmet food set out on several long tables ready to be consumed right after the ceremony. She was certainly impressed. The happy couple had gone great lengths to make this blessed event a sumptuous affair.

As darkness fell, Italian string lights draped around the property blinked on and off as the quintet ensemble finished their classical set and took a brief break. The guests began to slowly find their way to their seats. Ned's best man, Warren Ashmore, took his place down front, a few feet from Ned's business partner Charlie, who had recently been ordained a minister so he could officiate the wedding. Serena was going to go without a matron of honor after Poppy had gently turned down the request that she do the honors. Despite Serena's rewriting of history concerning their friendship, Poppy felt strongly that it would be hypocritical of her to pretend they were close friends, at least close enough for her to stand by her side at her wedding.

After the young flirtatious bartender handed her a white wine spritzer, Poppy turned to find herself face-to-face with Ned's children, Willa and Gavin. Both had morose expressions on their faces, as if they were wishing they were anywhere else on the planet.

"Cheer up, this is a wedding not a funeral," Poppy chirped.

"Feels more like a funeral to me," Willa mumbled.

"I know you have issues with Serena, but your dad loves her very much, and like it or not, she makes him happy, so why not just give him this one day?"

"Thank you for that incredibly helpful advice I did not ask for, or want to hear," Willa snapped, stalking off.

"Sorry, I guess we're just not in the mood to celebrate," Gavin muttered, pouting even more, if that was possible.

Ned bounded over to them, looking dashing in a blue blazer and open collar white shirt and gray slacks. The invitation had specifically stated Palm Springs casual although wearing shorts was frowned upon, at least on this occasion.

"I just got word from the bridal suite. Her makeup's done. We're good to go, so I'm going to ask you all to take your seats," Ned said, beaming.

"Sure, Dad," Gavin piped in, quickly plastering on a fake smile. "I was just telling Poppy how happy I am for you. We both are, me and Willa."

Ned clapped Gavin on the back. "I can't tell you how much I appreciate that, son. I know this has been hard on you kids, but you're going to grow to adore Serena. I'm willing to bet on it."

Ned noticed his partner, the minister, waving for him to join him at the wedding arch. "I gotta go." He clutched his tummy. "I'm so nervous all of a sudden. I've got all these butterflies in my stomach." Then he scurried off.

"That's probably his gut trying to tell him he's making a huge mistake," Gavin grumbled.

"Why don't you obey your father for once and sit down," Poppy huffed, spinning from him and walking away.

Poppy was halfway across the grass, heading down the middle of the aisle to her seat down front, when she noticed a man approach Ned and whisper something softly in his ear. Ned tensed up and looked around. Suddenly they all heard a woman yelling at the top of her lungs at someone to let her pass. Heads turned to see who was causing the commotion. It was Carina, Cecily's sister, pushing her way past several guests inside the house as they frantically tried to stop her. But Carina Loudon was hell-bent on shoving her way outside and breaking up this wedding.

Ned stormed past Poppy, and she heard him bark at a few of his friends, "We have to get her out of here before Serena finds out what's happening! It will ruin her whole day!"

"Killer! Killer!" Carina shouted.

She was gripped by the arms on both sides by an angry couple, friends of Ned, Poppy presumed, and steered back toward the front door. Poppy noticed Warren on his phone calling the police to report a trespasser. Carina's shrill screaming voice could be heard for several more minutes from the driveway out front until a police car arrived and she was ordered to leave the property immediately or be arrested. A car door slammed and everyone heard tires squealing as Carina finally retreated back to her home in the Thunderbird Estates to plot her next move.

When Ned, a little shaken but more determined than ever, returned and took his place next to Warren, Charlie the newly minted minister signaled the quintet ensemble, which finally began the "Wedding March" after that temporary delay.

Ned's eyes danced as he watched his bride-to-be slowly walk down the aisle in a lovely romantic vintage wedding dress with scalloped sheer sleeves and fine beading. And yes, it was white. Slightly off-white, but still white.

Despite Poppy's arched eyebrow at the color choice, she could not argue that Serena did indeed look beautiful.

Serena stopped at Ned's side and faced him as he clasped her hands with his own, mouthing to her, "You look beautiful." Poppy could see Serena's eyes glistening with tears. She had never seen Serena look so happy and content. She truly appeared to be madly in love with this man.

When the quintet ensemble finished and put down their instruments, Charlie began his spiel. "Dearly beloved, we are gathered here tonight to join this man and this woman in holy matrimony . . ."

It was a rather traditional ceremony except for a few jokes thrown in by Charlie about the advanced ages of the bride and groom. Ned laughed appreciatively. Serena just stared daggers. Everything went along smoothly until Charlie got to the part where he had to say, "If there is anyone here who has just cause why these two people should not be married, speak now or forever hold your peace." All eyes flicked to Gavin and Willa, who were sulking in the back row of chairs. When people turned to look at them, they tried hard to look cheerful and supportive, but very few were buying it.

Least of all Poppy.

"Then, with the powers invested in me by the state of California, literally twenty-four hours ago . . ."

Chuckles from the crowd.

"I now pronounce you husband and wife."

Everyone erupted in cheers as Ned bent over and kissed his brand-new beautiful bride on the lips.

As if on cue, a cascade of fireworks burst over the night sky in an explosion of colors to the oohs and aahs of the wedding guests. Even Gavin and Willa were impressed.

Ned Boyce was sparing no expense to celebrate this momentous occasion. And except for one ill-intentioned wedding crasher and two gloomy miserable grown children, he had pulled it off spectacularly.

Poppy profoundly hoped that much better days were ahead for Ned Boyce and Serena Saunders. But similar to Ned's nervous butterflies, Poppy was also experiencing an anxious feeling in the pit of her stomach. But hers was more a sense of dread as she wondered, after all it took for Ned and Serena to get here, what could possibly go wrong next?

Chapter 23

When Poppy pulled her car into the driveway of her home just after midnight from Ned and Serena's wedding reception, she found it odd that most of the lights were turned on in the house. Sam had taken to the guest room earlier to try to get some rest in order to shake this nagging cold he had caught, and so she had expected just one light to be on in the living room. That's when she spotted Sam through the window, fully dressed, checking his pockets.

Poppy jumped out of her car and marched inside, startling Sam as she slammed the front door shut behind her.

"Oh, I didn't expect you home so soon," Sam said, slightly startled.

"It's after twelve," Poppy said curtly.

"How was the wedding?"

"Fine. Are you going somewhere?"

"Yeah, I'm going to drive back to my cabin."

Poppy raised an eyebrow. "In Big Bear?"

"That's where it is."

"Sam, it's nearly a two-hour drive and you're not feeling well. Why can't you just wait until morning?"

"Because I can't sleep in the guest room. I've been tossing and turning for hours, and I don't want to move to your room so you can catch this miserable thing I've got. I just figured it would be easier if I just got in my truck and drove up the mountain. I'm thinking I just need to recover in my own bed where I can be grumpy and feel sorry for myself and not bother anyone."

"You're no bother, Sam," Poppy sighed.

"Have you seen my keys? I can't seem to find them."

"I last saw them on the kitchen table."

"Yes!" Sam shuffled into the kitchen and returned a moment later, keys in hand. He noticed the melancholy look on her face. "Something wrong?"

"No, it's nothing, I understand," Poppy blurted out quickly, wanting to kick herself for not being honest about what she was feeling in the moment.

But what would she say?

Would she ask if he was seeing someone else? How silly she would feel if she was wrong.

"I see you're wearing it," Sam said with a smile.

Poppy snapped out of her reverie. "Sorry, what?"

"The scarf I bought you for your birthday. It looks very nice on you."

She touched the pretty print scarf around her neck. "Oh, yes, it's lovely. Thank you again."

Now was the time to ask about the necklace.

She knew she must, or otherwise it would eventually drive her insane.

"Sam . . . ?"

Sam suddenly sneezed.

"Bless you."

He glanced at her with watery eyes and a runny nose. "Thanks. I need a tissue. Be right back." He then bounded into the guest bathroom, emerging seconds later, blowing his nose with a Kleenex. He checked the time on his phone. He obviously wanted to hit the road so he could get back up the mountain. Suddenly remembering, he glanced up at her. "You wanted to ask me something?"

Yes.

She most certainly did.

Who was that expensive necklace for?

Would he wonder why she had not mentioned it to him before? And why didn't she say that she saw him in the jewelry shop? Was she spying on him?

She opened her mouth to speak.

To finally ask him about it.

And then he sneezed loudly again.

This one caused them both to jump.

"Oh, I feel like crap," he moaned, sniffing and wiping his eyes, his voice raspy from a scratchy throat.

"Go home. We can talk in the morning when I call to check up on you."

"Are you sure?"

"Yes, it's not important. Promise to drive safe."

"Always."

She instinctively took a step forward to kiss him good night but he raised a hand, stopping her.

"We probably shouldn't. If we kiss and I give you this thing, I will never forgive myself."

She nodded.

He made perfect sense.

But it still hurt.

"Good night, Sam," she said tightly.

"Night," he said before shuffling out the door.

She stood frozen in place trying to figure out what had just happened as she listened to him get in his truck, start the engine, and drive away. She fingered the beautiful scarf he had given her that was hanging around her neck. She really did love it. But she could not stop her mind from contemplating just who was wearing that extravagant necklace at this moment, because it certainly was not her.

She could not keep a lid on this much longer.

Poppy knew she had to confront him.

And the longer she waited, the worse it would get.

She should have asked him when he was standing right in front of her, but she had chickened out. There was no point in prolonging the agony. She was going to call him right now and get to the bottom of this.

Just as she reached for her phone, it began buzzing.

She picked it up and looked at the screen, hoping it might be Sam. But it wasn't. It was Serena.

How strange she would be calling Poppy so soon after the wedding, during her honeymoon, no less. Ned and Serena had rented a large suite in a pricey Rancho Mirage hotel.

Poppy answered the call and asked tentatively, "Serena?"

She heard someone sobbing.

"Serena, is that you? Is everything all right?"

Now the person was heaving, trying to catch a breath to speak. "Pop-Poppy . . . Oh God!"

It was definitely Serena sobbing and wailing.

"No! No! No! No!" Serena screamed over and over.

"Serena, what's the matter? What's happened?"

Serena tried to talk but she was so distraught, so obviously in shock, her words were unintelligible as she blathered on, still crying.

"Serena, I can't understand you. You need to calm down and take a deep breath . . ."

She could hear Serena trying to follow her instructions with little effect.

"Just tell me where you are so I can come to you."

Finally, Serena managed to compose herself a little bit. "In Rancho Mirage . . . the honeymoon suite . . ."

"Is Ned there with you?"

A long pause.

"Serena?"

"Yes, he's here," she whispered, sniffing.

Poppy could hear Serena mumbling something, but she could not make out what she was trying to say.

"Serena, what's—"

Before Poppy could finish her question, Serena burst out with a loud anguished sob and screamed, "He's dead, Poppy! Ned is dead!"

Chapter 24

Poppy had tried to keep Serena on the phone as she jumped into her car and sped over to the rented honeymoon suite in Rancho Mirage, but when the police arrived, Serena had set the phone down to talk to them and Poppy could only hear muffled voices and some rustling sounds.

When she finally arrived at the suite, the young officer who had been at the previous crime scene at Ned's house blocked her from entering.

He held up a hand. "Sorry, ma'am, you're not allowed to go in there."

"But Serena is expecting me, she needs me."

The officer gave her an unsympathetic stare. "Just following orders, ma'am."

"You don't remember me from the last time?"

"What last time?"

"The last time we were all gathered around a dead body where Serena Saunders was right in the thick of things?"

There was a possible flash of recognition, then it went away as quickly as it had come. "No, ma'am, I don't."

Poppy sighed, frustrated, then spotted Detective Jordan

conferring with his colleague, Detective Higgins. She frantically waved at him. "Excuse me, Detective, it's me, Poppy Harmon!"

Jordan closed his eyes, annoyed, then slowly turned toward her. "Of course it is. Let me guess. Ms. Saunders needs your emotional support again."

"That's right! She must be feeling very vulnerable right now."

"So is her husband. At least Ms. Saunders is still breathing," Jordan deadpanned.

Poppy stared daggers at him.

Not funny.

"Please, Detective," Poppy pleaded.

Jordan shook his head, miffed but resigned. There was no getting rid of her. "Let her in, Officer."

The young officer stepped aside and Poppy blew past him and right over to Detectives Jordan and Higgins.

"So what happened?"

"Not that I am at all obliged to tell you, but my wife likes you, so I will say at the moment it looks like he died from an apparent heart attack."

"Heart attack? Then why are you here?"

"Because this is the second person found dead around Serena Saunders, so I'm not inclined to just take her word for it until we conduct a full autopsy."

"Makes sense," Poppy agreed. She flicked her eyes over to Ned's body lying on top of the bed, with no clothes on, as a paramedic pulled a white sheet over him. Serena sat slumped over in a chair in the corner, her hands covering her face.

Poppy turned back to Jordan. "What was he doing when it happened?"

Jordan cocked an eyebrow. "Do I really have to spell it out for you? It was their honeymoon. What do you think they were doing?"

"Oh," Poppy gasped, her cheeks flushing with embarrassment. "I see . . ."

"Well, if your heart has to give out, what a way to go," Higgins snorted, chuckling to himself.

Jordan did not crack a smile.

Higgins then quickly composed himself, wiping the grin off his face and trying to act serious. "Tragedy though, isn't it? Poor guy just tied the knot."

"Did Serena say if Ned had a history of heart trouble?" Poppy asked.

Jordan shook his head. "According to her, he had just had a complete physical and stress test before the wedding, and everything, including his ticker, checked out A-okay."

"Which makes you think there is more to the story," Poppy said, eyeing Jordan.

"We will wait and see what the autopsy report tells us."

"Thank you, Detective, I'm going to go over and see if there is anything I can get for Serena."

"How about a good lawyer?" Higgins joked.

Poppy failed to see the humor in his remark and told him so with her blazing eyes.

Jordan again remained stone-faced, making Higgins nervous again.

"Y-You know, in case something suspicious turns up in the autopsy report, like you said, Lamar," Higgins sputtered.

Poppy pointedly turned her back on them, hurried over to Serena, and rested a comforting hand on her shoulder. Serena lowered her hands from her face. Her makeup was smeared and her smudged mascara made her eyes look as if they belonged to a raccoon.

Serena flew to her feet and threw her arms around Poppy. "Oh, thank God you're here!"

"Serena, I'm so sorry. I can't imagine what you must be going through!"

"Why did this have to happen? And on our wedding night! When we arrived earlier, everything was perfect. There was a bottle of champagne on ice, caviar, rose petals on the bed. Ned had arranged all of it! It was the happiest night in my life, and then in the next moment, he's gone. It was so sudden, so unexpected. He thought it was indigestion at first, but then he just clutched his chest, looked at me funny, and was gone. I literally watched the life drain out of his eyes. It was so awful."

"Do you need me to call anyone? His kids?"

A flash of anger struck Serena's face. "No, of course not! This is all their fault!"

"What do you mean?"

"Those entitled ingrates have been hounding him for months not to marry me. They were so afraid he might cut them out of the will or something. They were constantly putting pressure on him, harassing him to the point where something finally had to snap! And it did!" Serena wailed, pointing at Ned's body covered with a white sheet on top of the bed. "This is on them! They did this! Those two money-grubbing spoiled brats are responsible for Ned's death!"

Poppy suspected Serena was just lashing out in her grief and would eventually come to the realization that Gavin and Willa were not directly responsible for Ned Boyce's untimely demise during his honeymoon.

Especially if the autopsy report revealed foul play.

A worrying possibility that increasingly made Poppy squeamish because the target of any murder investigation would focus squarely on the last person known to have been with the victim when he was still alive.

And that would be his loving wife of nearly five hours, Serena Saunders-Boyce.

Chapter 25

"Strychnine?" Poppy gasped.

Detective Jordan nodded solemnly.

"Good lord, then it wasn't a heart attack, it was—"

"Murder."

Poppy's head was spinning.

She had just finished breakfast and was about to call and check on Sam when she heard the doorbell and went to answer it, only to find Detective Jordan standing on her welcome mat. She knew this could not possibly be a social call. It was far too early in the morning. Plus the last thing in the world she would have ever expected was for stern, no-nonsense Detective Jordan to just drop by for a cup of coffee and a juicy gossip session, which she did a few mornings a week like clockwork with Iris and Violet.

After ushering him into the house and offering him a cup of coffee, which he predictably declined, Jordan plopped down on Poppy's couch as she sat opposite him in a chair, and true to form, he got right to the point.

"Preliminary autopsy results came back. The medical examiner worked through the night, did some lab tests, and found traces of strychnine."

And that's when Poppy began feeling slightly dizzy.

She had not been prepared for the shock of this news.

Of course her first thought went straight to Serena.

Had her Oscar-worthy performance the night before been just that? A performance? This new revelation certainly was not going to ease anyone's suspicion that she was not good for Ned Boyce.

Poppy managed to collect herself enough and flick her eyes back toward Detective Jordan. "I appreciate you stopping by to let me know."

"This is not a courtesy call, Poppy. I am under no obligation to update you on my investigation. I came here to ask you a few questions about Serena Saunders and how well you know her."

"We worked together in the nineteen eighties, and quite frankly, we did not get along. We only recently reconciled."

"From what you know of her, do you think she is capable of committing murder?"

Poppy's eyes widened. "No! Serena can be quite a handful, and she certainly is self-centered and quick-tempered on occasion, but *murder*? I hardly think so."

"Are you absolutely sure about that?"

"Well, no, I, uh, to be honest, I don't, I mean, maybe, but, but sh-she seemed to care for Ned, very deeply," Poppy stammered, flushed and flustered. "But it's true, she is also an actress . . ."

"Like you."

"Yes, Detective, but I am not being accused of killing anyone, or am I?"

"No reason to suspect you yet."

Yet?

Jordan leaned forward. "So what you're saying is, you don't know, but she *might* be capable of killing someone."

Poppy thought more about it. "I believe she really did love Ned Boyce. In the years I have known her, Serena has rarely shown a softer side, and whenever she was around Ned, she was markedly different, very happy and content. The two of them just seemed to have a very strong bond."

Jordan's face was unreadable. He just sat there listening to her prattle on. Poppy began to feel a little self-conscious.

She cleared her throat. "If you are so convinced Serena poisoned Ned, and you have the evidence to back it up, then why are you here instead of out there arresting her?"

"I never said I had the evidence. We only ruled Boyce's death a homicide less than an hour ago. I came straight here since you seem to know Ms. Saunders, pardon me, Mrs. Boyce best."

"Well, I simply don't believe she did it."

"What if I told you I spoke to Ned Boyce's lawyer on the phone before coming over here, and he told me that Ned revised his will just two days ago, leaving everything, and I mean everything, to Serena."

Poppy reared back in her chair, gut-punched.

She took a moment to reel from this latest unsettling bit of news before exhaling. "Do his children know?"

"Gavin and Willa? Nope, not yet, according to the lawyer. But they will . . . very soon."

"Oh, dear . . . This is undoubtedly going to get messy. What about Serena?"

"I spoke to her right after the lawyer. She claimed she had no idea Ned had changed the will. She was very convincing, lots of surprised gasps and well-timed sniffles. She's very good at what she does. I'm surprised she's never won an award for her acting."

"You obviously don't believe her. Whatever happened to innocent until proven guilty?"

"Oh, I fully intend to prove she is guilty so her next performance is behind bars in a real-life drama."

It was obvious Detective Jordan did not like Serena Saunders one bit. Poppy could certainly understand why. But she also did not think it was fair for him to be shutting the book on this case so early in the investigation because he was so confident Serena had done it.

Still, Serena could have easily slipped the strychnine powder in Ned's champagne when they toasted on their wedding night.

Then again, someone else could have stirred poison in one of Ned's drinks at the reception. Poppy had seen him downing several cocktails over the course of the evening.

No, Poppy decided, she was not going to convict Serena before further examining the evidence. Despite the fact that she and Serena had been mortal enemies for years, Poppy had grown more fond of her recently. Serena had very few friends to speak of, and now with Ned gone, it appeared she had no one on her side at all, coming to her defense, least of all Ned's friends and relatives.

There was only Poppy.

And she would not abandon Serena in her hour of need.

Despite the queasy feeling in her stomach that there was more to the story that had yet to reveal itself.

Chapter 26

"I would like to speak freely, if possible," Serena said, perched atop a stool in the Desert Flowers garage office. Poppy stood nearby while Iris and Violet sat on the couch and Wyatt at his desk in front of his computer. Matt was in LA for rehearsals before the start of shooting his movie directed by Warren Ashmore.

"Of course, Serena, consider this a very safe space," Poppy assured her.

Serena hemmed and hawed. "It's . . . It's just that what we have to talk about is of a very serious nature."

"Yes, we understand," Poppy said, not sure why Serena was so hesitant to speak candidly.

Her eyes flicked toward Wyatt. "A very serious, *adult* nature."

They all turned to Wyatt, who was listening intently.

Violet let out a giggle. "Oh, don't worry about my grandson. He knows more about what goes on in the world than all of us combined."

Serena was still unconvinced. "But what we need to discuss, what happened on my wedding night—"

"Ma'am, I'm fourteen. I've seen and heard it all. I have my own Netflix account," Wyatt sighed.

He was not happy to be called out on his tender age, especially given his remarkable talents as a computer programmer and, well, to be frank, world-class hacker. He was an invaluable resource for the agency, and Poppy, Iris, Violet, and Matt all took full advantage of his mad skills. They had no illusions that he was not well advanced for his age. As they all liked to point out, especially Poppy, age is just a number.

"Very well then," Serena said warily. "I called this emergency meeting because I would like to hire you."

Iris sat up, surprised. *"Again?"*

"Yes," Serena said, hands clasped in front of her on top of her lap. "But this time I want you to clear my name, prove to the police that I did not kill Ned."

The women exchanged concerned looks.

Poppy walked up behind her and put a comforting hand on Serena's shoulder. "Serena, I can't imagine what you must be going through, losing Ned like that . . ."

"I hear a but coming," Serena moaned.

Poppy circled around in front of her to address her head-on. "But I am not sure it's such a good idea for us to stick our noses in yet another one of Detective Jordan's investigations. He is already annoyed with me for poking around the night of your home invasion and inserting myself into his investigation of Justin Cambry's death."

"Which you proved was a random burglary and had nothing to do with Serena," Iris snorted. "The man should be grateful for your help. But alas, he is a *man*, so he obviously feels threatened by your success as a private investigator."

"I am not sure we need to psycho-analyze Detective Jordan. Most police detectives recoil at the thought of outside amateur help."

"You're *not* an amateur, Aunt Poppy, you are licensed in the state of California," Wyatt piped in.

The boy was right.

But she still did not think this was a good idea.

Serena could detect that Poppy was leaning toward accepting her case. "Do you know what I did last night, Poppy, which would explain my bloodshot eyes and why my hair looks like a rat's nest?"

She, of course, was exaggerating. Her appearance was impeccable. Maybe her eyes were a little red, but she looked very well put together and there was not a hair out of place.

"I was down at the Palm Springs police precinct all night, over seven hours, being asked the same questions over and over by Detective Jordan and a few of his cronies. I have filmed enough police interrogation scenes during the course of my long career to know they were trying to break me down, get me to admit I poisoned Ned because I only married him to get my grubby little hands on his money. They are totally convinced that I did it. Despite my claims of innocence, they refuse to believe a single word I have to say. We all know how this will end. They will not look into any other possible suspects, they will focus all their efforts on drumming up evidence proving I did it, that I somehow slipped strychnine into Ned's drink. They will get some district attorney up for re-election who needs a big high-profile win to indict me, even if they still don't have enough evidence for a conviction. I will continue to maintain my innocence, but then they will leak false information to the press to get the public on their side. I will be branded as some kind of black widow. The televised trial will drag on for weeks, everyone will speculate about how I only have ice water in my veins, and if the jurors are easily swayed, they will come back with a verdict of guilty and I will be shipped off to prison, probably until the day I die. Time will go by, people will forget about me, maybe Lifetime will make a movie about the whole sordid affair, and that's how my journey on this earth will end . . ." She paused. There was absolute silence in the office as everyone stared at her, not sure what to say, then she took a deep breath and continued. "An innocent woman sent to prison for a crime she did not commit. I can see it now, someday, maybe twenty years from now, a documentarian will take another look at the case, uncover hard evidence pointing to the real killer, and probably win an Academy Award for the startling new revelations that finally cleared the name of that actress who was accused of killing her husband on her wedding night all those years ago. But by then it will be too late. I will be either long dead and buried or in such a delicate mental state I won't even know or appreciate finally being cleared of the crime."

None of them knew what to say.

Serena stared at the floor a few moments, then raised her head and locked eyes with Poppy, who still stood in front of her. "I loved Ned Boyce with all my heart. I wanted to spend the rest of my life with him. But someone cruelly took him away from me, and I need you to find out who it was and bring that person to justice. Please, Poppy, please don't make me beg, you must do this for me."

Poppy believed her.

She could see the anguish and pain in her bloodshot eyes.

"Okay, Serena, we will take the case."

Serena jumped down off the stool and threw herself at Poppy, hugging her, sniffing as she fought back tears. "Thank you, thank you all for believing me."

Poppy was only speaking for herself.

She instinctively knew that Iris was most likely not

nearly as persuaded by Serena's dramatic soliloquy as Poppy had been.

Before she could stop her, Iris blurted out, "At least we do not have to worry about you coughing up our retainer fee now that you're a billionaire."

It had been a joke.

A very ill-timed and inappropriate joke.

Even Iris could read the room, so she decided now was a good time to change tact. "But luckily we don't have much on our plate right now, so why not?"

After thanking them profusely, Serena hurried out the door for a hair appointment, instructing them to keep her apprised of their progress.

Poppy turned to her team. "Well?"

"She's guilty," Iris said flatly. "This is just a ploy for her defense. If she has hired private investigators to find the real killer, it gives the appearance that she is innocent."

"I'm with Aunt Iris. She totally did it," Wyatt said, before spinning around on his own stool and pulling up a video game on his desktop computer screen.

Poppy turned to Violet. "And what about you? You're our eternal optimist, Violet. What do you think?"

Violet hesitated, glanced around at the others, then said meekly, "I have always thought Serena Saunders was a very good actress."

Poppy folded her arms. "I see, so you think she's guilty, too."

"I just think she's very convincing playing an innocent woman. But a case is a case and we should not be turning down clients, so what would be the harm in looking into it to see what facts turn up?"

Poppy figured she would be alone in this.

She could not blame Iris, Violet, or Wyatt for their hardened opinions. Serena had been found with two dead bodies in the span of a week.

Not a good look.

But on a gut level, Poppy strongly believed Serena was being sincere about her feelings toward Ned, and that she was incapable of hurting him, let alone murdering him.

Now she just had to prove it to everyone else in the world.

Chapter 27

Warren Ashmore's funny, touching, heartfelt tribute to his decades-old friend Ned Boyce at a Presbyterian church in Palm Desert was unfortunately marred by the histrionic antics of his grieving widow, Serena, who could not help hurling herself at the open casket, wailing at the top of her lungs, and at one point trying to crawl inside to lie next to him.

Warren quickly stepped down from the podium and, with Serena's fragile emotional state in mind, whispered something in her ear, trying to calm her down. Whatever he said seemed to finally do the trick, and Serena, still shaking, tears streaming down her cheeks, pulled herself together and managed to take her seat in the front pew. Her visibly angry and tense stepchildren moved farther down the row away from her when she plopped down, intent on keeping their distance.

Poppy watched all the drama unfold from the third row from the front, flanked by Sam and Matt, who had driven in from film rehearsals in LA for the memorial, or as Warren preferred to call it, "A Celebration of Life." To Matt's left sat Iris and Violet.

Warren returned to the podium to wrap up, ending with a funny story about him and Ned involving a weekend trip to Las Vegas when they were younger and running smack into a white Bengal tiger in the lobby of the Mirage Hotel Resort and Casino that had escaped from its cage right before Siegfried and Roy were scheduled to start their nightly performance. Ned's immediate reaction was not fear of being mauled but fear that he was allergic to cats.

Everyone in the church laughed appreciatively.

Everyone except Serena, who covered her face with her hands and continued to sob loudly.

Poppy could see Gavin and Willa turn to each other, rolling their eyes and shaking their heads, not buying this inconsolable widow act one bit.

Poppy chose to give Serena the benefit of the doubt.

When the minister finished the service with a short prayer and the mourners began filing out of the church, Serena remained seated in the front pew, quietly crying. Gavin and Willa walked past her toward the aisle without offering any greeting or condolence or even acknowledgement.

Poppy slipped out of the third row and made her way down toward the front against the flow of the crowd. She sat down next to Serena and put an arm around her sunken shoulders.

"If this is too hard for you, you don't have to attend the reception at your house. We can just say you're not feeling up to it and you can hide in your bedroom," Poppy suggested.

Serena unsnapped her black purse, plucked out a tissue, and blew her nose as she vigorously shook her head. "No, these people came out today to pay their respects to Ned, and as his wife, I need to be there for him."

"It's just that you have been through so much lately . . ."

Serena took Poppy's hand and squeezed it. "No, I have to do this. It's what Ned would want. Besides, if I don't at least make an appearance, I'm afraid Gavin and Willa will use my absence to poison everyone against me."

Poppy could not argue with that.

"All right, then, we'll meet you back at the house," Poppy said. "Is Warren riding in the limo with you?"

Serena nodded.

"Good, I'm glad you won't be alone."

There was no telling what she might do on her own.

As if on cue, Warren appeared at Serena's side and gently took her by the elbow to help her stand up. "You ready?"

"Yes, Warren, thank you," she sniffed as he escorted her down the aisle of the church to the limo waiting outside.

People were still milling around inside the church as Poppy joined Matt, Sam, Iris, and Violet.

"How is she?" Sam asked.

"Not great."

"She certainly knows how to put on quite a show," Iris declared.

"Please, Iris, not so loud," Poppy scolded.

"Everyone here knows it's all just an act," Iris huffed.

"Did it ever occur to you that maybe she really did love him?" Violet asked.

Iris snorted and laughed. "No! Not for one second! Serena Saunders has always been consumed with just one person. Serena Saunders! And I have seen nothing to suggest that any of that has changed. That pathetic crying jag we all just witnessed was exactly like the one she did in that Lifetime TV movie, the one where her grandson died of an opioid addiction. Covering her face with her hands, the wailing and sobbing, throwing herself on top of the

casket, it was like the perfect re-creation of her performance from that terrible movie."

Matt shrugged. "It looked pretty real to me."

"Yes, so did Meryl Streep playing Margaret Thatcher in
The Iron Lady, but news flash, Mr. Hollywood, she was
just *pretending*!"

"I'm with Violet, I think she really loved him," Matt
said firmly.

"She loved his money," Iris insisted. "And those poor
kids of his have no idea Daddy Warbucks has cut them
completely out of the will."

The blood suddenly drained from Poppy's face.

Iris had no clue that Gavin and Willa had been hovering
behind her just as the words came tumbling out of her
mouth.

"Iris . . ." Poppy warned.

Iris's body stiffened and she stared straight ahead at
Poppy and Sam and Matt as she spoke in a much quieter
voice. "You are going to tell me they are standing directly
behind me, aren't you?"

Poppy nodded and whispered, "Yes."

"And you're going to tell me that they're standing so
close there is no chance they did not hear what I just said,
aren't you?"

Poppy nodded again. "Yes."

Gavin tapped Iris on the shoulder. "Excuse me, what
did you just say?"

"I said nothing that concerns you. Mind your own business," Iris blatantly lied, hoping to avoid a scene.

"I distinctly heard you say something about our father
leaving his entire estate to Serena and cutting us out,"
Gavin pressed.

"I don't recall mentioning you by name. I could very
well be talking about someone completely different, not
you two, or your father, or your stepmother."

"But you're not," Willa growled. "You were quite obviously talking about *us*!"

Iris, in a rare moment, was at a loss for words. Then, quickly trying to recover, barked, "Is there an open bar at the funeral reception? I could use a stiff drink! Come on, Violet, you can carpool with me to the house."

Iris skirted away, embarrassed. Violet offered Gavin and Willa an apologetic smile, then scurried after her.

Willa turned to Poppy. "Is it true? Have we been cut out of Dad's will?"

Poppy tensed up. "You should really speak to your father's lawyer. He knows far more than I do."

"Oh God, it's true, isn't it? He left us nothing!" Gavin cried, now panicked.

"She somehow got to him, coerced him into changing the will, right before she killed him," Willa spit out.

"There is no evidence to suggest that Serena caused your father harm in any way," Poppy said defensively.

"Of course you would say that, you're on *her* side," Willa sneered. "I'm sure she paid you handsomely to render that opinion."

"It's not an opinion, Willa, it's a fact," Poppy said tightly. "Now you have every right to handle this situation in whatever manner you see fit, but my advice is, wait until tomorrow to get into the intricacies of your father's will, and allow his friends and family to mourn him properly, at least today. Can you do that, please?"

They both glared at Poppy.

Gavin, the less odious of the two, seemed to relent and offered a simple grunt.

"Fine," Willa seethed. "We had no plans to attend the funeral reception anyway. It would be too painful for us to have to watch Serena flit about playing the grieving lady of the house."

Gavin turned to his sister and whispered, "He must

have left us something. I can't imagine him just cutting us out completely. There has to be some mistake."

Ned had warned his children to shape up and start treating Serena better or he would do just that, but Poppy felt no desire to remind them of that uncomfortable fact at this moment. Luckily that too was the lawyer's job.

"Come on, Gavin, let's get out of here," Willa hissed, dragging him away like a misbehaved puppy. It would have been just as humiliating and emasculating if she had ahold of his ear while pulling him past a few stragglers and out the front door of the church.

Poppy noticed Sam loitering behind her, making a point of avoiding the drama. "You're awfully quiet, Sam."

"Just watching the fireworks," Sam said with a sly smile. "I'm going to go get the car and meet you outside."

And just like that, he was gone.

Poppy grimaced.

Matt put his arm around her. "Have you asked him about the necklace?"

Poppy looked at him, surprised. "How did you know about that?"

"A little birdie told me. Of German origin."

"That Iris, she just cannot keep a secret."

"It shouldn't be a secret. You should just be up-front and ask him about it."

Of course Matt was right.

Poppy knew she had been avoiding the inevitable.

"You're right. The longer I wait, the worse it's going to get. I'll talk to him right now."

Poppy followed Sam outside the church.

She spotted him strolling down the street toward his parked car and was about to run and catch up to him when suddenly she heard a commotion by the limo in front of the church. Her eyes flicked to a crowd gathered around. Warren was bent down on one knee, calling for everyone to step back and give them some space.

Then she saw the crowd part, revealing Serena collapsed on the sidewalk in a heap. She was not moving, which meant she was either unconscious . . . or dead.

Chapter 28

Two days later, after a battery of tests, including a very thorough psych evaluation, Serena was given the all-clear to go home, appearing in good health despite her fainting spell outside the church following Ned's funeral. Serena chalked the incident up to mental and physical exhaustion from the ongoing stress of recent events, especially the sudden loss of her husband. Poppy had heard through Serena's lawyer that Gavin and Willa had wasted no time in using her hospitalization as leverage in their quest to take over their father's estate, but Poppy knew they were just grasping at straws and had no consequential legal standing.

The doctor ordered more bed rest for Serena, who for once did not seem to put up a fight. She probably knew deep down that the doctor was right, and that if she had a fighting chance of getting back to her old energetic self, she should definitely take the time for a little self-care.

Now that Ned was gone, Warren had returned to Los Angeles to resume preproduction on his film, and Gavin and Willa had literally dropped her from their lives, Poppy knew she was about the only friend Serena had to lean on, and so she had volunteered to drive her home from the hospital. Once settled back in Ned's mountaintop house, which for all intents and purposes now belonged to her, Serena had dismissed Poppy, not wanting to be a nuisance.

Poppy told her in no uncertain terms that if she needed anything, anything at all, she should not hesitate to call her, day or night.

Serena thanked Poppy with a wan smile, assuring her that there was no need to bother her. She was just going to spend the next couple of weeks recharging her batteries and figure out what to do with her life without Ned, something she had not had time to contemplate since their wedding day.

"I had this vision of what the rest of my life would look like, traveling the world with Ned, enjoying each and every moment together . . . I guess it's true what they say— if you want to make God laugh, tell him your plans," she had said to Poppy when they arrived at the disconcertingly empty house.

"You will get through this, Serena. You're one of the strongest people I know," Poppy had told her, meaning every word of it.

Which was why she was so surprised just hours later, only a few minutes after midnight, when Poppy was awakened by her buzzing phone. She turned over in her bed, sitting up, adjusting the strap of her nightgown, as she reached for the phone on her nightstand to see who was calling so late.

It was Serena.

Poppy immediately answered the call. "Serena, are you all right?"

She only heard a rustling sound at first.

"Serena, are you there? Hello?"

Then, finally, an urgent whisper. "Poppy?"

"Yes, Serena, what's wrong?"

"I-I heard a strange noise..." she stammered. "I-I think someone is trying to break into the house!"

Again?

"Are you sure?"

"I can hear him walking around out in the living room!"

"Serena, where are you now?"

"My bedroom."

"All right, go lock the door, right now!"

More rustling and heavy breathing and then a click.

"Okay, I locked it."

There was a pause.

Then Serena gasped and frantically whispered, "I think he knows I'm here! I hear him coming down the hall!"

This was madness.

How could there be another intruder only a few weeks after the last one? What was so popular about Ned Boyce's house with the Coachella Valley crime element?

"Serena, are you still there?"

"Yes, yes, I'm here," she frantically whispered.

"What's going on? Where is he?"

Her voice went even lower. "I think he's standing right outside the door."

Poppy could imagine Serena staring at the door handle, waiting for it to jiggle as the intruder tried to bust his way inside.

Poppy's mind raced, desperate to come up with a plan.

"Serena, listen to me, I want you to go out the sliding glass door in your bedroom, walk outside to the pool area, through the gate, and then down the hill until you get to the nearest house. You can call the police from there... Serena? Can you still hear me?"

"Yes, I'm going now, I—"

There was a bloodcurdling scream.

"Serena! Serena! What's happening?"

Then another longer, even more terrified shriek.

Poppy raced outside to her car but knew it would take at least fifteen minutes to get to the house.

Anything could happen by then.

Poppy was behind the wheel and backing out of her driveway when she heard Serena's shrill, frightened voice through the phone. "It's him! He's standing outside by the pool! Oh my God, it's HIM!"

"Who?"

"Ned!"

Poppy backed right into a trash bin that had been set out for the garbage collector in the morning, knocking it over.

"What are you talking about?"

"I can see him clear as day! He's right there! Ned! Ned!"

"What's he doing?"

"He-He's just standing there, looking at me," Serena said softly.

Poppy gunned it to Rancho Mirage, slowing down only when she spotted a police car turning out of the all-night drive-thru window at Jack in the Box.

When she arrived at the mountaintop house, she jumped out and ran inside the house, calling for Serena. She found her sitting in the living room in a satin pink robe, staring straight ahead, nearly in a catatonic state.

"Serena, are you okay?" Poppy looked around. "Did you see the man who broke in? Did you scare him away?"

"I-I don't know, maybe, I didn't hear anything after a few minutes, and so when I came out to check, everything was back to normal."

"What do you mean back to normal?"

"There were no signs of a break-in, so I figured it had to be Ned."

"What do you mean it had to be Ned? Ned's dead, Serena."

"I know," she muttered solemnly before flicking her eyes toward Poppy, and said, dead serious, "It was his spirit. He came to warn me."

"Warn you? About what?"

"He told me to get out of this house while I still can."

"You heard Ned, I mean his ghost, say that?"

"Yes. He's very worried about me. He doesn't want me staying here any longer . . ."

"You're telling me that Ned is haunting the house and wants you to leave . . . ?"

"He says he is only trying to protect me."

"From what?"

"I don't know . . . Maybe there are evil spirits here that Ned is worried about. He always believed in the supernatural, much more than I ever did . . . until now."

This was bonkers.

But Poppy held her tongue.

"Stay put," Poppy ordered. "I'm going to take a quick look around."

She combed the entire house inside and out, searching the pool area for any clue that someone had been there, but turned up nothing. When she returned to Serena in the living room, Serena was making herself a drink at the bar.

Serena took a sip of her Manhattan. "Did you find anything?"

"No. You're sure you heard someone outside your bedroom door?"

"I think so."

Poppy sighed, frustrated. "You *think* so?"

"I was sound asleep. Maybe the noises were part of a dream. I'm not sure. When I was jolted awake, I thought it was real and grabbed the phone to call you."

"But when you were on the phone with me, you told me you could hear him coming down the hall."

There was a long pause.

"I did?"

"Yes, Serena, so now you're saying it might just have been a dream or your imagination?"

"No, I definitely heard noises. I just can't say for sure that it was an intruder. But I can promise you this, I did see Ned standing outside by the pool. And he did warn me to leave this house. That *did* happen. I swear I'm not making it up."

"Serena, that's impossible," Poppy said softly.

"I saw him with my own eyes, Poppy. He was real! I swear it!"

Poppy was curious to take a peek at the psych evaluation conducted on Serena when she was hospitalized because she was now worried about her current state of mind.

If this was not some sick joke or a result of her delicate emotional state, then the only alternative explanation was what she had so adamantly claimed, that she had just been paid a visit by the ghost of her late husband Ned Boyce.

It was right out of a plotline from a *Dark Shadows* remake Poppy had appeared in in the early nineties. Only in that poorly received TV movie that came in dead last in the ratings, the storyline was far more believable than the tale Serena Saunders was dramatically spinning tonight.

Chapter 29

"Iris, what are you doing?" Poppy asked after finding her hunched over, removing bottles from the liquor cabinet in Serena's mountaintop home.

"Hiding the booze," Iris said matter-of-factly, placing the bottles into several recyclable grocery bags.

"Do you really think that's necessary?"

"Of course I do! I believe Serena has been drinking too much and that's what is causing these mad hallucinations, so I am going to hide all the liquor out in the garage behind the water heater where she won't find it."

Poppy disagreed.

It was true Serena was known to have a cocktail or two to calm her nerves every day, but she was hardly a drunk. She did not consume enough gin to explain the recent sighting of her late husband's spirit desperately warning her to abandon their home.

When a thorough search of the property had turned up no clues that suggested an intruder of any kind, either in human form or a ghostly spirit, Serena still stubbornly stuck to her story about Ned's impromptu visit.

He had been there.

She had seen him outside by the pool as clear as day. And he spoke to her and his message was clear.

It was then that Poppy decided it might be a good idea for her to come stay with Serena and look after her for a few days. Serena balked at first, dismissing the notion that she required a babysitter, but when Poppy explained to her that if Ned's ghost was indeed haunting the house, then perhaps Poppy might be able to see the apparition too if she was staying there.

That remote possibility had sold Serena on the plan because she was intent on proving that she was not going insane. In fact, she also invited Iris and Violet. There were plenty of spare bedrooms in the massive house and there was always safety in numbers.

When the three of them had arrived, Iris claimed the biggest guest suite for herself and then immediately set about confiscating all the alcohol.

Violet made herself at home in the kitchen and prepared a light chicken dish for their supper, and Poppy set the table after browbeating Iris into leaving the one bottle of Chardonnay chilling in the fridge so they could have it with their meal.

When everything was ready, Poppy went to fetch Serena, who had been resting in her bedroom. She emerged with dark circles under her eyes, no makeup, and a rather disheveled appearance. Frizzy hair, wrinkled blouse, chipped nails in need of a manicure. The stress of the last few weeks were definitely taking its toll.

Serena was uncharacteristically quiet as they ate, complimenting Violet on the rosemary chicken after taking a few bites but leaving most of the plate untouched.

Iris took a gulp of her Chardonnay. "So do you think Ned might make an appearance tonight?"

Poppy shot Iris an admonishing look. "Iris . . ."

"No, it's fine. I know how it sounds," Serena muttered, swirling her cauliflower mash around with her fork. "You must think I am some kind of a kook."

"If we thought that, we would not be here," Violet assured her.

"I appreciate you all coming to stay with me. Just having you here makes me feel better."

"Of course," Poppy said. "We're happy to."

When they finished, Violet shot to her feet, noticing Serena had barely touched her food. "Did you not like your supper, Serena?"

"No. It was delicious, honestly. I just don't have much of an appetite. I'm sorry."

"No apologies necessary, just promise me you will at least try a bite of my Apple Crisp à la Mode. It's my specialty."

Serena wiped the corners of her mouth with her cloth napkin, set it down, and stood up from the table. "If it's all the same to you, I think I am just going to take a hot bath and go to bed early."

"Whatever you wish, Serena, and remember, we are all right here if you need us," Poppy promised.

"Thank you, good night," Serena said, slowly shuffling off to her bedroom.

"It's not even eight o'clock!" Iris snorted.

"Give the poor woman a break, Iris. She has been through quite a lot lately," Violet sighed.

"Fine, then. If she does not want her apple crisp, you can give me an extra-large piece and do not skimp on the ice cream!" Iris said.

"Coming right up," Violet said, clearing the dishes and heading into the kitchen.

Iris studied Poppy's face. "You look worried."

Poppy sat back in her chair and exhaled. "I am. I have known Serena Saunders for forty years, and in all that time, I have never seen her like this. She has always been in such total control. But now, it's as if she is hanging on by a thread and one tiny thing could trigger a complete breakdown."

"You are starting to sway me to your side. I was one hundred percent convinced that Serena did her husband in to get her hands on all his money. But now, being here and seeing her mental state firsthand, I am not so sure she is actually capable of something like that."

Poppy felt relief that she was not the only one coming to the belief that Serena was innocent of Ned's murder.

But that still left a very big question mark.

Who was?

Iris had just delivered the Apple Crisp à la Mode to the table and sat down to dig in when suddenly a piercing, eardrum-shattering scream filled the house.

Poppy, Iris, and Violet jumped up from the table and rushed to Serena's bedroom, flinging open the door. Serena's clothes were strewn on the bed, but she was not there. They heard water running in the bath and hurried in to find Serena, her pink silk robe wrapped around her, pressed up against the wall, her face a mask of terror, one hand clasped over her eyes as if she was trying to hide from something. Unable to speak from shock, she just kept pointing with a shaky finger at the large spa bathtub, which was filling with water but otherwise empty.

Violet crossed inside to shut off the water.

Poppy cautiously approached Serena, touching her arm. "Serena, what is it? What caused you to scream?"

It took her a moment to catch her breath as she continued pointing at the tub. "He-He was there in the bathtub, dead, someone had drowned him!"

Poppy took another glance at the tub. "Who?"

"A man. He was under the water, his eyes just staring up at me . . ."

"He's gone now. Why don't you take a look?" Poppy gently took hold of Serena's wrist to try to pry her hand away from her eyes.

Serena resisted. "No! No, I can't!"

"Come on, Serena, it's okay," Poppy said, tenderly pulling at Serena's wrist.

Serena finally gave up and allowed Poppy to remove her hand, but she kept her eyes firmly shut.

"Go on, Serena, open your eyes," Poppy said softly.

She took a few more moments, and then very slowly her eyes fluttered open and she looked down at the tub, now full of water and nothing else.

Her head snapped toward Poppy. "He was there, I swear!"

"I believe you," Poppy said.

But Serena caught the skepticism written all over Iris's face. "No, you don't, none of you do! You think I'm crazy! He was there! I saw him!"

Poppy put a comforting arm around Serena's waist and calmly led her back into the bedroom as Violet pulled the plug and drained the water from the bathtub.

Serena plopped down on the edge of the bed, staring into space, anguished. "What's happening to me?"

"You just need rest," Poppy said. "I think you should go to bed and get some sleep and things will look brighter in the morning."

At least she hoped that would be the case.

After a few more minutes of Serena trying to explain

that this was not her imagination, that she had heard an intruder, seen Ned's ghost and the dead man in her tub, Poppy felt enormous relief when she noticed Serena's eyes finally getting heavy. She began yawning, and after Poppy helped her climb into bed and slip underneath the covers, Serena mercifully fell into a deep sleep.

Poppy, Iris, and Violet tiptoed out, and after polishing off Violet's sweet and tasty apple crisp, decided to turn in themselves. Poppy set the alarm for six o'clock. She wanted to rise before Serena. She contemplated calling Sam before going to bed. Annoyed at his recent behavior, she ultimately decided against it, and after reading half a chapter of her Louise Penny novel, drifted off to sleep herself.

Another scream jolted her awake.

She flew out of bed, out the door, and down the hall toward Serena's bedroom. Iris and Violet popped out of their rooms and joined her as they tried the door handle and discovered it locked. Poppy began pounding on the door.

"It's two-thirty in the morning!" Iris groused. "Does Ned's ghost have to be so rude as to always show up in the middle of the night? Why can't he visit during normal daylight hours?"

"Iris, enough!" Poppy snapped, still pounding on the door. "Serena, let us in!"

They heard the lock click and the door opened.

Serena's spooked pale face peeked out at them.

Poppy pushed her way through to get into the bedroom. "Serena, what happened? Did you see Ned again?"

She slowly shook her head.

Poppy scanned the room. "Then what's wrong? What scared you?"

"Red Mitchell."

Poppy recognized the name.

He was an actor who had made a lot of Westerns in his day, including one with Serena where she played a saloon girl who fell in love with a gunslinger out to rescue his beloved horse from a marauding gang of cattle rustlers and horse thieves. All Poppy could really remember of that film was the amount of feathers on Serena's costume. There were feathers floating around in the air whenever she was on screen.

"Serena, Red is no longer with us. He died years ago," Poppy said in a hushed voice.

In 2002 of heart failure.

"I know, I know, I went to his funeral," Serena cried. "But I saw him."

Violet took a tentative step forward. "Was he here in the bedroom?"

"No, he was out there! Hanging from that tree!" Serena wailed, pointing to a large palm tree on the far side of the pool.

Poppy walked over and looked outside. "How is that possible, Serena?"

"I don't know! He just was! Why does this keep happening?" Serena sobbed, collapsing to the floor.

Iris and Violet rushed to her side, kneeling down to comfort her as Poppy returned her gaze back out the window.

There was no sign of anyone outside.

Least of all a former co-star hanging from a palm tree who had been dead for over twenty years.

After popping a sleeping pill, Serena finally agreed to go back to bed, and there were no further incidents for the rest of the night.

However, Poppy spent the next few hours tossing and

turning, unable to sleep, as she tried to comprehend why these scenarios Serena kept witnessing struck her as so familiar.

As the sun rose over the valley the next morning, it finally dawned on her. She quickly freshened up and dressed and joined Iris and Violet out in the kitchen, where they were having coffee.

"I figured it out," Poppy announced.

"What?" Violet asked, adding some sugar to her coffee and stirring it with a spoon.

"They're scenes from movies Serena Saunders co-starred in. The man in the tub was from *Dark Water: The Delia Weston Story*. It was a nineties Lifetime movie in which Serena played an abused wife who persuades her yoga instructor to help kill her husband so they can be together, and they end up drowning him in the bathtub. The man hanging from the tree, Red Mitchell, that was the last scene from a Western Serena appeared in called *The Tumbleweed Trail*. The gunslinger, played by Red Mitchell, gets caught by a gang of outlaws who stole his horse, and they hang him from a tree."

"That's the last scene in the movie? Remind me never to watch that one! What's so wrong with a happy ending every once in a while?" Iris snorted.

"Serena's character vows to take care of his horse on a farm she inherits from the owner of the saloon where she worked."

"Well, at least the horse lives!" Iris bellowed.

"So what does all this mean?" Violet asked.

"It means Serena is slowly descending into madness!" Iris concluded just as Serena appeared in the entrance to the kitchen, surprising them.

"She didn't mean that!" Poppy said sharply.

"No, it's fine. I certainly don't blame any of you for thinking it," Serena muttered. "Just listening to myself, I can hear how deranged I sound. I can't take it anymore."

"Would you like to speak to someone, a professional?" Poppy asked softly.

"No, I'm afraid they might have me committed on the spot. I need to figure out what's going on with me, but enough is enough. I can't do it here. I have to get out of this house!"

Chapter 30

Everyone thought it was a monumentally bad idea for Poppy to allow Serena Saunders to move in to her Palm Springs home, albeit temporarily. But when Serena had first broached the subject at breakfast, Poppy found it utterly impossible to refuse despite strong looks of objection from both Iris and Violet, who otherwise remained mum as they discussed it at Serena's kitchen table.

Serena had couched her request to move in with Poppy for just a few days, until she could "get her head on straight." When Iris mumbled under her breath that a herculean task like that would probably take a lot longer than just a few days, Violet had kicked her under the table, causing Iris to yelp.

But Poppy felt she had no choice.

Serena was falling apart staying at the mountaintop house, and Poppy could not imagine remaining there with her any longer than necessary, especially if it was weighing so heavily on Serena's admittedly fragile state of mind.

So the only solution appeared to be Serena moving in with her. The second Poppy gave her okay, Serena flew to her room, packing three giant suitcases, one just for her extensive and pricey jewelry collection. Despite a secure wall safe specially made for valuables on the premises, Serena had absolutely no intention of leaving her treasured jewels behind unattended. They were coming with her.

When they arrived at Poppy's house, Len, the neighbor across the street, was washing his car with a bucket of soap and a gardening hose in his driveway. He perked up at the sight of Serena sliding out of Poppy's car. He had already made a big show of pretending not to recognize Poppy when she moved in, even though it was quite clear he knew exactly who she was. But Serena had enjoyed a much longer career than Poppy, and not even Len could feign nonchalance when he spotted her. He bounded across the street to offer help unloading her bags from the trunk. At first Serena politely declined, but Len had insisted, nearly giving himself a hernia when he went to lift the bag stuffed with all of her jewelry.

Len proved useful, delivering all three suitcases to the guest room, then requesting a selfie with Serena to show his grandchildren, to which she kindly obliged. Although Poppy suspected the grandchildren had no idea who Serena Saunders was and the selfie was strictly for Len himself.

Serena had a long-standing habit of flirting with men. All men, really. She adored the opposite sex. And for the most part, they adored her. But today, with Len falling all over himself to be friendly, trying to prove his manliness by single-handedly carrying all three suitcases at once into the house, there was no trace of that side of Serena. She was gracious, of course, and grateful for his help, but there was no megawatt smile, or flipping of the hair, or intermittent touching his bare arm in a flirtatious, playful way. Serena just did not have it in her to be her typical coy, kittenish self with those come-hither eyes. In fact, Poppy noticed that Serena's eyes had completely lost their sparkle. She seemed to be just going through the motions.

After Len left, Poppy checked on Serena, who was in the guest room unpacking.

"I feel so awful. I enjoyed the luxury of staying at your palatial home in the mountains with its beautiful garden and pool and cavernous rooms and here I have shoved you into a guest room the size of a walk-in closet."

"It's lovely, really," Serena insisted. "Believe me, I would much rather be staying in this room than at that house. I'm never going back."

Poppy raised an eyebrow. "*Never?*"

Serena vigorously shook her head. "No! I will hire someone to clear out my things. I am going to put the house on the market the first chance I get."

"Where will you go?"

"I haven't a clue. But don't worry. I won't be in your hair long. Maybe I'll be a nomad and just go from Airbnb to Airbnb until I arrive at a place I can picture living in longer than a few weeks."

Serena sounded dead serious.

"I'm not worried. You can stay here as long as you like."

"Thank you, Poppy." She paused, then sniffed.

Poppy could sense she was starting to get emotional.

"You have been such a good friend," Serena said, choking up. "I cannot imagine having to go through all this without you."

Poppy smiled. "Who could have predicted the two of us would end up friends in our golden years?"

"I feel like we wasted so much time despising each other when we could have just buried the hatchet and been good friends a long time ago."

"It's never too late," Poppy said.

Her phone buzzed, and Poppy checked the screen.

It was a text from Violet.

Client meeting scheduled for 10. He is here early. Come when you can.

Poppy glanced up at Serena, who was sitting on the edge of the bed, taking a break from unpacking. "Serena, I have to go to work. I won't be gone long."

"I have no intention of disrupting your life. You go do what you need to do. I will be fine. Maybe I'll make us some dinner depending on what you have in the fridge."

"Call me if . . ." Poppy's voice trailed off.

"Ned decides to make another appearance?" Serena asked, chuckling. "Trust me, I will."

"Okay, make yourself at home," Poppy said, turning to leave.

"Poppy, wait . . ."

Poppy spun back around.

"I hope my being here doesn't cramp your style. I mean with Sam. I assume he stays here when he comes down from Big Bear, and I would hate to be in the way."

"You have nothing to worry about with Sam. Actually he hasn't been coming around as often lately."

"Oh, dear. So there is trouble in paradise?"

"I honestly don't know. Part of me thinks we might be taking a break from each other but he hasn't gotten around to telling me yet. He has definitely not been his usual amiable self lately, but I am done tormenting myself trying to figure out what's suddenly changed."

"You need to talk to him."

"Oh, I plan to, but it's been difficult to pin him down. Sometimes I feel like he's actively avoiding me."

Serena grimaced. "That's not right. If something is bothering him, he needs to tell you."

She was right, of course.

But it was disconcerting receiving relationship advice from Serena Saunders, who had gone through more husbands than Bluebeard went through wives.

After leaving Serena, Poppy drove directly to the Desert Flowers garage office two minutes before ten. She blew through the side door and stopped short at the sight of Warren Ashmore and Matt sitting on the couch. Iris and Violet sat opposite them. They all seemed to be waiting patiently for Poppy's arrival.

"Warren, Matt, I thought you two were in LA rehearsing for the movie," Poppy said.

Warren stood up to greet her. "We were, but I asked Matt to accompany me out here just for the day to see you. I have something urgent I wish to talk to you about."

Poppy gave him a brief hug and then sat down in the empty chair next to Violet. "Of course. How can we help you?"

"He wants to hire us," Iris blurted out.

There was a beat of silence.

Poppy nodded and turned her attention to Warren. "I see. And what exactly is it you would like us to do?"

"I want you to prove Serena Saunders murdered Ned."

The next beat of silence lasted a whole lot longer.

Matt cleared his throat. "Warren is pretty adamant that she's guilty, that she plotted the whole thing with the poison."

"But your cohorts here, Iris and Violet, they told me you don't necessarily believe she did it," Warren said, disappointed.

"As a matter of fact, I don't. I believe Serena was genuinely in love with Ned," Poppy said.

"So much so, now that he's dead, she is seriously cracking up badly, like next stop, the looney bin," Iris could not resist adding.

Poppy had grown weary of tossing admonishing looks in Iris's direction so she just chose to ignore her this time.

"As someone who directed her in a film, I can say with all certainty that she is a very talented actress," Warren spit out. "Come on, Poppy, you were on the set of *Valley of the Dolls* with us. You know what she's really like."

"Yes, it's true she was never the nicest person to be around, but I also happen to believe that this one time, when it involves Ned, whom she cared for deeply, she is *not* faking it."

"But you can't be one hundred percent certain that she didn't do it, can you?" Warren pressed.

"No, you're right, I can't."

"Then let's find out. Matt's going to be tied up with the film, but you ladies can look into this matter for me and get some definitive answers. I know I'm right about her. She's a manipulative, gold-digging, wicked monster, and I just need you to prove it."

"You sound like Ned's children."

"Did they try to hire you, too?"

"Yes, they did," Poppy said.

"And what did you tell them?"

"What I'm about to tell you. Serena was a client and is a friend. It would be a conflict of interest to investigate her. Especially since she has hired us to prove her innocence."

"And how has that been going? Come on, that's just a distraction. She's guilty as hell. Please don't tell me you're willing to let her get away with murder?"

"If she committed a crime, then the police will do their own investigation and arrest her."

"The police are useless in this town," Warren seethed.

"I happen to disagree. But whatever you may think, Warren, the answer is still no."

Warren's shoulders sagged slightly as it slowly began to sink in that Poppy was not going to accept the case. "Matt and I are staying one more night in town before heading back to LA tomorrow. I will be at home in case you change your mind."

"I won't," Poppy said in a clipped tone.

She wanted to make it clear the meeting was over.

Chapter 31

Serena sat back on Poppy's couch, swirling the last of her Chardonnay around in her wineglass and asked, "Do you ever miss it?"

Poppy used her fork to cut into a piece of key lime pie she had made for dessert, stopping before popping it into her mouth. "You mean Hollywood?"

"Yes. I know once I got my first break at twenty-one, a walk-on part as a prostitute on *T.J. Hooker*, it was in my blood. I just knew I would always be a part of the entertainment business."

"And you still are," Poppy noted.

"Yes, I've been very lucky. It's been a long, sometimes agonizing crawl, and there were many times I just wanted to walk away, but I stuck with it and endured and I have no regrets. But what about you?"

Poppy shrugged. "You have to remember, I quit decades ago, when I was just in my thirties. I was so tired of playing the game. I thought after *Jack Colt* was cancelled, I would have my pick of parts. I was a famous actress. I had been on the cover of *TV Guide*. But I did not realize that when you're not on America's television screens every week, Hollywood can forget you pretty quickly. I knew it was time when I got an audition for a feature film starring John Travolta. You can imagine how excited I was. The star of *Saturday Night Fever* and *Grease*! And it was a meaty part. The love interest. I prepared for that audition for a whole week. But when I got there, they told me I was not auditioning for the love interest. They wanted me to play his mother. He was thirty-eight at the time. Five years older than me. They wanted a twenty-two-year-old model to play his girlfriend. That told me it was time to get out."

"Not much has changed," Serena groused, swallowing the rest of her Chardonnay.

"I had met Chester by that point, and I knew he was going to propose. I was exhausted from begging for parts so I could keep my SAG health insurance. I craved stability. And Chester wanted to give that to me."

"And it all worked out for you."

"Hardly. In case you didn't hear, Chester turned out to be a hopeless gambling addict who siphoned off all our savings and left me penniless when he died suddenly."

Serena frowned. "I did pick up on a rumor going around . . ."

"But I have no regrets. That led me to getting my private investigator's license, and now I have the most fulfilling career I have ever had in my life."

"I envy you," Serena said, setting her wineglass down on the coffee table. "I have spent forty-five years struggling and fighting and scratching and clawing, and for what? Half the time I think casting directors call me in just to see how old I look now. It's a brutal business, but I was finally ready to let all that go, leave Hollywood behind me, and start a whole new life here with Ned, finally have some real security instead of having to hustle all the time."

"I'm so sorry, Serena."

"Truthfully, do you think I poisoned him?"

"No. You would not be here right now if I did."

"You're the only one."

"That's not true."

"I'm pretty good at reading faces. I can see Iris and Violet are convinced I am some kind of evil manipulative character, and Matt certainly has his doubts, probably because he has Warren Ashmore squawking in his ear."

"So you heard Warren came to our office today?"

Serena nodded. "Yes, I still have a few spies at Warren's production company. I will admit, that one did hurt. I thought Warren was an ally. He introduced me to Ned. He could see how much I loved him. I don't know why he decided to turn on me."

"You can't control what other people think."

"Poppy, when I met Ned, I honestly believed he was having financial trouble. He had the house his parents had left him, but I was led to believe that there were a lot of back taxes and that whatever money he did have was tied up in some failing stocks. He also alluded to the fact that his wealth management business was losing clients after the economic downturn."

"Perhaps he purposefully led you to that impression because he wanted to make sure you loved him for him and not his money."

"I did love him. More than any man I have ever met. And you know full well given my past that there were a lot of them."

They shared a giggle.

"I was as surprised as you to learn how rich Ned was, but it didn't matter to me in the least. I would have married him if he was a street sweeper or coffee barista because he was the first man I have ever dated who I did not get the sinking feeling was using me for some reason. To help him get an agent. Or invest in his start-up business. Or impress his fellow country club members by dating a well-known actress. Ned could not have cared less about what I could do for him. He just loved being around me. That made me feel so special." Her eyes welled up with tears. "And I miss him so much."

Poppy set her pie plate down and scooted across the couch to hug Serena for a long moment before Serena finally sat back and wiped her eyes, chuckling. "I suppose our Joan Crawford Bette Davis Divine Feud is officially over."

Poppy poured herself a glass of Chardonnay and refilled Serena's. "This calls for a toast. To healing old wounds."

They clinked glasses and both took a sip.

Poppy looked thoughtfully at her. "I promise you, Serena, I *will* find the person responsible for poisoning Ned."

Serena nodded. "I have no doubt, Miss Marple. I just hope they let me play myself in the TV movie version of this whole mess that will most likely get made."

The doorbell rang.

"Who could that be? It's almost ten o'clock," Poppy said, climbing to her feet. "Stay here. I will be right back."

Poppy crossed the living room and into the foyer to the front door. She peered through the peephole, then quickly unlocked the door and opened it.

Matt stood on the welcome mat.

"Matt, what are you doing here? I thought you were heading back to LA."

"I am," he said solemnly. "First thing in the morning. But I had to stop by here before I left."

Poppy had a sick feeling in the pit of her stomach. "What is it? What's wrong?"

Matt took a deep breath and exhaled. "I had dinner with Warren tonight at Eight-Four-Nine."

One of Palm Springs's trendiest restaurants in the uptown design district boasting a sleek white decor with pops of color and a New American cuisine menu.

"We were chatting about the production schedule over drinks when I suddenly noticed Sam at a corner table."

"Sam? But he's home in Big Bear," Poppy croaked, bracing herself for what was about to come.

"Apparently he's here in town and he wasn't dining alone. He was with a woman."

"Who?"

"I didn't know her. But she was much younger."

Poppy gulped. "How much younger?"

"Mid- to late twenties, maybe."

Her stomach would not stop tying up in knots.

She closed her eyes. "Were they on a date?"

"I couldn't tell for sure, but . . ."

"But what?"

"I was about to go over and say hello when he handed the girl a box with a bow on it, and then, she, uh, she opened it and was delighted to find a—"

"A necklace?"

Matt paused, staring down, unable to make eye contact with her. "A very expensive-looking necklace."

Poppy gripped the door handle to keep her balance. She felt as if she had just been sucker punched in the gut.

Chapter 32

Poppy had never considered herself an impulsive person. In fact, she was very much the opposite. She usually considered every angle of a problem before committing to a specific course of action. She rarely "flew off the handle" or "threw caution to the wind." It took her almost two years to pick out a new car, almost four to finally make a decision to put a down payment on her house.

So she was utterly surprised to find herself behind the wheel of her car, driving up the winding mountain road to Big Bear, where she planned to finally hash things out with Sam. This unbearable situation had gone on long enough. She should have confronted him weeks ago, pushed for him to explain his sudden change in behavior, this undeniable distance that had come between them. If Sam wanted to end things, he was going to have to bust a move today because she was done wondering what was going on in his mind. She deserved to know what he was thinking. Sam had never been the talkative sort; he was the kind of man who kept quiet until he actually had something important to say. And that was one of the qualities Poppy loved about him. But she knew there was something else going on with him, and today she had decided was the day she was finally going to get some answers.

Poppy turned off the highway up a gravel road toward Sam's cabin in the woods. As she got closer and the cabin came into view, Poppy suddenly pressed down on the brakes and pulled the car over to the side of the road. Up ahead she could see a red Camry she did not recognize. Sam's truck was nowhere to be seen.

Who did the Camry belong to?

As if on cue, the door to the cabin swung open and a beautiful young woman in her late twenties emerged, eyes glued to her phone. She was dressed in what appeared to be a flight attendant's uniform with gold wings clipped to a navy blue blazer, matching skirt, crisp white button-up shirt with a blue and gray scarf wrapped around her neck. Her hair was tied up in a bun, and she wore a beret that matched the colors of her scarf.

The dinner companion Sam had been with at Eight-Four-Nine last night.

It had to be.

The other woman.

And a flight attendant to boot.

It was such a cliché.

Poppy threw open the car door and shot out, marching the rest of the way down the gravel road toward the cabin. The woman was so preoccupied checking messages on her phone that she did not even hear her coming until Poppy was almost upon her.

The woman glanced up, startled, squeaking out a barely audible "Hello."

Poppy stopped, arms rigidly at her sides, hands clammy. "Is Sam home?"

"Uh, no, he's not. He went into town to pick up a few groceries—"

Before she could continue, Poppy interrupted her. "And who, may I ask, might you be?"

The woman smiled and extended her hand. "Oh, I'm Isabella."

The name sounded familiar.

But Poppy could not place her at the moment.

Still, she felt as if she had seen this woman before, perhaps in a photograph.

"I'm Sam's niece."

It suddenly all fell into place.

Isabella.

Of course.

The oldest daughter of Sam's brother Joe.

A flight attendant based out of Phoenix.

Poppy could feel her cheeks reddening with embarrassment, but she quickly tried to recover. "Isabella! I'm Poppy, Poppy Harmon, your uncle's . . ."

"Girlfriend. I know! I have heard so much about you. My dad has the entire *Jack Colt* series on DVD, all seventy episodes, and he loves to show all us kids the big Hollywood star Uncle Sam has been dating! I think he might be a little jealous."

"Sam never mentioned you were coming for a visit."

Otherwise she never would have made a complete fool of herself driving all the way up here and confronting this poor unsuspecting young woman.

"He didn't know I was coming. I picked up a Phoenix to Palm Springs leg with my airline with a two-day layover, so I thought to myself, why not surprise my favorite uncle?"

"How lovely. I wish I had known."

Why hadn't Sam told her?

Why hide it from her?

"Like I said, it was all very last minute," Isabella insisted. "And he told me how busy you are with your business as a private investigator, which is so cool, by the way."

Poppy could not resist prying a little further. "I certainly hope he did not keep you stuck up here in Big Bear the whole time you've been here."

"Oh, not at all. We went into Palm Springs yesterday and had a lovely day. We drove back up here after dinner."

"Knowing Sam, I am sure he took you somewhere nice."

"Eight-Four-Nine. I had never been there before. It was wonderful. The Plabano Chile Relleno was life-changing."

She wanted to ask about the necklace but did not have to, because Isabella was so forthcoming.

"And after we split a Baked Alaska for dessert, he even gave me an early birthday present, this stunning necklace I had my eye on from my last visit but couldn't afford."

"How thoughtful."

"I think Uncle Sam felt sorry for me. I recently broke up with my boyfriend, a pilot, which was my first big mistake, who it turned out was also married. Anyway, it's been a rough couple of months, and I think Uncle Sam wanted to find a way to cheer me up so he decided to splurge. I told him it was too much, I mean that necklace must have cost thousands . . ."

Twelve hundred dollars, in fact.

"But he insisted you only turn thirty once in your life."

"Happy birthday," Poppy said with a smile.

"It's not until next month, but since I was already here, he figured why not? It's so gorgeous. I'd show you, but it's packed away in my suitcase and I need to run. I still have to return my rental car and check in with the airline. I'm working a flight to San Francisco that departs in a few hours."

Poppy neglected to mention that she had already seen the necklace when Sam bought it at the jeweler's.

Isabella raised her phone and began tapping on the screen.

"Let me text Uncle Sam to let him know you're here! He will be so happy!"

Poppy shot out a hand to stop her. "No!"

The forcefulness of her voice caused Isabella to suddenly freeze.

"I can't stay, I have to get back to Palm Springs."

"But you came all this way. He's going to want to see you."

"I know, but I came up here to see another friend. I only stopped by to say a quick hello, I'm really pressed for time."

It was a fib.

Which was a softer way of saying it was a lie.

And Poppy felt guilty about it.

But she already felt ridiculous enough being up here.

Stalking Sam and his sweet and charming niece.

The idea of having to explain her presence was cringe-inducing. The best course of action now was to hightail it out of there and pretend it never happened.

"Isabella, do me a favor? Please don't mention to your uncle that I was here."

Isabella cocked her head to one side like a cute dog hearing someone at the door. "Oh. Okay."

"I just don't want him feeling slighted if he knows I was up here in Big Bear and didn't stick around long enough to see him."

Would she buy that weak excuse?

Poppy figured it could go either way.

"Sure, no problem," Isabella chirped.

And Poppy heaved a big sigh of relief knowing she had.

"It was sure nice finally meeting you in person, Poppy," Isabella said as she unlocked the door of the red Camry and slid behind the wheel. "I can see why my uncle thinks so highly of you."

And the guilt just kept piling on.

Isabella started the car, gave a little wave out the open driver's side window, backed up, and sped off, gravel flying up around the tires.

Poppy watched her go.

She felt silly and petty and stupid.

She had completely misread the situation.

But that still did not explain Sam's odd behavior.

And she was determined to get to the bottom of that and finally determine whether she and Sam Emerson had some kind of future together.

Chapter 33

Candy Sellers, with her loud, colorful print blouse, white Capri pants, teased out blond hair and ruby-red lipstick, was a real estate legend in the Coachella Valley. Her smiling mug could be seen all over Palm Springs from a billboard along Dinah Shore Drive to bus stops and even on the side of the buses themselves. Her hard-and-fast rule was to never represent any home under 1 million dollars. She was ruthlessly competitive and despised by her peers, but she had that magic touch when it came to selling houses. Multiple offers were common even after a housing market downturn. She just had a sharp instinct on finding the right buyer with an impeccable credit score or enough to buy the property outright with cash. So neither Poppy nor Serena were surprised when Candy called with the good news that she had an offer above asking price even before Ned's mountaintop home had gone on the market. The buyer only requested a speedy escrow, and Candy was firm on making sure the deal went through without a hitch. When she suggested Serena join her at the house for the inspection, Serena demurred, explaining that she had no intention of ever stepping foot inside that house again. But Candy was insistent, promising it would only take an hour or so and that it was important that she be there in case of any hiccups. Poppy offered to come along for moral support, and Serena had finally relented.

When they pulled up in front of the house in Poppy's car, Serena's hands were shaking and she had to remain in the car for a few minutes to calm her nerves and prepare herself before going inside. Poppy jumped out and circled the car, helping Serena out and guiding her by the elbow like a small child.

Candy greeted them at the door with a megawatt smile she had perfected over the years, waving them inside as if the home belonged to her and not Serena.

"The inspector is outside looking at the pool equipment," Candy explained, although neither of them had asked. "Can you believe I got over asking? Yes, I'm *that* good!"

"The sooner I unload this house, the better," Serena said flatly.

Candy grimaced slightly, yearning for more positive vibes in the room and much more praise for her efforts, but she quickly covered with that blinding smile. Her teeth were the whitest Poppy had ever seen. It was disconcerting how unnaturally white they were, as if they had been recently bleached.

"Barring any catastrophes from the inspection, like the place needs a new roof or something dreadful like that, I think we can close by the end of the month."

Poppy looked around, folded her arms, and asked, "Who's the buyer?"

"I am afraid I can't tell you that," Candy said, averting eye contact.

Serena suddenly snapped to attention. "What? Why not?"

"He or she, I'm forbidden to even talk genders, had only one requirement. That they remain anonymous. I did not think it would be an issue since you're so eager to sell."

"It's not," Serena said wanly, much to Candy's relief.

"Since escrow is speeding along at a clip, you will have to vacate all of your belongings sooner than later," Candy said.

"This is the last time I ever plan on coming here, but I will hire movers to pack up everything and put it into storage until I figure out a plan. I may just rent a furnished home for six months or so."

Poppy was about to offer her place for Serena to stay as long as she needed, but wisely refrained, given the possibility Serena might actually accept. Still, she would not kick her out anytime soon, since Serena seemed to crave her company.

"So I did some research on the place before deciding to take it on. I had no idea it had such a fascinating history," Candy gushed. "Alistair Boyce and Jean Harding built it way back in the nineteen sixties."

"Yes, they were my husband's . . . my late husband's parents. They came out to Palm Springs to shoot a movie and fell in love with the desert, so they built this as a weekend retreat," Serena explained, turning to Poppy. "Warren Ashmore directed the picture. He was just starting out, it was his first major film, he was in his early twenties. Ned was probably around fifteen. That's how they became friends."

"Well, I would say it's quite a palace considering this was just a weekend getaway retreat," Candy laughed, eyes twinkling.

"Unfortunately, according to Ned, his parents spent money faster than they could make it. It was not long after that when their fortunes took a turn for the worse, the parts dried up, and they moved out here full-time after they were forced to sell their Beverly Hills mansion to avoid bankruptcy."

"Oh God!" Candy cried.

"What? What is it?" Poppy asked, startled.

"The inspector is writing on his pad! I hope there's not an issue with the pool! I will be right back!" Candy roared, rushing out the sliding glass door.

Poppy turned to Serena. "Would you like me to help you pack some more of your things to take with you today?"

"Thank you, Poppy. There are a few beauty products that I left behind when I came to stay with you. I was in such a rush to get out of here."

Poppy followed Serena down the hallway to the main suite and into the bathroom. Serena plucked a travel case out of a basin drawer and began dropping in some perfume, lotions, and hairspray. By the time she was finished, Candy had returned and was waiting for them in the hallway next to the landscape mural.

"False alarm!" Candy crowed. "Nothing to worry about. The pool man just needs to change out the filters the next time he comes. I will make sure he does that." Her eyes flicked to the wall mural. "I sure wish this were an actual Dexter Holt original. It would increase the value of the house by nine million or so."

"As you can see, it's not signed," Serena sighed. "It's a total fake."

"But it just looks so real," Candy said admiringly.

As she clambered back down the hall, her red heels clicking on the tiled floor, Poppy hung back, noticing a slight tear in the wallpaper near the bottom left corner of the mural. She wondered if the inspector had caught it. She pressed the hanging piece back onto the wall, but it was so old, just her touch caused it to rip some more. She didn't want to fuss with it any longer, fearing she would just make it look worse, when she spotted what appeared to be the letter *D* underneath it. She carefully pulled the paper toward her, thinking she could just repair it with some adhesive tape, and then she gasped. In plain view was a *D* and an *E* and an *X*. The more she pulled, the more she could see a very distinct and recognizable signature.

Dexter Holt.

No. This could not be.

Did the knockoff artist sign the mural as some kind of joke? Or was this actually Dexter Holt's signature?

This could not possibly be an original, because if it were, the mural itself would be worth more than the cost of the entire house!

Poppy turned to Serena, who stared at the signature as well, not sure what she was seeing. "Poppy, is that . . . ? I mean, it can't be real, can it?"

Poppy just kept staring at the name, her eyebrows knitted together.

Dexter Holt.

The exact same signature she had seen dozens of times in museums all over the world.

Poppy could hear her heart in her ears, excitement pumping, as she turned to Serena, eyes drilling into hers. "Well, we certainly need to find out before you sell this house."

Chapter 34

Poppy dreaded having to look at the perpetual sour expression on Willa's face once again, but she had no choice. It was critical she speak to both of Ned Boyce's children. After Poppy called Gavin to request an in-person meeting, he had directed her to the Jackie Cooper Tennis Club in Palm Desert, where both he and his sister were members and Willa was at that moment playing a match. When Poppy arrived, Gavin met her outside and led her to the courts, where she watched a young upstart in pigtails, barely eighteen, trounce Willa in a shutout game. Willa hurled her racquet into the net and stormed off the court repeatedly hissing a four-letter word to herself. Poppy noticed her opponent had a self-satisfied smile on her face as she bounced away, happy in the knowledge that she had so soundly defeated such an obnoxious player.

Gavin waved at Willa to join them at a table near the outdoor bar, and she plunked down, pouting, not even acknowledging Poppy, which did not offend Poppy. She had so much distaste for this woman, it was preferable to have as limited interaction with her as possible.

Gavin was far more agreeable and ordered them some lemonades from the bartender.

"Make mine with vodka." Willa seethed.

There was an uncomfortable silence because it was not even noon yet.

"So what's so important you have to intrude on my day?" Willa asked.

"Poppy wanted to talk to us about the mural at Dad's house," Gavin explained to his sulky sister.

"What about it? The gold digger is apparently getting everything lock, stock, and barrel if our lawsuit is dismissed, so why should we even care?"

Gavin took a deep breath. "Poppy thinks the mural might be an original."

Willa froze. "Excuse me?"

"I was there yesterday and I noticed there was a tear in the wallpaper around the mural, and when I tugged on it, I found a signature underneath. Dexter Holt."

Their eyes widened.

"Dexter Holt?" Gavin whispered.

"That's impossible. I'm sure Dad would have known if it were an original," Willa scoffed. "I mean, the artist who actually painted it could have just signed Dexter Holt's name on a lark. Did that thought ever occur to you?"

"Yes, it did, which is why I have booked a flight later today to talk to the artist himself. He's still alive and living in Santa Fe, New Mexico. Did you ever suspect that the mural might be real?"

"Of course not," Willa sneered as if it were the most ridiculous thought in the world. "It would be worth millions now. And double that when Dexter Holt finally croaks. He must be well into his eighties by now. Surely Dad would have told us."

"Maybe he didn't know either," Gavin suggested. "Remember? He never liked that mural. He almost had it painted over when he inherited the place from our grandparents because he wasn't a fan of the style."

Poppy leaned in closer. "Do you remember why he didn't?"

Gavin nodded. "I think Uncle Warren talked him out of it."

Poppy's blood ran cold. "Warren Ashmore?"

"Yeah, Uncle Warren told him how much it had meant to our grandparents, and how preserving it would be like a nice remembrance, so Dad decided to just leave it the way it was and not touch it."

The waiter arrived with their drinks. Willa snatched hers up and gulped it down. Then she slammed the glass down on the table. "If it turns out that mural is an authentic Dexter Holt, we can't let Serena have it!"

Gavin frowned. "Dad's will was pretty clear, Willa . . ."

"I don't care! She doesn't deserve it! I won't let her walk away with all that money! We will just have to keep her tied up in the courts for years. I don't care how much it costs!"

"With no inheritance, I don't see how that's even possible. We'll go broke," Gavin sighed.

"We do not know for sure yet if the mural is a Dexter Holt original, so there really is no point in getting all worked up about it yet," Poppy said sharply. "Hopefully I will get some answers in Santa Fe."

Poppy could see both their minds whirring with activity. This was potentially a stunning, game-changing development. One that neither sibling could sit by and watch unfold without some plan to try to wrest possession of this possibly priceless piece of art. But they were at a supreme disadvantage. The house and all its contents were specifically willed to Serena. So they would have to get creative.

Poppy had no doubt they would do whatever was in their power to make sure Serena Saunders wound up the loser in a battle royale. And judging from the hate and fury in Willa's eyes, Poppy worried what extremes these incensed, disinherited kids might be willing to go to get what they wanted.

Chapter 35

It was midafternoon by the time Poppy arrived by taxi from the Santa Fe airport at Dexter Holt's Spanish Mission–style home on the outskirts of town. She had almost missed her connection in Phoenix because her Palm Springs flight had been delayed, but luckily, after a mad dash through the terminal, she had managed to board just as they were closing the doors and take her window seat in the exit row. She had planned on staying overnight at the iconic hotel La Fonda on the Plaza where she and Chester had once vacationed, spending a memorable week exploring the art galleries and spoiling themselves with massages at the famous Japanese-inspired spa Ten Thousand Waves. She had made a reservation but did not have time to check in before meeting with Dexter Holt, so she had simply lugged her small suitcase along with her.

After paying the taxi driver, she dragged her roller across the gravel to the covered porch, where a large imposing Native American woman with long straight black hair pulled into a ponytail and broad athletic shoulders waited on the doorstep to greet her.

Poppy offered her a bright smile. "You must be Nita."

The woman nodded. "Did you get my text?"

"No, when did you send it?"

"A few hours ago."

"I'm sorry, I must have forgotten to turn my phone back on when we landed. I grabbed my bag and went straight to the taxi stand. Is anything wrong?"

Nita grimaced. "I tried reaching you before you came all this way, but I'm afraid today is not a good day."

"What do you mean?"

"Mr. Holt is not himself today. It's the dementia. Some days he's as sharp as a tack and can hold a conversation for hours, play pinochle, complain about politics and the weather, and then other days he barely knows where he is."

Poppy's stomach twisted.

She could not believe she had come all this way and was not going to be able to question Dexter Holt.

Nita was his home caregiver in charge of his life. She was paid a yearly sum out of his estate by his lawyer to look after him and make sure he was comfortable. She had a nurse's degree but never liked working in hospitals. She preferred a more personal one-on-one touch with her patients. According to the lawyer who had put Poppy in touch with her, she had been with Mr. Holt for over five years. She was loyal, competent, and protective. Nita had warned Poppy through his lawyer that Mr. Holt was declining mentally and may not be able to give her the answers she needed, but since she did not object to her coming to see him, Poppy decided to just take the chance and get on the plane. Like her late husband, Chester, had done many times behind her back during their marriage, she had gambled and unfortunately made a bad bet.

"I am here until tomorrow morning. Perhaps he might be better by then," Poppy said hopefully.

"I doubt it, but you can always try," Nita said gruffly.

Poppy turned to see the taxi driving away. "It seems I am going to have to call for a ride back to town."

"You can wait inside. I'll make us some tea," Nita offered, leading her inside.

The home was breathtaking in its distinctive architectural Spanish Mission–inspired style with its arched doorways, brightly colored ceramic tiles, and exposed beams. What struck Poppy as odd was the lack of artwork on the walls, just textiles and clay pots and plants as decoration. Dexter Holt was a world-famous artist and there was not one of his paintings hanging in plain sight for anyone to see.

Nita led Poppy into the living room. "Have a seat. I will put the kettle on."

She disappeared down a cavernous hall. Poppy sat down on a brown leather couch. From the next room, she heard someone coughing. That had to be Dexter. She did not want to upset Nita by accosting the poor man, but she also wanted to make sure that what she was being told was true, that Dexter was not in possession of his faculties. She stood back up and tiptoed into what appeared to be a sitting room with a view of an enclosed courtyard. A man was rocking back and forth in a rocking chair, puffs of smoke floating in the air from the cigar in his mouth.

"Mr. Holt?"

He did not turn his head or acknowledge her in any way.

Poppy took a tentative step toward him. "Mr. Holt?"

Nothing.

Just rocking.

Back and forth.

Back and forth.

She could not resist getting closer and when she stepped in front of him, she recognized him immediately. His face was craggy, his cheeks sallow and eyes vacant. There was a grayness to his complexion that made her shudder. She knew instinctively he was probably not long for this world, which would explain why Nita allowed him to smoke a cigar and enjoy a scotch on the rocks that he clutched tightly in his bony, wrinkled hand. Toward the end, why not indulge in a few of life's pleasures?

She decided to try one more time, slowly bending down in front of him.

"Mr. Holt, my name is Poppy Harmon. Can you hear me?"

"I told you he's not himself today."

The sharp voice startled Poppy, and she snapped back up to see Nita holding a tray with a teapot and two flowery cups, some sugar packets, and a small carton of milk.

"I'm sorry, I heard him coughing in here, so I decided to check in on him to make sure he's all right."

"He's fine," Nita insisted. "Like I told you, he's just . . . elsewhere today, God only knows where."

Poppy watched him as he sucked on the cigar causing his froglike jowls to move up and down. His eyes were droopy and half-closed as he seemed to focus his gaze on a squirrel outside scampering up a one seed juniper tree.

This had been a huge waste of time.

But Poppy was not the type to throw in the towel and leave totally empty-handed.

"Nita, have you ever talked to Mr. Holt about his past?"

She shrugged as she set the tray down and poured the tea. "Sometimes. Not often. One lump or two?"

"Today is a two-lump kind of day."

Nita gave her a half smile.

"Did he ever talk to you about a wall mural he painted for a movie star couple in Palm Springs way back in the nineteen sixties?"

"Not that I recall. He had come in contact with lots of famous people in his heyday. Hollywood stars, famous politicians. He once mentioned partying with Mick Jagger in London, which I thought was kind of cool. Sometimes I don't know whether I should believe him or not. Maybe he's just imagining a past that didn't exist at this point, but I want to believe him. On his good days, he's a pretty nice fella. What movie star couple are you talking about?"

"Alistair Boyce and Jean Harding."

She seemed to roll the names over in her head and then shook her head. "Nope. Doesn't ring a bell."

Poppy blew on her tea and then took a sip. "Well, it was a really long time ago."

"Maybe we could look it up in his diary," Nita said offhandedly.

Poppy suddenly perked up. "Diary?"

"He kept a diary for years, the same way Andy Warhol did. He didn't like Andy Warhol. He thought he got too much attention at the expense of other up-and-coming artists like himself. He told me that once in one of his more lucid moments."

"Do you know where he keeps this diary?"

"Of course. There are hundreds of them stored in a room beneath the bell tower. He wants me to hand them over to a biographer when he dies to sort through them and write a book about his life."

"Do you think I could see them?"

Nita hesitated, scrunching up her face.

"Please, it's very important."

"I suppose. You did come all this way. But just be careful. Some of them are very old and I don't want them damaged any more than they already are."

Poppy swallowed her tea and set the cup down on the tray. "I promise. I just need to go through the ones from the late nineteen sixties."

"All right, then, let's go." Nita turned to Dexter. "I'll be back with another scotch, Mr. Holt."

He had no reaction.

He just kept his watery eyes fixed on the squirrel frozen halfway up the juniper, debating its next move.

Nita led Poppy out the door to the enclosed courtyard and across the property to an attached garage beneath the bell tower. She removed a set of keys from her belt and unlocked the door. It was dark and musty as they entered. Nita flipped on a light, and Poppy was amazed at the dozens and dozens of stacked boxes filled with writings and mementos. It took a half hour to locate the diaries from the 1960s, and another forty-five minutes to comb through them to find any mention of Alistair Boyce and Jean Harding.

"Eureka!" Poppy exclaimed, pointing at an entry from mid-1968. "Here it is!"

June 19, 1968. Had a stroke of good luck today. The starving artist won't go hungry, at least for a little while anyway. I got a job painting a wall mural at a new home being built by two actors named Alistair Boyce and Jean Harding. My parents love them. I think their movies are pretty dumb and they seem kind of full of themselves, but I'm getting paid two hundred dollars, so why not? Warhol does commissions. Of course he gets paid hundreds of thousands for his, but who knows? Maybe someday mine might be worth that. More even. I just don't get why everyone salivates over Warhol and his stupid soup cans. I don't really want to go to Palm Springs. I hear it's really hot this time of year, but the man who hired me really loves my work. He saw my show at the gallery on Robertson in LA. Apparently he is some wunderkind film director who just directed his first movie with these two actors and wanted to give them a housewarming gift. Fine by me. I don't mind pimping myself out if it means pocketing two hundred dollars.

Poppy read on. The next entry was several weeks later after he had painted the commissioned mural. He never mentioned Alistair Boyce or Jean Harding again.

But the identity of the wunderkind film director was obvious.

It had to be Warren Ashmore.

Ned Boyce had been wrong about his parents knowing who Dexter Holt was and commissioning a knockoff. The mural had been Warren's idea all along. Dexter Holt was just starting out when he painted it. His art was worth next to nothing back then. Just two hundred measly dollars. Ned's parents probably passed away before Dexter Holt became a household name. Only later did his work substantially increase in value. They never really knew what they had.

But someone certainly did now.

And the pieces of the puzzle were now falling into place.

Chapter 36

Serena wobbled on her feet, her eyes fluttered, and it appeared as if she was about to faint, so Poppy rushed forward to grab her by the elbow to steady her in case she fell backward.

Mr. Plemmons, the bespectacled, mustachioed art historian Poppy had hired to come evaluate the mural, blinked worriedly at Serena after delivering the shocking estimate of its worth.

"I-I'm sorry," Serena stammered. "How much did you say?"

"Around ten million," he said matter-of-factly, as if he was quoting the price of a dinner special from a restaurant menu board.

Serena swooned some more, gripping Poppy by the arm, her breath ragged. "A-Are you sure?"

"Oh yes, in fact, it's a rather conservative estimate. When Mr. Holt passes on, I suspect the price might double, if not triple."

Given the fact that Dexter Holt was in failing health, that day would probably come sooner rather than later.

Poppy had to be certain this mural was a Dexter Holt

original. Even though Holt himself wrote about painting it in his diary, she needed some kind of professional confirmation and so she had contacted Mr. Plemmons, who had come highly recommended from one of Iris's golfing buddies, an enthusiastic art collector in La Quinta. He calmly removed his glasses and wiped them clean with a white handkerchief, still studying the mural.

Poppy was flabbergasted at the insane value of the mural. And to think, according to his children, Ned had almost painted over it because he was not a fan of the style. It made her shudder. But luckily Warren Ashmore had talked him out of it at the last minute.

But now, in Poppy's mind, luck had played no part in it.

Because Warren Ashmore always *knew* it was an original.

He had commissioned the piece in the first place when the house was first built.

No wonder he had remained a loyal friend to Ned Boyce all these years. He knew what a valuable work of art Ned had in his possession and how much money it could fetch one day, even if poor Ned did not have an inkling what was on his wall.

Why should Ned even care? He was already loaded thanks to his late wife Cecily.

"This changes everything!" Serena whispered, pulling Poppy aside. "We have to call Candy and tell her. We can't accept the current offer, not when the house is worth so much more!"

"No, not yet," Poppy said.

"But you heard Mr. Plemmons! This wall alone is worth ten million dollars!"

"I understand, but I fear something else is going on here, and until we can determine exactly what, I don't think we should make this news public. I want you to give me a little more time to investigate."

The wheels in Poppy's brain were spinning fast. She grabbed Serena by the hand. "Come with me."

As she dragged her away, Serena called back to Mr. Plemmons. "We'll be right back!"

Poppy led her to the main bedroom, marching straight for the bathroom, the squish of the plush carpet under their shoes. Poppy turned on the light, stared at the bathtub for a long moment, then spun around, her eyes flicking up at the air vent. She took a step closer, peering through the vent. There was a small piece of electronic equipment with a tiny camera lens pointed through one of the grates.

"Just as I suspected," Poppy said.

"What? What is it?"

"A high-tech digital projector."

She then marched back into the bedroom, searched around for another vent, then grabbed a chair, placing it right underneath it. She discarded her shoes and stepped up on the chair, balancing herself before stretching up on her tippy-toes to peer into the vent opposite the door to the room.

"Here is another one," she said excitedly.

She hopped down from the chair and clapped her hands together. "And I bet if we search around outside, we will find a third one. I assume these projectors don't belong to Ned."

"No, of course not. He would have told me. Has someone been spying on us?"

"No, they're not cameras, they project images, like scenes from your old movies, a dead man in the tub, a man hanging from a tree outside . . ."

Serena gasped, suddenly realizing. "But what about Ned? I saw Ned standing right over there by the door."

"That could have been a video someone took of him when he was still alive."

"But he spoke to me. He told me to get out of the house."

"Probably a prerecorded voice. An actor posing as Ned. I'm sure you were so frightened by seeing his image that night, you may not have been able to detect that his voice might have sounded slightly different."

"But it all seemed so real to me," Serena said hoarsely.

"Someone went to a lot of trouble to make sure you believed it was real, all of it. You weren't suffering from hallucinations, Serena. Someone was trying to gaslight you, to drive you out of this house, and I believe it has to with the multimillion-dollar wall mural down the hall that no one had a clue was authentic."

It all made perfect sense.

The projection equipment undoubtedly belonged to someone who would know the tricks of movie-making.

Like a film director.

All the signs kept pointing in the direction of Warren Ashmore.

Chapter 37

Poppy had not expected to see Matt in Palm Springs when she arrived at the Desert Flowers garage office after receiving a text from Wyatt summoning her. She had been under the impression that Matt would remain in Los Angeles for the duration of rehearsals before the start of shooting in Wyoming in the coming weeks. But there he was, a troubled look on his face when she walked through the door, while Wyatt sat at the desktop computer, his back to her, furiously tapping keys.

Poppy's face felt stiff as her eyes locked with Matt's. "Is everything all right?"

Matt shook his head like a wet dog coming out of the water. "No, not by a long shot."

Poppy braced herself. "What is it now?"

Matt swallowed, his Adam's apple bobbing up and down. "Rehearsals ended early because there is a problem with the movie's financing. One of the investors pulled out and the production company had to shut down until we find more money."

"Oh, dear, that does not sound good. I'm so sorry, Matt," Poppy said.

"I decided to drive back to Palm Springs and wait it out, and when I swung by the office to check in, Wyatt had some interesting bit of news for me."

Poppy cocked an eyebrow and directed her attention toward Wyatt, who spun around in his office chair with a smile, smears of chocolate on his face from munching on a candy bar.

"You might want to wipe your face, bud," Matt suggested.

Wyatt used his bare forearm to remove the chocolate and then used his tongue to lick it off. "Grandma mentioned you had some questions regarding Warren Ashmore, so I decided to dig a little deeper, and I turned up something very interesting on IMDB."

The International Movie Database was a world-renowned Web site and app with a nearly complete record of every film, television series, and streaming project ever made.

Poppy thought she might need to sit down to hear this, but she remained standing. "Okay, what did you find?"

"*The Vegas Connection*," Matt interjected.

"What is that?" Poppy asked.

"A cheesy heist film made a few years back that was directed by none other than Warren Ashmore," Wyatt explained.

Matt jumped in, adding, "It was about six frat brothers who team up to rob a casino off the Vegas strip. The movie was shot on a shoestring budget and didn't make much of a splash. It never played in theaters and was sold directly to a free streaming service, probably for a song."

Poppy knew Warren's Hollywood career had faded long ago, that in order to keep working he had to pretty much accept anything that came his way, so it was hardly a red flag that he had accepted a low-rent *Ocean's Eleven*–type knockoff. After all, when she first worked for him in the 1980s, he was already relegated to TV movie remakes, and that was almost forty years ago.

"That's why he was so excited about this new project with you, it was a feature film with huge potential," Poppy said.

"Right. It was a big opportunity for him, and he knew it. He just wants to be taken seriously again, so that's why this latest crisis with financing was such a blow to him. He looked devastated when we all found out," Matt said.

Of course if he somehow got his hands on Ned's house with the ten-million-dollar mural, all of those financial pressures would simply evaporate, but Poppy did not bring up that fact to Matt and Wyatt just yet.

"So what is so interesting about *The Vegas Connection?* It sounds like dozens of other rip-offs of classic heist movies."

"It's not the movie itself, it's who's in it," Wyatt hinted with a sly smile.

The kid loved drawing out the suspense.

Poppy wanted to scream at him to just come out with it but thought it best to keep her lips pressed shut.

"Justin Cambry," Matt blurted out.

Wyatt sighed loudly and folded his arms, annoyed. "I wanted to tell her!"

"Sorry, kid, you were taking too long," Matt snapped.

It took a moment for the name to register.

But then it all came into focus.

"The man who broke into Ned's house, the one Serena shot to death," Poppy whispered.

"Yup. One and the same," Wyatt declared, beaming. "He had a small walk-on part in the movie playing a blackjack dealer."

"So Warren must have known who he was," Poppy said, slightly shocked.

"Why didn't he mention it?" Matt asked. "I mean that's such an odd coincidence."

"If it is actually a coincidence," Poppy said, one step ahead of them.

"Poppy, are you saying Warren and Justin Cambry were working together? For what purpose?" Matt wondered, plunking down on the couch.

Poppy shrugged, but she knew in her gut that they were without a doubt connected, and that she now had strong evidence of the whole insidious plot. Warren wanted Ned and Serena out of that house. He could not just admit to Ned that the mural was worth millions. Otherwise Ned would have sold the house and kept all the money for himself. He had to keep the secret for as long as he could until he figured out a way to get possession of it for himself.

He enlisted Justin to break into the house and terrorize Serena, perhaps to the point where she might persuade Ned to move to a home that did not trigger such a traumatic memory. It was a plausible if not probable theory. Then, when Ned was poisoned and Warren discovered the house had been willed to Serena, he used his filmmaking tricks to scare her half to death, an elaborate ruse designed to drive her out of the house for good, leaving the house open for him to snap up as an anonymous buyer.

He could finance ten comeback pictures with the windfall from that wall mural.

But she could not bring herself to lay it all out now for Matt. Her heart felt sore and heavy for him. He had worked so hard to get this role, and if the facts bore out, then not only would this film project be on the verge of collapse financially, it would also most certainly lose its director.

But there was one very troubling concern Poppy was mulling over. If Warren Ashmore was capable of procuring a two-bit hustler to assault Serena Saunders and attempting to gaslight her, if he had no trouble doing any of that, did he also have it in him to murder his best friend?

Chapter 38

When Candy Sellers burst through the front door of the mountaintop house, her face filled with panic, Poppy braced herself. She knew it was showtime. A plan had been set into motion to lure this mysterious anonymous buyer out into the open. Serena had called Candy, who at the time was getting her hair done in Palm Desert, and calmly informed her that she had run into an old friend at a swim aerobics class who happened to mention that she was in the market for a new home. The friend had long admired the Alistair Boyce–Jean Harding home and was especially excited about purchasing a place with a Hollywood history since she had missed out on an opportunity to snap up a house in Las Palmas once owned by Sidney Sheldon, the best-selling novelist and creator of TV classics *I Dream of Jeannie* and *Hart to Hart*. When Serena had told her that she was selling the Boyce–Harding house, her pal jumped at the chance to see it and had just arrived with her own real estate agent for a tour.

According to Serena, there had been a long dead silence over the phone as Candy processed this news. Then, in an agitated tone, Candy had tried to explain that they already had an offer, a good one, well over asking price. Serena lowered her voice almost to a whisper and said, "Well, wouldn't it be nice if we found ourselves in a bidding war?"

Poppy had smirked as Candy apparently ditched her hair appointment and broke speed records to race to the mountaintop house. She was out of breath, her bottled blond hair a frazzled mess as she stormed inside, insisting on speaking with the realtor who at the moment was threatening her sizable commission. It appeared that the mysterious anonymous buyer did not have his own real estate agent and had agreed to allow Candy to broker the deal for both buyer and seller. The dollar signs in Candy's eyes were unmistakable, now replaced with abject fear at the thought of losing half what she was expected to rake in from this sale.

Candy marched up to Iris and Violet, who were relishing their undercover assignments as real estate agent and prospective buyer, respectively. "Which one of you is the realtor?"

"That would be me," Iris said loudly, pressing a business card she had Wyatt make up earlier that morning into the palm of Candy's hand.

Candy studied the card. "I have never heard of Desert Flowers Realty."

"We're new," Iris said with a pleasant smile. "This is my client, Violet Hogan, a retired school principal from Boston, who recently came into some money after the death of a wealthy cousin back east."

"How lucky for her," Candy muttered before realizing her faux paus. "The money, not the dead relative."

Poppy suppressed a smile. They had come up with Violet's backstory on the car ride over, and Iris felt necessary to get it all out while she still remembered it.

Candy blinked, not sure how to handle any of this. She quickly turned to Serena, who was standing off to the side with Poppy, whose reason for being there was for moral support, if her presence was questioned. "Serena, I already told my buyer we were going to accept their offer."

"Why would you do that?" Serena asked stiffly.

Candy's face tightened. There were dark rings around her eyes and a redness in them. This scene was definitely causing her a lot of duress. "Because you told me you wanted to get rid of the house as soon as possible and this buyer had offered a number over asking price. It would be unethical to back out now."

"But escrow has not even started. Why can't I change my mind?" Serena asked, folding her arms, eyes drilling into poor Candy, who was about to melt on the spot.

She took a deep breath. "There is no escrow because they have agreed to pay the price in *cash*."

"Then it should be no problem entertaining another offer if there is no paperwork yet, right?" Iris offered helpfully.

Candy glared at Iris, lips pursed.

"How much did your buyer offer?" Iris asked.

"I cannot disclose that, but it was well over the asking price," Candy mumbled, sweat now forming on her wrinkled brow. She turned to Serena, desperately trying to reason with her. "I really think we should stick with the original offer because it would be wrong—"

Ignoring her, Serena turned to Iris. "We were going to ask two point five million, well below its actual worth, just to unload it, and her buyer offered three million."

Violet dramatically stepped forward. She had been rehearsing this part all night. "I will give you four."

"F-four million?" Candy stammered, stunned.

"Yes," Violet snorted. "I believe that would be a sufficient sum to iron out any lingering problems you may have with your disappointed buyer, don't you?"

Serena's face lit up. "I certainly do!"

Candy fumbled a bit, as if the room were spinning and she were about to faint. "Excuse me, I need to make a phone call. I will be right back."

Then she fled out the sliding door to the pool and clamped her phone to her ear as she frantically paced back and forth past the patio furniture.

Poppy, Serena, Iris, and Violet all exchanged exhilarated looks. The plan was working brilliantly.

"Do you think he will make a counteroffer?" Serena asked.

Iris scoffed. "Of course he will! He knows the wall alone is worth ten million!"

Poppy touched Iris's arm. "Shhhh, she's coming back."

Candy nearly banged into the glass before taking a quick step to the left and through the open door. She clutched her phone like it was a lifeline and took yet another deep breath in a vain attempt to get her rapidly pounding heart under control. "I just spoke to my buyer. They're willing to go to four point two."

"Five million!" Violet blared, not missing a beat.

Serena excitedly clapped her hands. "Five million? That's far more than I ever thought we would get! Isn't that wonderful, Candy?"

Candy stared slack-jawed at Violet. "Just how much did you inherit from that relative?"

"Enough to keep this bidding war going all day if I have to," Violet said with a smug smile.

Iris beamed from ear to ear. "Would you like to call your buyer back and see if he or she is willing to up the offer to six or seven?"

Candy thrust out her hand. "Wait, I need time to think."

"What's there to think about, Candy? Just focus on how much commission you will make with a *five million* dollar sale."

But there was something else going on in Candy's mind.

She had made some type of agreement with the anonymous buyer. Perhaps she even secretly knew about the true value of the wall mural.

"I just . . . I just need . . ." Candy moaned.

She was spiraling.

"An hour. Give me one hour. Let me go talk to the buyer and see what they want to do."

"Why not just call them like before?" Iris suggested. "They're clearly waiting by the phone."

Another hateful look from Candy.

Iris was relishing this moment.

She loved playing a high-powered real estate agent with the upper hand. "I honestly do not see the problem here. My client obviously has much deeper pockets than yours. You will still come out with three percent of the sale if we split it. That's three hundred thousand dollars. If I were you, I would not be hesitating right now. I'm sure you will find your buyer another lovely property to call home."

Candy despairingly turned to Serena. "Please, Serena, let's not be too hasty . . ."

"You know where I stand, Candy," Serena said sharply.

Candy nodded.

She knew money talked.

That was her whole game.

"Okay, you're the client," she said, resigned.

After setting out a purchase agreement for Violet to sign, at least in the short term for as long as they needed to run this scheme, Serena popped open a bottle of champagne to celebrate. Candy awkwardly stuck around long enough for the toast, and then made up some quick excuse to bow out, something about another showing all the way out in La Quinta that she had to get to soon, and then she rushed out.

Poppy set her half-empty champagne glass on the table. "That's my cue."

She hurried out of the house, leaving Serena and her undercover superstars Violet and Iris to pat each other on the back for a job well done. She saw Candy's candy-colored Porsche roaring off down the road toward Highway 111. Matt's Prius pulled up, and Poppy hopped in the passenger's side. He slammed his foot down on the accelerator to catch up with Candy.

"Everything play out the way you wanted?" Matt asked.

"And then some. She left practically hysterical. And if my hunch is right, I know exactly where she's heading."

They followed her back into Palm Springs and toward the toney Las Palmas area of town. Matt saw Candy suspiciously glancing at her rearview mirror at one point, so he slowed down, allowing a Jeep Grand Cherokee to pull in between them for a few blocks. But then she seemed to get distracted again, ignoring a flashing red light and nearly mowing down an elderly woman in the middle of the crosswalk.

Finally, turning off Palm Canyon Drive, Candy sped down a side street, turning right, then left until she screeched to a stop in front of a more modest midcentury modern home and crawled out. Matt slowly drove by the house, then parked a couple addresses up the street but still close enough for them to have a clear view of the house.

Candy marched up the front walk to the door, dabbing at the sweat on her face with wet tissue. The door opened before she could even reach out to ring the doorbell.

A man stepped out, his face red and blotchy from stress or hives or maybe even shingles. But still, he was easily identifiable. It was exactly whom Poppy had expected Candy to come calling on.

Warren Ashmore.

The anonymous buyer.

Chapter 39

The crushing disappointment on Candy Sellers's face almost made Poppy feel sorry for her.

Almost.

"I-I don't understand, what are you saying?" Candy stammered outside at a patio table by the pool.

"I have decided not to sell after all," Serena said matter-of-factly, taking a sip of an ice-cold glass of lemonade. "Oh, this is delicious."

Candy blinked, confused. "But what about the bidding war? That Hogan woman was ready to plunk down five million dollars."

"I know, but after thinking it over, I'm just not ready to make such a big change. I read an article that said you should not make any big life-changing decisions for at least a year after a major trauma like losing your spouse."

"B-But you were so eager to sell. You thought the place was haunted . . ." Candy said in a trancelike state, almost as if she were floating above her own body, watching the mystifying conversation unfold below.

Serena cackled. "Yes, I was in quite a state. But my doctor prescribed some antianxiety medication, and since I began taking it, the hallucinations have stopped. I'm starting to feel like my old self again." She frowned at Candy's disbelieving look. "I thought you would be happy for me. I said I'm feeling much better."

Candy forced a smile onto her otherwise shattered face. "Yes, yes, of course I am. If you're not ready to sell, you're not ready to sell . . . When do you think you might be?"

"I may never sell. The place has started to grow on me. It meant a lot to Ned, so therefore it means a lot to me."

Candy was desperately trying to process what was happening. None of this made any sense to her, and she had no clue she was being used as a pawn.

Poppy, who had been sitting quietly at the table, watching Serena's incredibly focused performance, took a sip of her own lemonade, and finally decided to speak up. "Oh, you're right. This is delicious."

Candy did not appreciate the interjection. Her eyes flicked toward Poppy, who caught the flash of anger before she returned her attention back to Serena, now more doe-eyed.

"I appreciate all the hard work you've done, Candy, and rest assured, I will be recommending you to all my friends looking to enter the housing market," Serena chirped.

"Thank you," Candy answered in a clipped tone.

Poppy could not resist adding, "Although who knows how long before the real estate bubble bursts and the prices in Palm Springs start to plummet again!"

Candy bit her bottom lip, refraining from comment.

Serena leaned forward with a wide, friendly smile. "Would you like some more lemonade, dear?"

"No, I've had quite enough. The sugar from that one drink will go straight to my hips," Candy practically snarled as she stood up to take her leave. "You have my number if you decide to change your mind again."

"Of course," Serena cooed. "But I won't."

Those last words hit Candy like a brick to the head.

She was done playing nice, having lost all patience with this client who it appeared had been giving her the run-around.

"Good-bye!" Candy marched back inside the house and out the front door, slamming it hard behind her to make the point she was not pleased with how any of this had turned out.

Serena turned to Poppy. "How was I?"

"Emmy-worthy."

She winked at Poppy. "Just an Emmy? I was going for an Oscar. Meryl has three. I don't see why I don't deserve at least one!"

They both laughed.

Serena clasped her hands together, resting them on the table. "So what happens now?"

"We give Candy time to deliver the bad news to Warren, allow him a few days to process it all, then we set the stage for your next performance."

There was much for them to prepare.

They had to pull a whole show together in just under three days.

But Poppy was confident they would get it all done by the time Serena picked up her phone that Friday just before midnight and called Warren Ashmore.

He picked up on the first ring.

"Serena? What's wrong? Why are you calling so late?"

"Warren, it's happening again!" Serena wailed

She had her phone on speaker so Poppy and Matt could listen in on the call.

"Ned! He's here! In the bedroom! He's warning me to get out of the house again!"

There was a long strained beat.

"Are you kidding me?"

"No! No! I swear! And I saw the dead man in the bath-tub again! Please, I need help! I can't take this anymore!

Why does this keep happening? This whole house is haunted! I just want to light a match and burn the whole place down!"

"No! Don't do anything rash!" Warren cried. He was undoubtedly envisioning flames engulfing and destroying the precious Dexter Holt wall mural in the hallway. "I'm coming over!"

"Hurry, please!"

Another long pause.

"Warren, are you still there?"

Matt glanced at the phone screen and whispered, "I think he hung up. That was brilliant, Serena."

Serena lowered her phone to her side and smiled.

Poppy checked her watch. "He should be here in about fifteen minutes. Places everyone!"

Matt bounded outside while Poppy and Serena turned off all the lights in the house. Then Poppy opened the front door and escorted Serena out to the guest house on the far side of the property, where she could watch everything on a television monitor. They had placed cameras and microphones all around the house in order to capture everything.

It had only been twelve minutes when they heard Warren's car roaring up out front. Then they watched as he rushed up to the door, noticing it open and poking his head inside. "Serena?"

Dead silence.

He took a tentative step inside the foyer. "Serena, where are you?"

Nothing.

He looked around cautiously, then slowly made his way down to the main bedroom, surprised that Serena was nowhere in sight. "If you're hiding, there is nothing to be afraid of, I'm here now."

Then, as if out of thin air, Justin Cambry, the young

man who had broken into the house, appeared by the doorway, startling Warren. His eyes widened with fright at the
sight of him. "W-What? What's going on? You're dead!"

Warren suddenly realized and spun around, staring up
at the vent where Poppy had found the first digital projector.

That's when Matt started pumping music through the
speakers set up outside. A song from one of Alistair Boyce
and Jean Harding's first pictures together. A memorable
serenade made famous by the movie. It had even been
nominated for an Oscar for Best Original Song in the early
sixties. And on cue, the image of Alistair and Jean—him in
a dapper tuxedo and her in an Edith Head–designed gorgeous white evening gown—appeared, and they danced
and danced around the pool.

Warren angrily charged out through the bedroom's sliding glass door and yelled into the night, "I don't know
who put you up to this, but I know what you're doing!"

Of course he knew.

Because they were using his own tactics against him.

Poppy watched Warren's wild meltdown for a few more
moments, then she squeezed Serena's hand and walked out
of the guest house. It was time for her own role in this
over-the-top melodrama. The music suddenly stopped and
her heels clicked on the patio concrete, alerting Warren to
her presence. He whipped his head around, his face a
mask of confusion and fear.

"You!" Warren growled, pointing a finger in her direction. "I figured you must be a part of this! Okay, so you
found the projection equipment and thought it would be
funny to turn the tables. Bring Justin and the Boyces back
from the dead."

"It was a challenge finding an image of Justin Cambry
from the one film he did with you. It was such a brief, in-
nocuous part."

"It was bigger before I had to cut it down. The kid was a terrible actor."

There was no point in denying anything.

It was clear Poppy knew everything.

"Okay. What's really going on here? You found out I was the anonymous buyer and I didn't want Serena to get the house so I played a few dirty tricks to scare her off. So what? Even if they do charge me with trespassing, I'll probably never do time. First offender and all that. What's the big crime here?"

"How about first-degree murder?"

"Lady, you're cracked. Serena was the one who shot Justin Cambry three times in the chest, not me!"

"What about Ned?"

His face flinched slightly but he kept his cool and spoke evenly. "Ned Boyce was my best friend. Why would I have any reason to cause him harm?"

"I can think of ten million reasons."

This time the facial flinch was a little more pronounced.

"I have no clue what you're talking about."

"The wall mural. The Dexter Holt original. I flew to Santa Fe and spoke with the artist himself."

"I heard he's got dementia. You can't possibly take anything he says seriously!"

"He wrote it all down in a diary. Every detail right there in black and white. How you hired him to paint the mural when he was a starving artist. And then, quite unexpectedly, Dexter Holt became world-famous. Sadly Alistair and Jean didn't live long enough to see him become a legend in the art world. But you did. You knew the value of that mural had skyrocketed and will again when Mr. Holt dies in the not-so-distant future. Your career has been on the downslide for years, and the rumor mill is full of stories about your unfortunate gambling problem and head-spinning massive debt, most likely to some pretty shady

characters who are not known for their patience. Am I getting warm?"

"You know nothing about me!"

"My late husband suffered from the same addiction, so
I'm good at reading the signs now. I can see the despera-
tion in your eyes. But if you bought this house and all the
contents within, you'd be swimming in money and all
your problems would just float away, poof, like a puff of
smoke."

"Now you've got me curious. Just what do you think
my evil master plan was?" Warren sneered, his forehead
crinkling.

"First, you had to stop Ned from marrying Serena. Ned
trusted you and would listen to you. He might have even
given you the house. He was that caring and kind. But Serena was more of a wild card. Once she was on the scene,
Ned was less amenable to your needs. He was too much in
love with her to pay you much mind. So you had to get rid
of her. When Ned went out of town on business, you hired
Justin Cambry, a small-time thug you knew from working
with him on your film, to take care of her. But Serena was
surprisingly more self-reliant than you ever imagined and
shot him dead before he had the chance."

"You got this all wrong, but keep going. I find this little
conspiracy theory of yours mildly entertaining."

"Like so many of your movies."

That one hit its target.

Warren actually looked wounded.

"Unable to stop the wedding, you had to change course.
So your next plan was removing Ned and framing Serena.
With Ned dead and Serena in prison, it would be much
easier for you to get your hands on the deed to this house.
You spiked Ned's drink at the wedding, causing a heart attack on his wedding night when he was with Serena, who
by your calculation would most likely go down for the

crime. I'm sure Ned confided to you that he cut Gavin and Willa out of the will and everything was going to go to his new bride. That gave Serena a clear motive. But then that plan didn't work either. She was a suspect, but there was no proof she had committed the crime. The fact was, Serena genuinely loved Ned with all her heart. It was obvious to everyone she was emotionally distraught from her loss. So you staged this very impressive Hollywood production to drive her out of the house, making her believe that she was seeing ghosts and slowly going insane. And what do you know? The third time was the charm. It worked. She put the house up for sale and you were waiting in the wings to make an offer as some anonymous buyer. No doubt with more borrowed money, you could pay back after the sale went through and the mural finally belonged to you."

"If this were a film script, I'd toss it in the recycle bin as too ridiculous and unrealistic! Where's your proof?"

"It's all guesswork at this point."

"See, you've got nothing!"

"But I am confident the police who were issued a warrant to search your home in Las Palmas a few hours ago are combing your residence as we speak, and might find, oh, I don't know, something to implicate you, maybe even the poison you used in Ned's drink, who knows?"

Warren had not been expecting that. "T-The police are at my house . . . now?"

"You were in such a rush to get over here, fearing an unstable Serena might damage that priceless mural, you probably didn't have the chance to get rid of any damning evidence."

She could read his stricken face.

The poison was there.

He would be caught red-handed.

Warren gaped at Poppy, not sure what to do. And then,

in a split second, he turned and bolted out of panic, dashing straight for a side gate that would lead back out front to his car. Unfortunately, Matt was blocking his escape near the gate. Warren hurled a punch at him, which Matt effortlessly dodged from years of stage combat classes. Then his hand shot out, grabbing ahold of Warren's arm and twisting it hard behind his back as Matt spun him around and wrapped his free arm around Warren's neck.

Warren struggled in Matt's tight grasp for a few seconds, but he was no match for the much younger man. He stopped squirming all together when his eyes fell upon Detective Jordan and a few officers slowly walking toward them. They had been hiding outside behind the guest house all along, eager to make an arrest.

Warren cranked his head around toward Matt and hissed, "I only hired you for my movie so I could keep tabs on the Desert Flowers outfit, to make sure you didn't get too close to the truth! You were never going to be the lead in my movie! I think you're a rotten actor!"

Matt snapped back, "And I never really liked any of your movies. Except the one with Poppy in it."

He winked at Poppy and grinned.

She blew him a kiss as the police officers relieved him of a sulking, defeated Warren Ashmore.

Chapter 40

Two Bunch Palms, a contemporary wellness resort located in Desert Hot Springs, California, was an oasis in the desert once owned by gangster Al Capone before it became a world-class spa, with six-hundred-year-old soothing and therapeutic natural mineral springs. The property also boasted a full-service spa with massages, facials, herbal wraps, and body scrubs and a vegetable-forward Southern California–inspired menu at the world-class restaurant. It was the perfect weekend getaway. And Poppy was so grateful that Serena, as a show of thanks, had insisted on treating her to a ladies' weekend. They were sharing a luxury two-bedroom suite near the palm and hammock grove. Poppy had just finished up with an Adaptogen Wrap and was feeling tired. She had told Serena she was planning on relaxing in the mood-enhancing mineral pool for a spell after her appointment and perhaps attend the Sage Cleansing Workshop at noon, but she was having trouble keeping her eyes open because she was so sleepy. So instead, she headed back to the room, where Serena had supposedly gone after her ninety-minute Deep Tissue Massage with her strapping masseur, Jace (Greek for "healer").

Poppy used the key card to enter and was just inside the

suite when she heard urgent whispering coming from Serena's room. She was obviously not alone. Moments later,
Serena, her hair tousled, her lipstick smeared on her face, a
peach-colored silk robe thrown on and tied at the waist,
hustled out of the room, eyes wide with surprise. "What
are you doing here? I thought you were going to take some
time in the mineral pool and then do a workshop."

"I was, but I got very tired after my facial, so I thought
I would just come back here for a nap before lunch."

Serena's eyes nervously flicked toward the bedroom.
"Oh. Okay."

Poppy arched an eyebrow. "Is someone here?"

Serena shook her head. "No, I was watching something
on my iPad."

She was lying.

Poppy was reasonably certain Serena did not even own
an iPad. But there was no television in her room, so she
had to come up with something.

Serena stood frozen in place, waiting for Poppy's response. Instead of confronting her, Poppy gave her a thin
smile and said, "Well, I will let you get back to it. Wake
me up when you want to get a bite to eat. I've been daydreaming about that grilled brioche toast with the straw-
berry compote and chantilly cream we had yesterday."

Serena finally nodded, wrapping the loose satin robe
tighter around her bosom.

Poppy retreated to her room but made sure to leave the
door open just a tiny bit. She waited, peering through the
crack to see who exactly Serena had hiding in her room,
although she had a pretty good idea already.

As she predicted, Serena's twenty-three-year-old masseur Jace tiptoed out of the bedroom in his tight shorts,
shirtless, clutching his Two Bunch Palms yellow Polo shirt
in one hand. Serena escorted him to the door as he padded
barefoot behind her, dangling his pair of leather sandals in

his other hand. The six-foot-two Adonis bent down to give Serena a deep good-bye kiss, but she was so focused on getting him out before Poppy saw him, he barely brushed her lips with his own before she hoisted him out of the suite with all her might. Then she quietly closed the door, leaned up against it, and breathed out a heavy sigh of relief, secure in the knowledge that Poppy was none the wiser.

Poppy stepped away from the door, then sat down on the bed. She was hardly surprised that Serena was enjoying the company of a much younger man. She had always had a taste for strapping young bucks. And a leopard rarely changed her spots. Still, in the end, she did choose the more age-appropriate Ned Boyce to marry, and despite what she had just witnessed, Poppy still sincerely believed that Serena had loved him at the time she married him.

When she and Serena went to the Two Bunch Palms restaurant for lunch, Serena prattled on about every topic under the sun except for her dalliance on the Two Bunch grounds with her hunky masseur. Fraternization between guests and spa employees was strictly forbidden. When they passed Jace on the trail back to their room after lunch, he gave them both a warm smile and friendly greeting, pretending he had not snuck out of their suite just two hours earlier.

Once back in her room, Poppy noticed a text from Matt on her phone, urging her to call him. She had purposely not taken it to the restaurant, as they discouraged cell phone use in the common areas. She closed her bedroom door for privacy and quickly called Matt back. He answered right away.

"Poppy! Sorry to bother you on your spa weekend, but I thought you would want to hear this."

"No, I'm happy you called. What's happening?"

"I spoke with Detective Jordan this morning. Warren Ashmore has confessed to Ned Boyce's murder in order to make a plea deal for a life sentence with the possibility of parole."

"He should feel lucky. A jury could have doled out the death penalty."

"But there is one hitch."

Poppy braced herself. "Which is?"

"Jordan says Warren gave a full-throated confession to everything, Ned's poisoning, Serena's gaslighting, the whole enchilada, except he claims he never enlisted Justin Cambry to go to the house to harm Serena. He swears he had nothing to do with him being there that night."

"He expects us to believe a man he hired to act in one of his films just coincidentally picked his best friend's house to rob? I find that highly suspect."

"He doesn't deny knowing Justin. But other than introducing Justin to Ned and Serena at a party some months ago, he had no further contact with him."

"Wait. So Justin Cambry had met Ned and Serena before?"

"Just once, according to Warren. He thinks maybe Justin did his research on them, with the intent to find a rich target, and hit the house on a night he thought they both would be out."

"But Warren was already desperate to get his hands on the house and mural. It makes sense he would hire outside help to get rid of Serena."

"Yes. He knows how it looks. But at that point, he was just trying to talk Ned out of marrying Serena, like when he managed to talk Ned out of painting over the mural years earlier. Ned listened to Warren. He was Ned's best friend. But Warren knew that once Serena moved into the house as his wife, that would make it doubly hard for him to get them both out. And Ned would not budge about Serena. He truly did love her. Usually Warren could talk his good buddy into anything, but not in this case."

Warren knew Serena was not going anywhere, so he had to formulate a new plan. Poison Ned and make it look like Serena had done it. Then they would both be out of the picture, making it easier for him to get his hands on the house. Gavin and Willa would be more pliable. They did not care one whit about that house. They just wanted lots of cold hard cash. It would be a breeze for him to snap it up in a quick sale.

Warren Ashmore would rot in prison for betraying his best friend and cutting his life short. It was a just punishment.

But Warren confessed to every crime he was accused of with the exception of one. Why lie over one detail when you're willing to take ownership of everything else? Because it suggested he was telling the truth. And Poppy was now sure of one thing. This story was far from over.

Chapter 41

Kal sat back in his plastic chair at the table in the visiting room of the Riverside County Jail, with a look of defiance. "I'm not sayin' a word to you two. You're the whole reason I'm stuck here. You could be wired, for all I know."

"Neither of us are wired, Kal," Poppy assured him. "We just want you to tell us the truth."

"So it can be used against me during my trial? Forget it!" Kal scoffed, folding his arms across his broad, muscled chest.

"The cops have you dead to rights. The case against you is airtight. Talk to your lawyer," Matt said. "She insinuated when we called and requested this meeting that the DA might be willing to offer a plea deal *if* you cooperate with us."

"I don't believe you!" Kal bellowed.

"She thought you might say that," Poppy said calmly, placing her phone faceup on the table and sliding it over so Kal could see the screen. "She texted me the details."

Kal glanced down at the phone. What he saw caught his attention. His lips moved as he silently read what she had written. When he finished, he slowly looked back up at

Poppy and Matt, who sat opposite him. Poppy noticed one of the guards ready to march over and snatch her phone away, since giving an inmate anything, especially an electronic device, was strictly prohibited. But since Kal never touched it and Poppy had already picked it back up and shoved it deep inside her purse, the guard decided to stay put.

"Not a bad deal, if you ask me," Matt said. "Of course the detective handling your case, who is working with the DA making that offer, is a close personal friend of ours. He would be forever grateful if you just told us what we want to know."

"The thing is, I already told the cops that Justin had nothing to do with . . ." Kal flicked his eyes suspiciously around to make sure no one was listening, ducking his head down and whispering under his breath ". . . our extracurricular activities at the gym."

He desperately wanted to make sure he did not use words like "illegal" or "blackmail" or "extortion" when he spoke about the scheme just in case either Poppy or Matt was indeed wired with some kind of recording device.

"But if he did work out there, and was around the trainers who were actually involved, maybe he got a sense of what was going on."

Kal shrugged. "I don't know how. We were very discreet. Both the guys and their clients. That was the key to everything. Nobody wanted any of it to get out. The only way Justin could have known what was up would be if one of my guys talked. But I'm telling you, Nicholas, Mick, Julio, Amir, none of them would have blabbed to anybody. They knew the risks about what would happen if the wrong person discovered what we were doing."

Matt leaned forward. "Was there anyone else aware of your little side operation?"

Kal shook his head. "No. It was mainly me and those four guys." He thought about it for another moment. "Wait. There was another trainer who we thought about bringing into the fold. Mick chatted him up to see if he might be the right fit for us. But he had a big mouth and an even bigger ego, and we decided he was too unpredictable, too much of a hothead from all the steroids he was injecting into himself."

"Do you remember his name?"

"Clint somebody. I can't remember his last name, but it will most likely be in the gym's directory, which I'm sure the police already have in their evidence file."

"Anyone else come to mind?" Poppy asked.

"Nope. That's all I got. After Clint, we didn't try to recruit anyone else . . . that is, until Zac Efron here showed up with his six-pack abs and million-dollar smile."

Matt blushed.

Poppy suppressed a smirk. "Do you know if Clint ever crossed paths with Justin Cambry?"

"Beats me. It was a small gym, though, as you know. Everybody pretty much knew everybody."

"Thank you, Kal," Poppy said as a bell rang indicating the visiting hour was over.

Kal hauled himself to his feet, moaning slightly. "They don't let me work out as much as I'd like. My body's getting a little soft."

He still looked like a Mack truck, although Poppy saw the beginnings of a paunch.

"So you'll let your detective friend know I was helpful so we can get this plea deal in motion?"

"Absolutely," Poppy promised.

Kal paused. "You know, what we did, it was a two-way street. Those women knew what we had to offer and they all went for it. They would've gladly paid us for the services we provided, and I'm not talking about cheering them on while they did bicep curls."

"Unfortunately, you did not give them much of a choice," Poppy reminded him. "Which is exactly why you are in here."

She had spent enough time talking with Kal and was ready to leave him and his crimes behind for good.

Poppy turned on her heel and walked away, Matt close behind, leaving Kal scowling after them.

Kal had been right about one thing.

Clint Barker was a monster on steroids.

Veins popping out all over his body.

He was permanently red-faced with a perpetual angry expression, his foul mood a side effect from the steroid injections. His arms and legs were also dotted with acne, another known side effect.

Wyatt had had no trouble tracking him down. He already had his own downloaded copy of Muscle Buddies's employee and client directory and had pinpointed Clint Barker's address before Poppy and Matt had even finished asking for it.

He was living in a one-bedroom apartment just off Araby and Highway 111. He also had a police record for dealing illicitly obtained anabolic steroids without a valid prescription, which was illegal. Now out on bail, he was hanging out in his apartment whiling away the time watching daytime TV until the start of his own trial.

Poppy had left him a few phone messages, but he had declined to return any of them. So Poppy and Matt decided to just show up at his door one late afternoon, hoping to find him at home so they could talk to him in person.

When he flung open the door, eyes wild with rage, they instantly regretted that impulsive decision.

"I don't want whatever you're sellin', so just go away!" Clint hollered, knuckles white from his tightened hammy fists.

Poppy and Matt took a wary step back.

Matt raised his hand. "We're not here to sell you anything. We just want to ask you a few questions."

"I got nothin' to say!" Clint snorted, trying to shut the door. Matt stuck his foot out, stopping it from closing.

Clint's nostrils flared. "You better move that foot before I break it."

Matt gulped.

He knew Clint could easily snap him in half like a twig in his steroid-induced state.

Poppy, fearful he was about to start banging the door on Matt's foot and cracking bones, quickly stepped forward. "Mr. Barker, we are not here to cause you any trouble. We just want to know about your time at Muscle Buddies." She reached into her purse and drew out a hundred dollar bill. She could tell from the bareness of the apartment with hardly any furniture inside that Clint could probably use some extra cash.

He eyed the bill warily, not sure if he should grab it out of her hand. That's when she pulled out a second one hundred dollar bill, tantalizingly rubbing the two together.

It was more than he could bear.

With the speed of a lizard's tongue, he reached out and snagged the two bills, crumpling them up and sealing them inside his massive hand. "You got two minutes and you're not coming inside. We do it right here."

That was definitely a relief.

The last thing Poppy had any desire to do was step inside this man's smelly, dank apartment with used needles and empty cartons of McDonald's takeout.

"Okay," Matt agreed. "Did you have any idea about

the blackmail ring that was operating out of the gym with some of the trainers and clients?"

"Yeah, I heard some things. Mick offered up a few details, so what? I had nothing to do with any of that business! Ask any of those guys. They'll tell you. Read my lips. I was not involved! Ever! I don't do that sort of thing!"

Poppy suspected his moral compass could have easily been corrupted if he had only been asked to join in on the scheme, but she decided not to press that particular point at present. They still needed to ask him more questions.

"We know. We spoke with Kal," she said with a bright smile.

"Then what else do you need to know from me?" Clint growled. "You got less than a minute left."

"Did you ever speak to anyone else about what you knew they were doing, say a client or a fellow trainer?"

He thought about it. "Yeah, maybe."

"Justin Cambry?" Poppy asked.

There was a light of recognition behind his otherwise dead eyes. "How did you know that?"

"It's our two minutes. We ask the questions. How much did you tell him?" Matt asked.

"I don't know, he started pumping me one day. He knew the other guys were up to something and he was curious to know what, so I told him what I knew. Luring in older clients, showering them with attention, then hitting them with the insurance scam part of it. He seemed real interested."

Apparently Clint Barker was not exactly the King of Discretion.

"Do you think he wanted to become a part of Kal's team?" Poppy asked.

"No, he only cared about how they were pulling it off. He told me he was dating an older woman on the sly and that she was loaded, always rewarding him with designer clothes and expensive watches."

Poppy's heart leapt into her throat. "Did he ever mention a name to you?"

Clint went deep inside his tiny little pea brain but unsurprisingly came up blank. "Nope, not that I remember. Now time's up. Move your damn foot."

Matt obliged.

Just before closing the door, Clint stopped. "Wait. I do remember him say at one point that she was famous. Well, not super famous, just semi-famous, like I wouldn't have heard of her. Now that's all I got, so adios."

And the door suddenly slammed shut in their faces.

They could hear the lock clicking into place.

Poppy was more than happy to say good-bye to the off-putting Clint Barker. Matt turned to her as they headed back to Poppy's car.

"Semi-famous? Like an actress anyone under thirty probably won't remember?"

He was dead-on.

It was an apt description of one Serena Saunders.

Chapter 42

Matt snickered as Poppy reached deep into the lower registers of her voice to perfect her imitation of Serena Saunders's scratchy, smoky natural voice. "Hello, this is Serena Saunders calling."

They were at the Desert Flowers garage office, and Poppy was laser focused on perfecting every intonation and tone she had picked up from years of listening to Serena both in person and on-screen for the receptionist at Grand Life Insurance.

The perky, friendly receptionist seemed to buy her performance. "Oh, yes, Ms. Saunders, I will patch you through to Maggie right now."

Maggie had to be Serena's insurance agent, who was quite aware of all the policies and claims of her client, so this conversation would probably require more than a little finessing.

Matt gave her an enthusiastic thumbs-up as the call was transferred and the phone trilled twice before someone answered.

"This is Maggie Brandt."

Poppy paused, psyching herself up, and then just went for it. "Hello, Maggie, Serena Saunders."

"Oh, Serena, I have been meaning to call you. I heard about what happened to your poor husband. Please accept my sincere condolences."

"Thank you, Maggie," Poppy sniffed. "Much appreciated. It's been a very difficult time."

"I can only imagine," Maggie lamented, mustering up as much sympathy as she possibly could. As an insurance agent, she was trained in displaying just the right amount of empathy for a house destroyed in a fire, a car totaled in an accident, and of course in the case of a life insurance policy, the death of a loved one. "I am so sorry I could not make the funeral, but the company sent flowers, did you get them?"

Poppy had no idea whether Serena had received them or not but just decided to go with, "Yes, they were beautiful."

"Oh, good. I know how much you love lilacs," Maggie said cheerfully. "So, how can I help you today?"

"I'm calling about my policy," Poppy said, taking a stab in the dark and hoping Maggie might shed some more light on the subject.

"Yes, we're reviewing the terms of your husband's life insurance policy, and so far we don't foresee any hiccups, so you should expect a payout in the coming days."

Poppy paused. If Warren Ashmore had not just confessed to poisoning Ned, this certainly would have raised a red flag. A life insurance policy was always the strongest motive to commit murder. But it also made sense for Ned to take out life insurance when he got married in order to protect his beautiful new wife in case the unthinkable happened.

Which unfortunately it had.

"Thank you, but that's not the policy I'm calling about." Poppy decided to take a chance and make an educated guess. "I wanted to discuss my last claim."

"Oh, you mean the ring?"

Bingo.

"Yes, the ring."

Poppy's throat hurt as she struggled to maintain Serena's raspy voice.

"Was there a problem with the check we sent over?" Maggie asked with just the right amount of concern.

"Oh, no, everything was fine in that department."

Maggie decided to try again. "Don't tell me you finally found it?"

A lost ring.

An insurance payout.

None of this was surprising given what they had learned about Justin Cambry picking up on the key details of Kal's Muscle Buddies blackmail operation.

"No, unfortunately not. It's still missing. But I have recently come into some information suggesting it might not be lost at all. It may have been stolen."

Maggie gasped. "Really?"

"Yes, and I have an idea who might have done it."

"Oh my!" Maggie cried.

Poppy could picture Maggie salivating at this news. If they recovered the ring, they could recoup the insurance payout.

Poppy winked at Matt to signal him the plan was working. "It's just a hunch, but I have hired the services of a local private investigation company to look into the matter."

"That's wonderful news, Ms. Saunders. I know how much that ring meant to you."

"The detectives want to review my policy, so that is why I wanted to get in touch with you."

"Not a problem. I can email you a PDF of the policy right now," Maggie said, tapping the keys of her computer.

"I was hoping you might email it directly to the detective agency to save time."

There was an uncomfortable pause.

"I'm afraid it's against company rules to email a client's policy to a third party."

"Oh dear. I am on the set of my latest film project and they're about to call me to do a scene so I don't have time to forward it and they need it right away."

"You're making a movie? How terribly exciting!" Maggie gushed.

"The detective I have employed is my best friend. She was once an actress herself, Poppy Harmon?"

"Oh, I loved *Jack Colt*!"

"Poppy and I go way back, so you can see it's all in the family!" Poppy took a beat. "Wait, hold on, Maggie. What's that? Oh, dear. Maggie, I'm needed on set. I have to go. Can you please just shoot that email over to Poppy as a personal favor?"

Maggie struggled for a brief moment, then threw caution to the wind. "Of course. You go. Break a leg!"

After rattling off her own email address, Poppy hung up and Matt jumped to his feet, giving her a standing ovation.

"That was a master class performance!" Matt declared.

The policy arrived in less than a minute.

The ring was a Van Cleef & Arpels, frivole between the finger ring, rose gold, diamond, valued at over twenty-two thousand dollars and insured up to its full value.

Serena had put in a claim for the supposedly missing ring one week before she shot Justin Cambry three times in her bedroom, killing him.

Given what they knew now, that had to be more than just a coincidence.

Chapter 43

When Poppy and Matt arrived at Poppy's house, they found Serena's bags packed by the front door. She was sitting in the kitchen eating some leftover soup from the night before. When they walked in, she lit up with a bright smile. "Oh, you're home. I thought I might miss you."

"Are you going home?" Poppy asked.

"Yes, I don't want to put you out any longer. Now that I know I am not going crazy and the house is definitely not haunted, there really is no reason for me not to go back there."

Even if the house was haunted, there is not a ghost frightful enough to keep Serena away from that ten-million-dollar mural, Poppy thought to herself.

Serena slurped the last of her soup, stood up from the table, and carried her bowl and spoon to the sink to rinse them off. With her back to them, Poppy signaled Matt, who bounded over next to Serena. She had just turned on the water. He took the bowl from her. "Here, let me do that."

Serena giggled coquettishly. "Well, aren't you sweet?"

"No sense getting soap all over those beautifully done nails."

She giggled again, then cranked her head around toward Poppy. "Where on earth did you find this one? He's absolutely adorable."

"Isn't he though?" Poppy replied with a wink.

"Before you go, I was hoping I might talk to you about acting. I so admire everything you have done, especially that Hallmark Christmas movie where you played Mrs. Claus. You were so committed, you almost made me believe in Santa again, and I was twenty years old when I saw you in that."

"That movie was so silly. I'm surprised anyone even remembers it."

"Well, the movie wasn't that good, but you certainly were. Seriously, if you have a few minutes, could we sit down and chat over a cup of coffee? I would love to hear some of your stories. It would mean a lot to me as I'm really just starting out in the business."

Serena, flustered and blushing, giggled yet again. "I don't see why not. I have nothing pressing on my calendar today, I mean, nothing I can't put off until tomorrow, so yes, if Poppy doesn't mind us taking over her kitchen."

"Not at all. I have some bills to pay in the other room, so you two talk," Poppy said.

Matt, with his hand placed gently on Serena's lower back, guided her over to the table where she sat back down. "I'll put some coffee on for us."

Poppy could see Serena checking out Matt's backside as he ambled over to the counter, took the pot from the coffeemaker, and began filling it with water. That was her cue to make a hasty exit.

Of course the bills to pay was just an excuse. Poppy was always organized and paid every bill immediately as it came in. No, she and Matt had prearranged this ruse to keep Serena busy. Matt was a master flirt, and luckily Serena was an easy mark given his youthful good looks and sparkling personality. The plan was to keep her occupied so Poppy could search her belongings. If they had arrived home ten minutes later, they would have missed her altogether, making this task all the more difficult.

Poppy hurried over to the two suitcases by the front door. She knew which one contained Serena's prized jewelry collection. She got down on her knees and set the case down on its side and unzipped it. There were expensive-looking necklaces and earrings but no rings. She rummaged through it, stopping occasionally to make sure Matt still had Serena fully engaged with questions in the kitchen. Another girlish giggle confirmed he had her in the palm of his hand. Not finding the ring, she was about to zip the case closed and move on to the larger suitcase when she noticed a side pocket. She dug her hand down in it and felt around, her fingers touching a small box.

She pulled it out and smiled to herself.

A velvet ring box.

She popped it open and inside was a Van Cleef & Arpels, frivole between the finger ring, rose gold, diamond.

Exactly as described in the insurance claim report.

And everything suddenly became crystal clear in Poppy's mind. Serena was having an affair with Justin Cambry all along, behind Ned's back. Poppy still believed Serena loved Ned—she was not that good of an actress—and Poppy could see how deeply Serena cared for him. But she also had a very strong physical attraction to much younger men. Ned gave her love and security. Men like Justin fed her ego and could take care of her other needs. She had met Justin through Warren Ashmore, and the two began a secret relationship. Justin, an opportunist, had learned all about how to take advantage of older women from his pals at Muscle Buddies, and decided to start his own game of blackmail with Serena by threatening to expose their affair to Ned if Serena did not pretend to lose an expensive piece of jewelry and then file an insurance claim stating it had been lost.

A twenty-two-thousand-dollar payout was enough to buy his silence. But unfortunately, he never lived long enough to spend any of the money. They had purposefully gotten together that ill-fated night and something went terribly wrong. An argument, perhaps. Maybe Serena changed her mind about paying him. Whatever happened remained a mystery, except for the fact that Serena had shot and killed him.

With the only witness now dead, Poppy knew that to find out what really happened, they would need to hear it from Serena Saunders herself.

Chapter 44

Clint Barker, in handcuffs, was led inside the small dingy room at the Riverside County Jail with its peeling paint and dusty floor by a large Black detention officer. The police had just arrested him hours earlier on more charges. Poppy, Matt, and Detective Jordan were seated at a scuffed metal table with one leg annoyingly bent, which made the table rock every time Matt rested his elbows on it, causing Jordan to sigh in frustration. Poppy tried not to laugh at the detective's exasperation. The officer unlocked Clint's handcuffs and then pushed him down in a rickety chair opposite them.

Poppy reached into her purse and pulled out a pretty white lily-embroidered handkerchief with scalloped edges, balled it up, and shoved it beneath the bent leg of the table, effectively preventing it from rocking anymore. Matt knocked the table with the bottom of his elbows and much to Jordan's relief, the table finally remained steady.

"Thank you," he sighed.

"I will be right outside if you need me," the officer said before taking his leave and shutting the door behind him.

Detective Jordan leaned forward, eyes locking with Clint, who defiantly stared him in the face, refusing to be intimidated. "I assume you have spoken to your lawyer."

Clint nodded.

"I need you to say yes or no."

Clint scowled. "Yes."

"So you understand that if you do this and plead guilty, the judge will take a reduced sentence into consideration?"

Clint shifted uncomfortably in his seat, then threw his head back, looking up at the ceiling and sighing. "Uh huh."

"Yes or no!" Jordan barked, slamming a fist down on the table hard, causing everyone to jump.

"Yes!" Clint hissed.

"Okay, then. Let's get started," Jordan said a little more lightly as he slid a phone across the table in front of Clint. "That's a burner phone. Can't be traced. You will use that to call her."

"What if she hangs up on me?" Clint asked.

"Then you keep calling until she's willing to talk to you. Just remember, you get the deal only if this works. If you screw it up, you get nothing."

"I got it, I got it," Clint sneered.

"Good," Jordan said, unfolding a slip of paper and tapping it down next to the phone. "That's her number. Make the call."

"We understand if you need a moment to prepare," Matt said, trying to be helpful.

Jordan rolled his eyes. "He's not an actor about to go on stage, man. He's just a born liar. I'm sure he can wing it."

Poppy had to cover her mouth before a burst of uncontrolled laughter escaped her lips.

Clint stared at the phone for a moment, his right leg nervously bobbing up and down, then his hand snapped out, grabbed the phone, and he began typing in the number on the piece of paper.

"Don't forget to put it on speaker," Jordan instructed.

Clint did as he was told and they all heard the phone trilling a few times before someone answered.

"Yes?" a woman's voice said.

"Is this Serena Saunders?"

"Who is this? I don't recognize the number," she replied curtly.

"My name is Clint."

"I don't know anyone named Clint. Only Clint Eastwood, and your voice is way too high to be him."

Poppy saw Matt smirking.

"I'm a friend of Justin Cambry. You knew him, didn't you?"

There was a long pause.

"Yeah, I'm pretty sure you knew him. In fact, I have it on good authority that you two were *very* close," Clint said with an ominous chuckle.

"What is it you want?" Serena snapped.

"Before the poor sod wound up with three bullet holes in the chest courtesy of you, Justin just happened to mention the little scam he had going on with you."

"I am sure I do not know what you are talking about."

"Filing a false insurance claim about a lost ring, the twenty-two-thousand-dollar payout to keep his mouth shut about your affair? Is there something else I'm missing?"

"You know nothing!" Serena spit out.

"That's where you're wrong, lady. Justin was a good buddy. We shared everything. What's mine was his and what's his was mine. So I'm calling to collect that twenty-two grand."

Serena let out a throaty laugh. "You can't be serious."

"I'm dead serious. I want that money. Today. Or I will come and get it."

"You step one foot on my property and I will plug you full of holes just like I did to your friend. It will be a clear case of self-defense. Now, you listen and you listen good. Even if Justin was blackmailing me, and I am not admitting that he was, my husband is dead. You no longer have any leverage over me. I have no reason to pay you a dime. You can go straight to hell. I'm hanging up now. Don't you dare to ever contact me again!"

"There's a video!" Clint blurted out before she had a chance to end the call.

Another pause.

"What did you say?" Serena asked in a raspy whisper.

"Justin recorded the two of you together one time with his phone and kept it as his own insurance policy, in case you refused to be cooperative."

"You're lying. There is no video."

She was right.

This was a ploy Clint was improvising that could backfire on them in a spectacular fashion if she insisted on viewing it herself.

"I can text it to you right now."

"No! I don't want to see it!"

"Fine. Just know I have it and can send it to the police whenever the mood strikes. Hell, I might even post it on Instagram. You're kinda famous, after all, aren't you?"

"You're sick," Serena seethed.

Poppy could hear the sheer panic in her voice.

"I'm sure after the cops watch it, they will start questioning your rock-solid self-defense claim that it was a simple break-in and you were afraid for your life. Because, trust me, you hardly look scared in that video."

"If I fork over the twenty-two grand, I want that video deleted permanently, do you understand me?"

"You can watch me do it when you bring me the money. You will never have to worry about it ever again."

Another long beat.

Then Serena finally spoke, defeated. "Where should we meet?"

Clint rattled off the location Detective Jordan had coached him to say, then a time.

"Tonight. Eleven o'clock sharp."

Serena hung up without saying another word.

Matt turned to Detective Jordan. "You were wrong about one thing. Clint is definitely an actor. A pretty good one. That was a terrific performance."

"I wasn't wrong," Jordan insisted. "He was just being himself. I'm sure he's had conversations just like that many times before."

Clint glared at him.

"You should be happy," Jordan said. "You just shaved at least two years off your sentence." He stood up and walked over and rapped on the door.

The officer opened the door and poked his head in.

"Get him out of here," Jordan growled.

The officer marched over, snapped the handcuffs back on Clint's wrists, and then escorted him toward the door.

"Thank you, Clint," Poppy said.

He grunted an unintelligible reply.

And then he was gone.

Poppy and Matt exchanged hopeful looks.

The trap had been set.

Now they just needed to catch the prey.

Chapter 45

The parking structure behind the Regal Cinemas on Tahquitz Canyon Way, south of downtown, had very little lighting after dark and was the perfect late-night meeting spot for anyone wishing to keep a low profile. Poppy was ducked down between two parked cars left in the lot overnight, well hidden from view. She could see across to where Matt lingered in the shadows, dressed in jeans and a gray hoodie pulled up over his head to hide his face. It was ten minutes past eleven, and Serena so far was a no-show. Poppy feared she might have gotten cold feet. But then, at seventeen minutes past the hour, she could see a pair of blinding headlights approaching as a car turned into the parking structure and pulled into one of many empty spaces. The lights flicked off, and there was a moment of silence until the driver's side door opened, a woman stepped out, and then slammed it shut.

Serena Saunders took a step forward. She was carrying a blue gym bag and was wearing a heavy gray sweater and dark pants, which Poppy found odd given the warm evening temperature. Poppy could make out her eyes nervously scanning back and forth. Poppy crouched down even farther, fearing Serena might spot her. After another painstakingly long silence, Poppy peeked up over the hood of the car she was hiding behind to see Serena still standing in the middle of the lot. Her face was drawn, and she appeared more than a little agitated.

"Is anyone here?" Serena hissed.

That was Matt's cue.

He stepped out of the shadows, his face unseen from the hoodie. "Over here," he said with his best impression of Clint.

Serena tensed up.

Poppy could tell she was scared.

Matt slowly walked toward her, looking down, making sure his face remained hidden. "Did you bring the money?"

Serena raised the gym bag. "Right here." Then she tossed it over to him. It landed at his feet. Matt bent down and unzipped the bag. He started rifling through the stacks of bills. Serena sighed. "You don't have to count it. It's all there. I don't want to be here all night."

Matt plucked a wad of cash out and thumbed through it until he was satisfied. Then he stuffed it back in the bag and zippered it shut.

"And how will I know you will delete that video so no one ever sees it?"

Matt popped back up to his feet with the gym bag in hand. "It's already done."

"You could be lying," Serena growled.

"You have my word."

Serena scoffed. "Somehow that does not give me much comfort."

"Trust me, I have no interest in drawing this out any longer." He raised the gym bag in the air. "This is pretty much all I need to go away and never contact you again. My policy is one and done, so no worries." Matt was doing a bang-up job posing as Clint. "Just one question," Matt couldn't resist asking.

Serena's eyes narrowed. "What?"

"Do you feel any guilt over shooting Justin?"

"*Guilt?*" Serena scoffed. "Are you kidding me? He was a two-bit scam artist who tried pulling a fast one over on me. *Me!* How dare that scum try to play me! He had to pay for his sins. I feel nothing. No remorse whatsoever. I did the world a huge favor erasing him from this earth."

Poppy shuddered listening to Serena. She had always suspected there was a dark side simmering beneath the surface, but the rage on Serena's face, the bile spewing from her mouth, the hate filling her eyes, was stunning to behold.

"I have dealt with diabolical Hollywood monsters for decades. I was never going to allow one thick-headed pretty boy hustler to get the best of me." Serena reached underneath her gray sweater and yanked out a handgun stuffed in the front of her pants. She pointed it right at Matt. "Correction. Make that two pretty boy hustlers."

Matt slowly raised his hands in the air. "Now hold on, let's not do anything rash—"

"If you honestly thought I was going to allow you to waltz out of here with all that money, *my* money, then you're dumber than Justin ever was!"

Suddenly there were flashing blue lights everywhere as three squad cars squealed into the parking structure. Matt dove out of the way as Serena panicked and started firing wildly in every direction. One bullet lodged into the other side of the car Poppy was hiding behind. She could hear Detective Jordan's commanding voice. "Put the weapon down on the ground and raise your hands in the air!"

Serena, caught off guard, stood frozen in place, eyes wide with surprise, still gripping the gun by her side.

"I am not going to tell you twice!" Jordan roared.

Poppy feared the police might start shooting if Serena refused to surrender, so from her hiding place, she called out, "Do what they say, Serena! I don't want to see you get hurt!"

Serena's head snapped back at the sound of Poppy's voice. "Poppy, what are you—"

"Now, Ms. Saunders!" Jordan ordered.

Serena dropped the gun, and it clattered to the cement pavement. Then she did what she was told and raised her hands in the air. Within seconds, police officers were swarming all around her. Her hands were pulled behind her back and she was handcuffed. She seemed to be in a daze, still not quite processing what was happening. Her head kept spinning around as if she were a possessed Linda Blair in *The Exorcist*. An officer attempted to read her her rights, but she interrupted him. "Poppy, come out where I can see you!"

Secure in the knowledge that it was safe now that Serena was in police custody, Poppy slowly stood up and walked out to where Jordan and his officers were holding Serena. Matt also emerged, lowering his hoodie, and moved toward them. Serena's eyes flicked from Poppy over to Matt. She emitted a surprised gasp as she recognized him. Then the full weight of the realization that she had been conned struck her all at once and her shoulders sank.

"I would applaud your bravura performance, Matt, but as you can see, I am indisposed at the moment," Serena said, gesturing toward the handcuffs on her wrists.

"It's fine." Matt shrugged, folding his arms. "I don't need your accolades."

Matt's dismissive tone obviously stung her.

She was an actor herself after all. And it was no secret that all actors craved people to like them. In Poppy's decades of experience, adoration was a big motivating factor when it came to becoming an actor in the first place.

And many spend their lives pretending to be someone else so they never have to be their true selves.

Serena gave Matt a feeble smile, and then she turned to Poppy. "I underestimated you."

Poppy glared at her. "How so?"

"I never thought you had the brains to figure all this out. When you started this whole private detective venture, I will admit, I laughed at you behind your back. I thought it was an insane idea and that you would never make it. But I guess I was wrong. You surprised me, Poppy."

"You surprised me, too. I always thought you were a good actress. I just never knew how good. You actually convinced me that you cared about me, that we were going to be close friends. Your performance was stellar, a true triumph, Serena."

Serena studied her for a long moment, not sure what to say.

Detective Jordan was growing impatient. "Come on, it's late. Let's book her and go home."

The officer took Serena by the arm and started leading her away to a nearby squad car, but she stopped in her tracks, twisting her head back around toward Poppy. "Wait."

"What now?" Jordan sighed.

She paused, her eyes brimming with tears as they fixed on Poppy. "It was not all an act. I loved Ned. With all my heart. I was devastated when he died. I did not know how I would go on. I actually believed I was falling apart mentally when Warren tried to gaslight me. All of that was real. I wasn't acting. I just wanted you to know that."

"And our friendship?" Poppy spat out.

Serena opened her mouth to speak, but no words came out. She just could not admit any genuine feelings toward the woman she had always deemed a bitter rival back in the day.

Jordan had heard enough. He testily waved at the officer with Serena. "Let's go."

The officer dragged Serena off.

She left without saying another word.

Matt appeared at Poppy's side and affectionately put his arm around her. "She won't admit it, but frankly, Poppy, I think Serena surprised herself with just how much she liked you."

Poppy rested her head on Matt's shoulder. "I guess we will never know for sure."

Chapter 46

Poppy was somewhat surprised when she had arisen the next morning after an exhausting late night witnessing Serena Saunders's arrest for the murder of Justin Cambry and received a text from Sam. He had sent the message a few hours earlier at five o'clock, which was early even for him.

The text was simple and to the point.

Dinner tonight? John Henry?

John Henry's Cafe was their favorite spot in town, a hidden gem off Tahquitz Canyon and Sunrise Way, owned by their dear friends Alfredo and Luis, a spot locals called the town's "best kept secret." Alfredo had started out as a busboy and had worked his way up for twenty years until he was able to buy the place when the original owner, John Henry, and his partner, Angelo, decided it was time to retire. The eclectic menu boasted a wide variety of modern and classic American-European fare, from macadamia nut-encrusted sole to a hearty chunky beef stroganoff, which happened to be Sam's go-to dish. Its charming outdoor patio setting with its trees and string of lights was the perfect spot for a romantic evening for two. Poppy and Sam had gone there on their first official date, and Alfredo had made sure they always sat at the same table every time from that fateful night they had dined there. But given Sam's recent remote and disconcerting behavior, Poppy wondered if Sam would be so cruel as to end their relationship at the same place where it had first begun.

Poppy texted back that she would meet him there. She had a full day at the Desert Flowers office wrapping up the Saunders case and meeting with potential new clients. Sam pushed back a bit on the plan, texting that he was happy to pick her up, but Poppy was annoyed just enough by him lately that she quickly shut him down, insisting they just meet at the restaurant.

Sam finally agreed, having made the reservation for seven-thirty, which would give Poppy enough time to go home and shower and change before dinner.

Her last meeting of the day ran late, and so she found herself rushing home to get ready. She did not put much thought into her appearance, brushing her hair back into a ponytail, putting on minimal makeup, and slipping on a casual kaftan with green undulating palm trees. It was the best she could come up with since she had been so busy she had yet to do the big pile of laundry in the hamper. She jumped in her car and sped to the restaurant. After greeting Alfredo with a kiss on each cheek, she was led her to her usual table where Sam was already seated, his phone clamped to his ear. As she sat down opposite him, he raised an index finger to signal her he would be just a moment longer.

She felt anger rising up within her.

She had arrived on time.

Get off the phone already.

As if reading her thoughts, Sam quickly wrapped up his call and put his phone away. "Sorry about that. I have been getting a deluge of calls from mutual friends ever since Warren Ashmore was arrested for murdering Ned Boyce.

Nobody can believe it. I mean, I have known the man for decades, just like you. We hung out at bars together, went hunting together. I mean I get that we lost touch over the years, but I thought I knew the guy. I guess I never really did after all."

Sam had just said more to her in this one moment than over the course of the entire past few weeks. And it rankled her. Why was he all of a sudden a chatterbox? She was done guessing.

"Sam . . ."

"I never could imagine the lengths Warren would go to to become obscenely rich. He never gave a hint of that side of himself to me or to any of his other friends for that matter. We are all just so shocked. I mean, he *killed* a man. His best friend."

Poppy paused thoughtfully as Sam stared at her for a response, then said, "Well, you two did meet in Hollywood, and those types of friendships usually stay on the shallow end of the pool."

Sam chuckled. "That's a pretty cynical attitude. But I guess I don't blame you after what happened with you and Serena."

"So you know everything?"

"It's all over the news and social media. Kind of hard to avoid it. I mean, I knew she was a calculating diva, but I never suspected anything like that!"

Poppy had no interest in discussing Serena Saunders anymore. She wanted to talk about where she stood with Sam. They had been avoiding the topic for far too long now.

She tried again. "Sam . . ."

"How about drinks?" said Hugo the waiter, dressed in all black. Poppy and Sam always requested that he serve them when they dined at John Henry's. He was sweet and kind, a great waiter, and also for Poppy's benefit, very easy on the eyes. He turned to Poppy first. "House cab?" Poppy smiled and nodded. Then he turned to Sam. "Whiskey sour?"

"Yes, thanks, Hugo," Sam said.

Hugo scooted off.

"Sam, we need to talk."

He stood up from the table.

For a moment, it looked as if he was going to walk out on her.

"Wait," he said nervously. "I have to do this now."

"Do what?"

He came around to Poppy's side of the table and took a small box out of his front pants pocket.

Then he got down on one knee.

Poppy emitted a short gasp.

He took her by the hand. "You may have noticed I haven't been my usual self lately. That's because I have been working up the courage to do this for weeks now, it's something I have wanted to do for a long time, but I have been a bundle of nerves, worried this might not be what you want for us. I was so scared I was making a huge monumental humiliating mistake. I bought you this very nice necklace for your birthday, thinking I would just put this off awhile longer, but then I told myself not to be such a wimp, if I want it then just go ahead and take the risk. So I gave the necklace to my niece, who had her eye on it anyway, and went back and got a proper ring so I could finally take a flying leap knowing you could still say no. Anyway, Poppy, I want you to know that I love you with all my heart, and I would be so happy if we finally made this official, and closed the deal as they say in Hollywood."

Poppy noticed the din of the other diners had faded away. There were no clattering of silverware or scraping of plates. All the neighboring tables were watching this scene unfold with rapt attention. Even the restaurant staff were all frozen in place, not serving or clearing tables.

The entire restaurant was completely silent.

Sam cleared his throat and then raised his eyes expectantly, fixing them on Poppy. "So . . . will you marry me?"

Poppy's mouth dropped open, flabbergasted.

For a moment, she thought she might faint.

But ever the actress, knowing she was center stage in front of a riveted audience, with tears pooling in her eyes, she gladly said the word they all wanted to hear.

"Yes."

There was thunderous applause.

"Yes, Sam, I will marry you."